The
McCloud Home for Wayward Girls

The
McCloud Home for
Wayward Girls

WENDY DELSOL

BERKLEY BOOKS, NEW YORK

THE BERKLEY PUBLISHING GROUP
Published by the Penguin Group
Penguin Group (USA) Inc.
375 Hudson Street, New York, New York 10014, USA
Penguin Group (Canada), 90 Eglinton Avenue East, Suite 700, Toronto, Ontario M4P 2Y3, Canada
(a division of Pearson Penguin Canada Inc.)
Penguin Books Ltd., 80 Strand, London WC2R 0RL, England
Penguin Group Ireland, 25 St. Stephen's Green, Dublin 2, Ireland (a division of Penguin Books Ltd.)
Penguin Group (Australia), 250 Camberwell Road, Camberwell, Victoria 3124, Australia
(a division of Pearson Australia Group Pty. Ltd.)
Penguin Books India Pvt. Ltd., 11 Community Centre, Panchsheel Park, New Delhi—110 017, India
Penguin Group (NZ), 67 Apollo Drive, Rosedale, Auckland 0632, New Zealand
(a division of Pearson New Zealand Ltd.)
Penguin Books (South Africa) (Pty.) Ltd., 24 Sturdee Avenue, Rosebank, Johannesburg 2196,
South Africa

Penguin Books Ltd., Registered Offices: 80 Strand, London WC2R 0RL, England

This is a work of fiction. Names, characters, places, and incidents either are the product of the author's imagination or are used fictitiously and any resemblance to actual persons, living or dead, business establishments, events, or locales is entirely coincidental.

PRINTING HISTORY
Berkley trade paperback edition / August 2011

Library of Congress Cataloging-in-Publication Data

Delsol, Wendy.
    The McCloud Home for Wayward Girls / Wendy Delsol.—1st ed.
        p.   cm.
    ISBN 978-0-425-24131-8
    1. Teenage mothers—Fiction.   2. Unmarried mothers—Fiction.   3. Mothers and
daughters—Fiction.   4. Hotelkeepers—Fiction.   5. Bed and breakfast accommodations—
Fiction.   6. Birthfathers—Identification—Fiction.   7. Wake services—Fiction.
8. Family secrets—Fiction.   I. Title.
    PS3604.E4474M38 2011
    813'.6—dc22
                                                                                    2011008455

PRINTED IN THE UNITED STATES OF AMERICA

10 9 8 7 6 5 4 3 2 1

For Bob, Ross, and Mac

ACKNOWLEDGMENTS

Again, I thank my agent, the whipsmart Jamie Brenner of Artists and Artisans. Jamie has boundless energy and an infectious enthusiasm. I'm incredibly lucky to have her on my team.

I am indebted to my editor, Kate Seaver, for offering a home to my wayward girls and for strengthening their story. Kate's savvy edits coaxed the very best from my characters.

I thank my critique group—Chantal Corcoran, Dawn Mooradian, Kali VanBaale, Kim Stuart, Mia James, and Murl Pace—for their input, fellowship, and friendship. For medical advice and terminology, I thank Dawn Mooradian, MD, and Lynn Rankin, MD.

To my greatest supporter and champion—my mother, Elaine Peck—I owe much more than this fleeting mention. I thank her for a lifetime of selfless encouragement and unconditional love. I am grateful to my sisters, Jennifer Peck and Valerie Devine, for their friendship and company on this wondrous journey called life. To that end, I thank my extended Jones and Peck relations for a trove of wonderful memories, grist for the writer's wheel.

Finally, love to my husband, Bob, and sons, Ross and Mac. Perhaps because my own family life is tranquil, I am forced to invent dramas and scandals. I thank them for this luxury.

CHAPTER ONE

Jill

Tuesday Morning

"Jesus! Jasper. Are you trying to scare me to death?" Jill said, steadying herself against the creaky door of the antique armoire. Jasper Cloris, the local undertaker, loomed in front of her. His pallid demeanor had always given her the creeps, as if he took his work home with him.

"Hope not. Business is fine. No need to recruit."

It didn't help that he took his job, and death in general, lightly.

"I wanted to discuss some arrangements with you in person," he continued, tucking a strand of his long side-swept hair behind his right ear.

Jill shuddered at the indigo black contrasted with the pale orb of his lobe and wondered, as always, why a funeral director would choose to dye his hair such a ghastly color. She lifted a stack of linens from a shelf and clutched them to her chest.

She didn't have the luxury of letting him distract her. "Can you talk while I set up?" She snapped a tablecloth open and sailed it over a four-top.

"I bear bad news and good news," he said.

"Oh. Okay."

He stood as if somehow waiting on her.

"Well?" she asked.

"Hester Fraser is dead."

"What's the bad news?" Jill asked, regretting the words instantly. Hester had been the kind of mean that only old money and generations of entitlement could afford, but trashing the still-stiffening had to be the sort of bad karma that crossed all cultural barriers. A run-of-the-jungle cannibal probably knew better. Jill felt a tingle down her spine. Damn, Jasper gave her the willies.

He sent her one of his canned smiles as if her gaffe made them pals. "I've been retained by her nephew, Keith, an old acquaintance of yours—I believe—to handle the arrangements." He spoke slowly, obviously enjoying himself. "We're expecting a rather large crowd for the wake. I was wondering if your dining room and lounge were available."

Jill chewed at the inside of her cheek. So this was why Jasper had come in person. He wanted to see her reaction. Not just to the news of Hester's death, but of Keith's involvement. It wasn't enough to be the town ghoul; he wanted to be the town gossip as well.

She looked straight into Jasper's gray eyes, hoping to quell, somehow, the twitch that was snaking across her brow. "We were more than just acquaintances, surely you know that."

"As they say in my business, careful what stones you turn over." He cleared his throat. "I thought it best not to pry."

Looking about the room, Jasper ran his fingers up and down the lemon-yellow and powder-blue striped tie that matched his pale blue linen suit. It was a point of honor with Jasper that he never wore black. He would affably proclaim it his job to brighten, in any small way, that which was inevitably bleak. Jill had never been fooled. His big loopy grin and Willy Wonka suits didn't change the fact that a sworl of black matter lingered about his person.

Jill sailed another cloth over a two-top.

"Keith arrives this evening from Boston," Jasper said, so intent on reading Jill's reaction that he leaned forward. "He may, in fact, be in need of a room."

Jill pulled her face into a smile, forced but inscrutable. "What night were you considering for the wake?"

"Thursday."

Jasper knew better than to ask for Friday. She hosted a weekly wine tasting with parlor games for her guests on that night. "And how many were you thinking?"

"A hundred or more," he replied.

Jill's inn often accepted local catering jobs. Since the dining room was only open for breakfast, it was available for small parties. In fact, in light of her current financial situation, she was in need of the revenue. She didn't normally like to include the lounge. She liked to leave it open for her guests to settle into the old leather club chairs; mingle informally; and enjoy the views to the garden, pond, and woodlands beyond. A party of a hundred would require the additional space, however. She'd have to set something up for her guests on the patio and hope for dry weather.

"I think I can handle the group. Are you sure, though, the choice of venue is appropriate? Does the family approve?" Jill was fully aware old Hester Fraser didn't have any remaining "family," besides Keith, whose name refused to dislodge itself from her brain's self-preserving censor.

"Probably not in its past incarnation." Jasper flopped the point of his tie up and down. "Though I, myself, never knew it as a home for unwed mothers, I can scarcely imagine it was the sort of place one would have opened up to functions." He smoothed the tie over his starched white shirt. "But in its current capacity, there could be no objections."

Though Jill ached to defend the home's past lives, plural—Jasper presumably unaware of its first—she resisted. He wasn't worth the energy it would take to string together nouns and verbs. "I wasn't referring to the house itself, rather the strained relations between Hester and my parents."

"Ah. Yes. That. Hester jilted."

Jill exhaled. "Yes. That."

"Surely an involvement long forgotten."

"Surely." *An involvement long forgotten.* Jill looked at her watch. The conversation had set her back. Just as she felt a small burn of panic begin in her tummy, the door to the kitchen swung open and Borka and Magda bustled in. Borka with a steaming pot of coffee in one hand and a pitcher of orange juice in the other, and Magda with a tray of mugs and glasses. Jill wondered if it was bad form to be thankful for the crushing Soviet domination that had sent the Kovacs sisters into exile. "I really do need to get ready. How about we talk by phone later today?"

With Jasper dispensed of—if only temporarily—Jill stepped into the kitchen, pulling in a deep calming breath and savoring the morning smells: bittersweet coffee, smoky bacon, and freshly squeezed orange juice. A large platter of sliced fruit sat atop the old marble countertop. Jill didn't know what she'd do without the two sisters, both solid fiftysomething women who had been working at her side for almost fifteen years. Magda was as unruffled as an Amish collar, and Borka a contrary being who began at least one sentence a day with something along the lines of "In Budapest, we don't do like this." They could whip up a breakfast for twenty and have the kitchen scoured, linens changed, bathrooms sanitized, and corners swept for three o'clock check-in.

Borka, who'd filed into the kitchen on Jill's heels, dipped her head toward the harvest table that ran down the center of the kitchen. "Ruby made a mess."

Jill snatched up the canvas and a paint jar. "She must have had a bad night. You know she paints when she's agitated." Ruby, Jill's mother, had been painting a lot lately. Yet another thing that Jill, like any good storm tracker, put on the watch list.

"Your mother," Borka said, "she like the story of the lady who paints so many pictures she can't find the window. Myself and my sister, we're too busy—our whole lives—for pictures."

Jill didn't know how to reply. Granted, Ruby idled away a great deal of time on her watercolors. Nonetheless, Borka was hardly anyone's definition of an art critic; nor did she understand the complex situation that had converted their home for pregnant teens into an inn and saw Jill take over the helm, after burying her father and tending to her grief-stricken mother. Besides, Ruby put in her hours. When recovered from the breakdown following the death of her beloved husband, Daniel, Ruby had declared herself the "face of the inn." She wore dresses, stockings, and pearls daily and greeted the guests with such a disarming mixture of poise and spunk that more than one walked away in a state of bemusement. Ruby's free-time hobby was fine by Jill; not only was it therapeutic, but it also—ideally—kept her out of trouble. Jill chalked Borka's annoyance up to apples begrudging oranges their bright peel. Though the discord nettled Jill, it didn't faze her regard for Borka, who—for all her gruff—was a friend. Jill would never forget the compliment Borka once, and only once, paid her. That Jill could remember it verbatim was testament to how dearly she'd treasured it. Years ago, and quite randomly, Borka had said, "You good person, good worker, a keeper." With those few no-verb-required words, as efficient as Borka herself, Jill had felt even her hair lift.

Jill managed to get through breakfast without the distraction of Hester's death and Keith's imminent arrival causing any damage to herself, her staff, or her guests. Her daughter, Fee, however, seemed to sense her disquiet. Jill was bunching linens into a sack to be picked up by the laundry service, when she found Fee staring at her with her hands on her hips.

"What's wrong with you this morning, Mom?"

"I learned of someone's death just before breakfast."

"Who?"

"You wouldn't know her. She was very old. She'd lived in a nursing home for almost ten years." Coming up with that figure was as simple as making change for a twenty. Fee was fourteen now. It was the Labor Day weekend, just two weeks before Fee's fifth birthday, when Hester suffered that massive stroke and was moved into a facility.

Jill and Fee had, in fact, visited Hester in the home once. It had been unintentional, of course, and Fee wouldn't remember. Her third-grade class had made valentines for the home's residents and Jill had volunteered to chaperone. The kids had shuffled through the corridors shell-shocked and horrified, handing their artistic labors of hearts and flowers and rainbows into the bony clutches and sunken eyes of the half dead. In the lounge, a darkened room with sagging chairs enlivened only by the fuzzy blur of an old TV, Fee and her classmates had dutifully handed over the last of their cards. They were about to leave when something about a woman who sat away from the others drew Jill's attention. She was in a wheelchair and balled into such a messy array of gray hair and bones that she looked like something a snake would cough up after crossing paths with a mouse. Even in that weakened state, Hester's presence had filled Jill with dread. She had ushered Fee out of the room, spooked into a jittery haste by the haunting green eyes, tracking her retreat.

"What was her name?" Fee asked.

"Hester Fraser."

"I've heard of her. Wasn't the Climbing Ivy once her house?"

"Yes. It used to be. It was sold after she got sick."

Hester's stately Victorian mansion had become the Climbing Ivy Restaurant years ago. It was a popular eatery that offered a bar and casual dining on the first floor and formal dining upstairs. The removal of walls, tin ceilings, and period wallpaper had been controversial at the time. Keith's already tarnished image had suffered further damage by his decision to act as power of attorney during the sale of the home that had been in the Fraser family for four generations.

In hindsight, Hester's years in assisted care couldn't have been cheap. Jill had a brief encounter, the only one in almost fifteen years, with Keith just days after Hester's stroke. She ran into him walking down Main Street and might not have even noticed him except for his companion, a strikingly attractive woman whose stylish red leather coat and long black hair stood out amid the everyday garb—faded denims, drab wools, and muted flannels—of small-town Scotch Derry, Iowa.

It had been awkward. The woman was introduced as simply Meredith, a prefix of girlfriend or wife was not offered, but Jill could sense Meredith's displeasure and intuited that Keith had omitted a title, most likely the former. She'd have heard had he married. They talked mostly about Hester, her condition, where he'd placed her, and about the "For Sale" sign on Hester's front lawn. And as much as Jill had labored to appear calm and collected, internally she'd fought a balefire, the heat of which had tinged her cheeks scarlet and choked her voice ragged. Meredith had glared so openly that Jill had invented an appointment to disentangle herself.

"I don't get it. Why does it bother you if she was old and sick?" Fee asked.

"She wasn't a nice lady, but she was very well known in this town once upon a time. I guess it just signifies the end of an era." Jill swung the sack of linens over her shoulder with the ease and practice of a merchant marine. "I've agreed to have the wake here on Thursday night, so don't make plans. I'll need your help." She headed into the kitchen. Fee followed.

"Do I have to?"

"Yes. And we've already talked about this. I'm expecting a lot of help from you this summer."

Fee groaned.

"I mean it. You'll get paid, but I need to know I can depend on you. I'm short-staffed since Marcie quit. Can I trust you? This event is important to me."

"Yes, Mother."

"And do me a favor," Jill said. "Don't tell Booboo about Hester."

Ruby had refused to be called Grandma, and toddling Fee couldn't pronounce the *R* in Ruby. Booboo was the result.

"Why?" Fee asked.

"They didn't get along."

"And?"

"I'm not sure how she'll react." Ruby was, almost daily, growing into what would politely be termed "feisty"—less politely, "ornery." She'd always had moxie complemented by an enviable ability to disarm gossip with a breezy indifference. There were recent outbursts and barbs, however, that were uncharacteristic—and a complete contradiction to her mind-your-own-bees-please policy. And Ruby's sudden interest in men, grizzled old geezers, had Jill completely baffled.

"Well, lately, the littlest nothing and she acts all crazy." Fee opened the back door for her mother. "Maybe something big and she'll act normal."

"One can always hope," Jill said.

CHAPTER TWO

Jill

Tuesday Late Morning

"Fee, are you ready?" Jill called, car keys firmly in hand but patience slipping away. Fee was on the phone, again. Actually speaking. Not a good sign. It indicated a drama whose scale outstripped the ability of Fee's wickedly quick texting thumbs. Or worse: one for which no electronic trail would remain. Jill had hoped Fee's fallout with her friend Marjory would have blown over by now. Judging by Fee's moodiness and clandestine conversations, it hadn't. Friends soothed Jill with reminders that all teens had dramas, but Jill had a sense that this one had really wounded Fee. Despite everything else going on—money concerns, Ruby's erratic behavior, and now Keith coming to town—Jill had already resolved to focus on her daughter this summer. Another potential funnel for eye-on-the-sky Jill to watch.

Standing in the home's foyer—now the check-in area—Jill

crossed her arms and stared at the wall of McCloud family memorabilia: the crest bearing the family motto, "Hold Fast"; a glass-encased tartan kilt and sporran; and photos, one of which, in particular, always caught her eye. Jill's aunt Rose, her father's sister, was the original wayward in whose memory the home had been repurposed. Rose, from whom Jill inherited her russet hair and petite stature, was fifteen at the time of the photo and bore a postwar charm and confidence. Posed in front of the house, she wore a fitted white cotton dress with a square neck and belted waist, and had a head of curls that she'd probably rolled in rags or socks to achieve the corkscrew spirals so fashionable back then. Jill shivered to think of the horrors which led to Rose's death one short year later on some makeshift operating table in a back-alley clinic. To this day no one knew much, except Rose's pious father would never have accepted an out-of-wedlock pregnancy.

The clearing of a throat just inches from her left ear yanked Jill back to reality. Mr. Nitpick, Room 202, stood before her, fingering one of the local maps she provided. "If I might have a word," he said.

She knew, all too well, he wouldn't keep it to one. It had taken three phone calls, long, laborious conversations, just to make the reservation. Of foremost importance was the mattress. Two conversations were required to confirm that the inn offered Dux mattresses, genuine Dux mattresses, not some cheap Nanking knockoff, but the real deal—king size. In a moment of complete insanity, Jill had been talked into the luxury beds during the inn's remodel, two years prior. Fifteen beds, at over seven thousand dollars each; it was a ridiculous business decision with no proof of return, except for the carper in 202. She, herself, slept on a Serta, circa 1990.

"How may I help you?"

"Are any of the nearby breweries organic?"

Not with the organic again. The reservation process was all
the warning Jill needed and she had taken great care to ready
Room 202 before his arrival. No one tucked a tighter bed corner than Borka, Jill would bet the land on it. And Jill, an
admitted neat freak, had given the room her seal of approval.
At check-in, he'd handed Jill a large shopping bag. "If you
don't mind, I prefer my own sheets," he'd said. "Egyptian cotton, fifteen-hundred thread count." No guest had ever checked
in with their own bedroll before and Jill had been startled.
She'd reassured him that the inn's linens were of the highest
quality. He'd shaken his head from side to side and asked,
"Ah, but are they organic?" As, no, Jill could not guarantee
that some WWII bomber hadn't been retrofitted for a Nile
Valley flyover of DDT, she'd graciously taken the sheets and
Borka had remade the bed.

"Big Falls Brewing Company is organic." She pointed to a
spot on the map. "About thirty minutes north of here."

"And do they craft traditional cask ales, unfiltered and
unpasteurized?"

"I think you'll be pleasantly surprised," Jill said. "And make
sure you see the falls. They're only a fifteen-minute hike from
the gates. Well worth the effort."

Jill sent her guest off with binoculars and a backpack pro-
visioned with a water bottle, Amana blue cheese, crackers, and
a handful of locally grown apricots. She then put in a quick
warning call to Max at the brewery.

Fee finally emerged with cutoff jeans and a T-shirt shrugged
down and over one bare shoulder. Her legs were long and
strong and Jill wondered whether Fee could have sprouted

overnight. She was taller than the other McCloud women by at least four inches, with a solid athletic build and chestnut-brown hair. Jill had always coveted Fee's smooth-as-corn-silk hair. Jill favored her father's side of the family, the Scottish side, with wiry red hair and parchment-white skin that freckled under anything over sixty watts. Fee, on the other hand, was already tanning nicely.

"I'm ready," Fee said, flipping her hair back with a flick of her wrist. "Let's not be all day at it either. I have soccer later."

Jill straightened Fee's shirt with a swift tug.

It was a beautiful morning and Jill ambled along. She shopped the farmers' market every Tuesday while it was in season. The impatient Fee had already been dispatched to the far end of the market for raspberries. The inn was sold out through the weekend with four new bookings coming in less than an hour after Jasper's visit. In anticipation of a full house, Jill had a long list of required items; still, she was enjoying the festive atmosphere. Her rolling cart was laden with bouquets of delphinium and gerberas, crisp green cucumbers, bright yellow peppers, trays of lush, red strawberries, and a bag, the large size, of kettle corn, which she was shoveling—by the fistful—into her mouth.

She wiped a sticky hand down the back of her Capri jeans and adjusted the Iowa Cubs cap down over her freckled nose as they worked their way along High Street, formerly the posh-est residential area in town and currently an artery of the expanded downtown. Besides the Climbing Ivy Restaurant, there was the Perry Home, now an antiques store; the Milton Home, a hair salon and day spa; and the old Graystock Home, now the Graystock Bed and Breakfast. Jill grabbed another handful of popcorn and peered into the Graystock's windows

in an effort to gauge whether her competition was also enjoying a flush of bookings. Both inns were of similar size and
rating. The Graystock offered more of an in-town experience
with its proximity to restaurants, shops, and the newly reno-
vated opera house. The McCloud Inn boasted a country escape
with its neighboring horse farm, access to hiking trails, and
views of the pond and surrounding woods. She wondered if
the owners of the Graystock had her same financial constraints:
a crushing spate of repairs and renovations, winter business
slow as a hobbled mule, and a newly adjusted home equity
loan muscling for command of the monthly ledger.

As she stood there, staring, the front door opened and a
tall man with wavy bay-brown hair stepped out to the large
covered porch. He paused, surveying the scene with one hand
shielding his eyes from the sun's glare.

Jill tugged her cap down to her eyebrows and moved as
quickly as her rolling cart would allow between the pop-up
canvases of a local baker and an asparagus vendor before she
arrived, flushed and breathing hard, in front of the Harmony
Farms stand. She took a deep bracing breath and bellied up
to the checkered tablecloth.

"Jill, I was hoping you'd stop by. I have new pictures of
Leo." Susannah, goat-cheese maker extraordinaire, crouched
below the table to rifle through a basket.

Jill took the blissfully quiet moment to scan the selection
of cheeses. For all the subtle flavors Susannah could finesse
into a silky goat cheese, she was a conversational tidal wave.
A gold-medal gabber who could cudgel from one unfinished
thought to the next without the need of a transition, preposi-
tion, or—for that matter—respiration.

Susannah popped to a stand, holding a stack of photos.

"Did you see that the guy from Missouri is back with peaches again this week? And Maddie thinks Leo could be left-handed. And major-league material the way he pitches that bottle back across the room."

Maddie, Susannah's daughter, had moved to Minnesota only a few short months following the death of Susannah's husband. The sudden loss of her spouse, daughter, and only grandchild had rendered the already chatty vendor starved for conversation. Many market regulars were since making do with Gouda or cheddar. The more others scattered, the more Jill remained loyal. Susannah was sweet and well meaning, if a whopping time suck.

"Heard you're hosting old Hester's wake," Susannah said, pressing the top photo into Jill's hands. "Look at this one. Have you ever seen such a sweet patootie?"

"Sweet patootie?" asked a male voice from behind Jill. "Are we talking potatoes or posteriors?"

Jill turned to find Keith Fraser smiling like he was as much a fixture at the weekly market as Ma's Muffins. "Keith. Oh my goodness, Keith."

"I thought that was you a minute ago," he said, lifting both arms, a possible prelude to a hug.

Jill extended her right hand. They shook. Noticing a sag in his shoulders, she regretted not stepping into the hug. She dropped his hand, but held his gaze. He'd aged well, damn him. A full head of hair and perfect teeth. His smile had always buckled her knees.

"I'm sorry about your aunt," she said, while internally chanting *stay cool, stay cool*. Her physiology was not cooperating. Muscles tautened, her epidermis flamed, and long-abandoned neural pathways cleared with a dizzying tingle.

"She lived a good long life." Looking down at Susannah's photo, he added, "Posteriors it is. Bare at that."

She relaxed. The fact that for the past fifteen years she'd imagined hundreds of run-in scenarios with Keith but not a single one involving the naked bottom of a gabby goat herder's grandchild somehow settled her nerves. She handed the photo back to Susannah. "My friend's adorable grandson."

"Yes, adorable," he said, nodding to the proud grandmother. "Can I walk with you?" he then asked Jill.

A bubble made its way up her throat. "Yeah. Sure." She stacked four tubs of Susannah's labors onto her cart. "Okay if we settle up next time?" she asked.

Susannah waved her away with a "Yes. Yes. Shoo now," in what was quite probably Jill's quickest transaction with Harmony Farms. Ever.

"I'm glad I ran into you," Keith said. "Jasper has spoken to you, right?"

"Yes. He came by this morning."

"And it's not too much trouble. I mean, it's not asking too much . . ."

"Not at all," Jill said. "There's no reason . . ."

"I wasn't implying . . . It's more that we haven't given you much notice."

"It's nothing we can't handle." Their stutters and stammers had her wishing they could start again. Were it only possible, she thought, to go back to the very beginning. She stopped, finding herself once again in front of the Graystock Bed and Breakfast, the hotel he'd apparently chosen over hers. "And how lucky we ran into each other."

"Funny enough, I just called your place a little while ago,

I left a message for you," he said, grinning. "Could I possibly have spoken to someone named Borka?"

"Yes." Jill tried very hard not to return the smile. Way back when, Borka would have easily made their "monikers of doom" list. Keith had a theory about names and their role in an individual's destiny. It had all begun with his uncle Claude, who tripped over his size-thirteen shoes and ended up hurtling—like a bowling ball—down the escalator at Marshall Field's, and striking holiday shoppers left and right. He managed to break three legs that day, only one of which was his. Keith also liked to cite his friend Skip, who had been passed over for promotion, twice. Jill, he had believed, was the name of a faithful sidekick, as in Jack and Jill. So much for his theory.

"I'd like to come by sometime," he said. "Go over the arrangements."

Jill wished she had some sort of smartphone or electronic date book that needed checking first. The truth was, everything went onto a huge paper calendar on her desk. "How about tomorrow at four?"

Keith spread his hands, as if it had all come too easily. "Tomorrow it is then. Four o'clock."

Surely there must be something else to say, Jill thought. About the passage of years, roads traveled, or, in her case, weeded over. Fee's long legs striding into view provided a welcome interruption.

"Fee. Honey." Jill waved with her right arm high over her head. "Over here."

Fee approached, looking from Jill to Keith and back to Jill.

"Keith, this is my daughter, Fee."

"Very pleased to meet you," he said, shaking Fee's hand.

"Keith is an old . . . friend of mine," Jill said to Fee. "The wake we're hosting is for his aunt Hester."

"Oh," Fee said, still volleying looks between the two of them.

"Speaking of which," Jill continued, "we'd better get back. It's a busy week."

"See you tomorrow," Keith said.

They both held their ground for a moment before Keith signaled himself off and turned to walk away. Jill had forgotten about the way he waved, arm and hand held firm and fingers splayed wide. She got about five paces along before Fee was at her elbow with eyes the size and shine of two brass portholes.

"Was that an old boyfriend?"

"Why do you think that?"

"Because you hesitated between the words *old* and *friend*. A dead giveaway."

Jill picked up the pace.

"So?" Fee asked, catching up with Jill and the squeaky cart.

"Yes."

"Really?"

"Don't sound so surprised."

"It's just . . ."

"Just what?" Jill asked.

"He's not bad looking," Fee said. "So when?"

"Around the time of your grandfather's death."

"But that'd be around the same time as . . ."

"I knew Keith just after . . ." Jill steered the unwieldy cart over the gravel surface of the parking lot.

"But, then, you must have been . . ."

"Only just. And I certainly didn't know it."

Fee fluttered her lashes, obviously processing the information. "What happened?"

"He left town," Jill said in an end-of-discussion tone. As much as she knew that this was a missing piece to the mousetrap assembly of timing and events surrounding Fee's birth, Jill was reluctant to elaborate. Over the years, Fee had naturally had questions. Jill's story of a college boyfriend, an Al Thomas, had always been vague. Having left school to assist with her dying father, a preoccupied and in-denial nineteen-year-old Jill had waited too long to track down the transferred-by-then, out-of-state student with an all-too-common name (was Al short for Alan, Albert, Alfred, Alexander, Alvin, or some unusual moniker like Alonso or Alphonse?).

"Because . . . ?" Fee asked.

"Because of a lot of things. Bad timing most of all." The topic reminded her of a loose end. "Let's go. I need to get home and phone your aunt Jocelyn."

CHAPTER THREE

Jill

Tuesday Afternoon

Jill edged the last of the farmers' market items—a flat of strawberries—onto the crowded countertop, casting a wary glance at the kitchen handset wedged between two jars of blackberry preserves and a bundle of asparagus. She wasn't looking forward to the conversation with her sister. There was a part of her that wanted to wait until evening, have a bracer glass of wine first. Then again, it was always best to have your wits about you when dealing with Jocelyn. Besides, if Jill waited until evening, Jocelyn might already have two or three drinks in her, even allowing for the two-hour head start an Iowa Happy Hour had over California.

Just get it over with. She looked at her watch: a Swiss-made work of precision and industry that had been her father's. In the fifteen years since his death, she'd had three cars, two washing machines, five vacuums, but only one watch. It was an Art Deco piece, rectangular in shape with applied Arabic numerals and golden arrow-shaped hands. She particularly liked the sub–second hand in the six position, a tireless minidial that measured out seconds in simple, sluggish lunges forward. Jill remembered the last time she'd taken it in for cleaning. The loop-eyed jeweler, new to the shop, had marveled at the antique piece, claiming, "A 1930s Gruen Curvex. They don't make 'em like this anymore." Jill had bent over the counter to take a peek. She'd never, in all the years it had guided her through the minutiae of her day-to-day, seen its intricate machinery. "Wow," she'd said. "It's so complicated. You'd never know by looking at it."

Jill took a deep breath and called Jocelyn at home. She wasn't surprised to catch her at home on a weekday. Jocelyn, a former hairstylist, was now a highly regarded, and well-paid, massage therapist and color therapist—whatever that was—for the swish crowd of L.A., but work was as fickle as a Hollywood husband.

"Hello."

"Jocelyn, it's me." Never one to waste time, Jill pinched the phone between her shoulder and chin as she carried perishables to the fridge.

"Hey, stranger. How's the wayward gang?"

Jill had always bristled at the term *wayward*, a descriptive that had been deemed pejorative and dropped from the home's name in the late seventies. Even with the more open-minded McCloud Home for Girls title, theirs had been an unusual family life and living arrangement, to say the least. Jill and Jocelyn had grown up surrounded by young women "in trouble." People, the elderly in particular, seemed to step backward in their footprints at the mere mention of teenage mothers.

For her part, Jocelyn had always been cavalier about the whole thing. She used to joke that they ran a home for "little mothers who got goosed." She had never dared say that in front of their father, though. Even she, the family rebel, had respected his dedication to the home.

Though the religious zeal of his father had soured Daniel, Jill's father, to organized religion, it had instilled in him a great respect for life. He had always grieved the nephew he lost to the back-alley clinic, as well as his beloved sister. With the more relaxed morals of the eighties, Jill had witnessed her father's great joy in aiding the willing and able among the girls to keep their babies. Over the years, a few had returned with fat-cheeked bundles or into-everything toddlers. In those moments, seeing proud, unwiped tears roll down her father's cheeks, she understood his passion.

Their mother had always dramatized, and even glamorized, the situation. She had an uncanny knack of remembering every girl's name as well as the individual story that landed her on their threshold. From time to time, Ruby would talk about her own path to the home: the football-player sweetheart named Josh, his tragic demise in an automobile accident, and the stillborn baby Janine.

"I have news," Jill said. "Hester Fraser is dead."

"No shit."

"Yep." Jill filled her arms with pantry items.

"I guess her pact with the devil ran out," Jocelyn said.

"Had to sometime."

"So is he?" Jocelyn asked.

"Is who?" Jill shelved a bag of raisins with the other dried fruits.

"Keith."

"Is he what?" Jill said, knowing exactly what Jocelyn was after.

"Is he coming for the funeral?"

"Already here." Jill stacked a plastic container of clover honey under another.

"Holy shit. I'm booking a flight."

The last thing Jill wanted was Jocelyn underfoot. "I don't know if that's a good idea."

"Why not?"

"Because it will be awkward enough without you."

"I was thinking of coming for a visit anyway."

"Yeah, right," Jill said.

"I was. I'm not working right now. Plus, it'll be nice to see Fee while she's on summer break."

"Come in July or August."

"We both know it would take a restraining order to keep me away."

"If it comes to that."

"So have you seen him?"

"Yes. Briefly."

"What were you wearing?"

Jill looked down. "Jeans, blue top." She swapped cardamom and cayenne on the alphabetized spice rack.

"Blue?"

"Yes."

"Of course, blue. You never listen to me, do you?"

Jill exhaled loud enough for it to transmit over the phone. "I happen to like blue."

"It's all wrong for you. Blue is the throat chakra. It controls our ability to communicate. For whatever reason, you don't process blue well." Jill heard Jocelyn stifle a laugh. "You clammed up, didn't you?"

"No."

"Come on."

"Not really."

"I've told you this before: green is the heart chakra; green is your color."

"I don't believe in that stuff."

"It's light refracted at different wavelengths and vibrations. Hard—cold—science. What's not to believe?"

Jill huffed at Jocelyn's definition of science, one that had about as much in common with true branches of knowledge—like physics, chemistry, or biology—as did the Church of Scientology. Besides being a "color therapist," Jocelyn fancied herself some kind of relationship savant. She liked to call it her "sexth sense," an ability to detect pheromones between two people, to know when they belong together, and how to charge or manipulate the atmosphere if and when they're too clueless or stubborn to do so themselves. Jill and Keith had always been Jocelyn's biggest "stumper," on par with other scientific anomalies like spontaneous combustion or ball lightning.

"Seriously, I don't think you should come. I haven't even told Mom yet and you'll just make things worse."

"You haven't told Mom?"

"No."

"Jesus, Jill. Take the friggin' blue off and vent a little."

"Go to hell."

"Shouldn't that be 'come to hell'?"

"Don't," Jill said.

"Come on. It'll make my year."

And ruin mine. Jill could already picture the uncomfortable reunion between herself, Keith, and Jocelyn. *Just perfect.* One could always count on Jocelyn to add cayenne to an already five-alarm chili. Jill hung up, fearing yet another storm front on its way.

CHAPTER FOUR

Jill

Tuesday Afternoon

"Was that Aunt Jocelyn?" Fee asked, startling Jill as she exited the pantry carrying two jars of expired peaches.

"Yes."

"Why didn't you let me say hi?"

"I didn't know you were there. Besides, you can talk to her in person. She's coming for the funeral."

"Woo-hoo." Fee broke into an impromptu, celebratory shimmy.

"I'll need help cleaning up the spare room." In the year since Jocelyn had last visited, the extra room in the family's ground-floor, private quarters had piled up with boxes and files.

"I'm on it," Fee said, bounding away.

Jill clapped one arm over the other. Jocelyn was the parade that prevailed despite the gloomiest of forecasts. Remembering that awful Christmas fifteen years prior, Jill wondered at her sister's ability to carry on while everyone around her could barely cope.

Jill fumbled with Scotch tape while pinning a roll of holiday wrap under her left arm. She heard a rustle at the front door and turned for a better view. The roll of paper tumbled onto the floor and opened into a red carpet of Santa caps and Rudolph noses stretching all the way into the foyer. Jocelyn stopped the procession with the toe of her boot.

"Where have you been?" Jill asked. "It's after midnight."

"Jesus, Jill, I may still live at home, but I'm under nobody's watch. Or should I make a point of calling your dorm room on Saturday nights to make sure you're all tucked in?"

"Nobody knew where you were," Jill said, scrunching her brow at how often such a phone call would go unanswered.

Jocelyn unfurled her winter scarf with languid movements, as if its wet, scratchy wool were fine silk or cashmere. She held it against her cheek with a look of reverie. "Anyway, I was out. And it was absolute bliss."

Jill cut the paper in four angry snaps of the scissors. It was so like Jocelyn to be off enjoying herself when everyone else was miserable. "Dad had a doctor's appointment. He's in his office, and Mom's been in her room crying ever since." She began rerolling the wrapping paper. It crumpled and bunched in an unsalvageable mess. "And Keith called for you twice."

Jocelyn hung her jacket on the oak coatrack and stepped into the library. She wore a too-tight cream-colored sweater that was all but transparent.

"Where's your bra?"

Jocelyn reached into the front pocket of her jeans and pulled out a wad of white lace, which she unfurled with a snap. She quickly shrugged off her sweater, standing before Jill with an impressive endowment. Jocelyn then deftly hooked her bra behind her back; lifted the straps over her shoulders; and adjusted her breasts into the voluminous cups. "Is that better?" she asked, before tugging the sweater back over her head and fluffing her honey-blond hair.

Jill had, of course, seen her sister's breasts hundreds of times. They shared a bathroom. She had, however, never seen them so conspicuously displayed. Jocelyn had always compared herself to Jill with a "You got the brains, and I got the boobs" summary. It had never really bothered Jill that Jocelyn was more buxom, partly because she also had to worry about her weight. In that moment, though, seeing Jocelyn so carefree, she felt a barrage of attacking emotions: shock, anger, embarrassment, and a nasty-tasting dollop of pea-green envy.

"So, what did the doctor say?" Jocelyn asked.

Jill blinked back tears. "He said to go home. Enjoy Christmas. Get his affairs in order, but there's nothing more they can do." She tucked the ends of the paper around the rectangular box in three efficient swipes of her thumbs; taped them down; and flung the package across the table.

"What does that mean?" Jocelyn asked.

"A couple of months, at the most."

Jocelyn dropped into a chair. "What are we going to do?"

Jill sank into the seat across from her. "Mom's a mess. She can barely get herself dressed in the morning. Never mind help with the staff and girls. She just keeps muttering, over and over, 'Life is too short. Life is too short.' I'm really worried about her."

"That doesn't sound good," Jocelyn said.

"When you think about it, she never knew her father. Her mother died when she was very young. Her first boyfriend died in a car wreck, and their baby at birth. Plus the miscarriage before you. That's an awful lot to bear before you're even fifty."

Jocelyn brought her fist to her lips and tapped her mouth. "And now Dad."

"I've made a decision," Jill said, ignoring the bluntness of Jocelyn's statement. "I'm not going back to school after break. I don't even know how I'd concentrate with everything that's going on here." She tugged at a thread that had come loose from the arm of the upholstered chair. "I'm going to take a semester off."

"What?" Jocelyn said. "You're overreacting. Mom will pull it together. The two of us will hold things together around here, until . . ."

"What about your job at the salon?" Jill asked. "Are you going to cut your hours?"

"I couldn't," Jocelyn said. "I couldn't afford to. Besides, I've finally built a solid base of clients. If I weren't there, they'd find someone else. I'd lose them."

"I want to be here," Jill said. "Mom's going to need me. Dad will, too. He'll need help putting things in order. And maybe if I were here, we could start taking on girls again. Mrs. Lawrence from the Chicago shelter called just this evening to see if we were resuming operations. The hiatus has implications beyond just our finances, you know."

"Don't." Jocelyn swung her head from side to side. "Mom doesn't want to. Besides, if you did, you'd never get back to school. You'd be stuck here. Is that what you want?"

Nobody wanted to be "stuck" anywhere, Jill supposed, but what an awful way to describe duty and obligation to family, to her father, moreover—a man who had dedicated his life to the care and protection of girls in trouble, a man who lived for his family, a man who lived by the words of the McCloud clan motto: "Hold Fast."

"I'm not sure what I want matters right now," Jill said.

Jocelyn fidgeted in her seat. "Figures. I had the most perfect evening of my life, and then I come home and it all crashes."

"What was so perfect about it?"

"John Foley."

"Who?" Jill asked.

"John Foley. He's the new bartender at Mick's Pub. He gave me a private tour of the back room." Jocelyn hoisted her right hip to the side. "I think I got a splinter in my butt from the wooden crate he backed me into." She laughed. "It was worth it, though. I think I'm in love."

Jill was speechless. Jocelyn had started dating Keith Fraser in September. The entire fall, during Jill's weekly calls home, all Jocelyn could talk about was Keith. How handsome he was. How smart he was. How he'd gone to Dartmouth and had already worked in New York. Plus, his family had money, which made Jocelyn practically purr with contentment. "What about Keith?"

"What about him?" Jocelyn replied.

"I thought you two were going out."

"We are."

Jill blinked and shook her head. "So what's with this John guy?"

Jocelyn jutted her chin out. "I'm twenty-two, not forty-two."

She held up her left hand. "And it's not like there's a ring on this finger."

"So did you and Keith agree to see other people?"

"No."

"Jocelyn, that's rotten."

Jocelyn stood. "It's not rotten." She flipped her hair back behind her shoulder. "It's fun. Besides, guys do it all the time, so why shouldn't we?"

Jocelyn left, and Jill finished wrapping the few gifts that remained, but she felt no holiday cheer. She didn't want to think about her father. After the doctor's appointment, he was shaken. His hand had trembled as he tried to grasp the mug of weak tea she'd set before him, atop a spread of bills and papers. At a time when he should be taking care of himself, he was worrying about other things: the girls they were declining, the consequent lack in funding, and even his wife. Jill had only been home for winter break for four days, but was already seriously alarmed at the state of her mother's nerves. She had no focus, was forgetful, and, at times, was short with the girls and staff. When Glenda, an old friend of Ruby's, had invited her for a drink, Daniel had encouraged the outing, arguing that a night out and a little girl talk would be a good diversion. Though it had recharged her mother's spirits and even, ironically, her father's, such selflessness had only saddened Jill.

Jill was also disappointed in Jocelyn. Keith was a nice guy and didn't deserve to be cheated on. Moreover, rumor had it that his family was going through a rough patch. Keith's mother had left his father for another man. Reeling from the split, Keith's father, William, had come to town to stay with his sister, the infamous Hester Fraser. Keith had arrived soon after, fed up with the craziness of New York and hoping to console his father. Keith was working as a waiter, but Jocelyn had bragged he didn't need the money, just wanted to learn the restaurant business.

Jill switched off the lights in the library and, in the foyer, lifted Jocelyn's scarf from the floor where she had dropped it, her carelessness encompassing both the animate and inanimate. In many ways she was the perfect big sister. So proud of Jill and always the first to announce her baby sis as the "smartest girl both sides of the Mississippi." Jocelyn had no interest in college herself, but had shown absolute glee when, two years ago, Jill had fanned a selection of college brochures across her bed. Jill respected Jocelyn's decision to skip college. She made decent money at the hair salon, plus she liked her job. But Jill just couldn't wrap her mind around the way Jocelyn treated guys.

Continuing down the hallway, alongside the staircase, she found lights left on at the back of the house, too. She switched off a lamp in the lounge and the chandelier over the dining-room table. In the kitchen, it wasn't the fluorescent overhead she found most glaring. It was, rather, the open jars of paint, dirty brushes, and a half-finished canvas that was so alarmingly slapdash it would have brought even Pollock to his knees.

Jill was crouched, pulling serving trays from a low cupboard, when Fee popped back into the kitchen.

"I got the bed cleared off," Fee said. "Most of the boxes fit in the closet. Some I had to stack on the floor."

"Good enough," Jill said, groaning to a stand. "Can you put clean sheets on the bed?"

"I guess. But are we still going to have time to go to the mall?"

The mall. Fee, bones lengthening virtually by the hour, had been promised new summer clothes. With everything that had come up, Jill had forgotten. "Probably not until after the weekend, now. It's just too crazy."

"But Aunt Jocelyn's coming. I'll need something to wear."

"Hon, she's your aunt, not your date."

Fee stomped off, leaving Jill to remember the kind of tricks Jocelyn played on dates.

Jill pushed aside the "Happy New Year 1996" banner and scanned the crowd in the living room. No Jocelyn. She moved into the kitchen. Jocelyn wasn't there either. Where the hell was she? Jocelyn had begged Jill to come to the party. She lent her a dress; did her hair and makeup; and even promised to leave before midnight, if Jill wasn't having fun. Jill had argued that she'd be the third wheel to Jocelyn and Keith's cozy duo. Jocelyn persisted until Jill finally relented, thinking maybe she should get out. Her dad had enjoyed a good couple of days. Christmas at home had buoyed his spirits. At Sunday dinner, Jill had caught her dad looking around the dining table at his wife and daughters, and Keith, with a nod of misty-eyed approval.

It was so like Jocelyn to talk Jill into something, paint an elaborate portrait, and then junk her like an old fridge. Jill took a sip of the cheap champagne. Her plastic glass had lost its stem, which prevented her from setting it down. She had to cup it in her hand, which made the cloyingly sweet beverage warmer by the moment. She took a few steps toward the sink, edging around a couple clamped in a passionate embrace, and dumped her drink down the drain.

"Have you seen Jocelyn?" Keith held a bottle of beer in each hand.

"No. I was looking for her, too."

"Oh well. You want one?"

"Sure." She sipped the beer and rejoiced as the cold, bitter brew washed away all taste of the sweet wine.

Keith glanced sideways at the entwined couple and shook his head. "You wanna go outside?"

It was a mild evening for winter, but still somewhere in the low thirties. Jill appreciated the clean, crisp air, but couldn't help shivering.

"Too cold?" Keith asked.

"I don't know how long I'll last," Jill said. "But it's actually kind of nice. Too many smokers in there."

"I'll say. I could feel cancer cells forming in my lungs." Keith suddenly went ashen, obviously realizing his casual use of the C-word. "I'm sorry," he said quickly. "That was a stupid thing to say." He patted his hair down, which only made it clump in a tuft of woolly brown. He had the kind of curls any woman would have coaxed and pulled into some sort of order. As a guy, though, he got away with a crop of unruly brown sprouts. She hadn't found him attractive at first. Possibly because everyone, and Jocelyn the loudest, was proclaiming him such a hunk. He was tall, probably six two or three, and big, but she had thought him a little lumbering in his movements. She now noticed his soft brown eyes and dark lashes.

"It's okay," Jill said. "He doesn't have lung cancer; it's prostate."

"I know, but it was still insensitive." He rolled his shoulders, a gesture one would expect from a much younger boy, a teen still getting used to his own bulk. It was hard to believe Keith was twenty-four, a college grad who had already worked on Wall Street. It wasn't that he lacked confidence; it was more that he had an air of reserve, with even a hint of self-deprecation. Jill had overheard him describing his job in New York as grunt work that any eighth-grade dropout could have performed.

Jill looked back at the house. She was getting cold, but the prospect of returning to a crowd of loud drunks wasn't appealing. "I should have stayed home."

"You're not having a good time?"

"I'm not really into big parties." It was one of the things she didn't get about student life at Iowa. There were endless frat and dorm parties where everyone squeezed into a tiny space, and stood around drinking warm beer and listening to hard rock so loud her heart took a free fall on every downbeat. Ironically, Jill's favorite part of most nights was the time she and her roommates spent primping and getting ready with Whitney Houston belting it out, and a bottle—or two—of wine open on the counter. Or when they had a few guy friends over for poker, or euchre, or a Sunday spaghetti dinner.

He nodded. "Me neither. Jocelyn begged me to come. I just wanted to go out for dinner and watch the ball drop on TV."

"She begged me, too," Jill said.

He scratched at his head. "Let's look inside again. It's not that big of a house."

They searched the first-floor main rooms that were thick with bodies and thumping with sound. Upstairs, they moved along a hallway. One bedroom—a teen's, judging by the Pearl Jam and Nirvana posters—had its door ajar and was occupied by a mashing couple. Another—the master judging by its size and muted decor—opened onto a red-eyed, smoke-shrouded circle of kids. One guy held a joint up between his thumb and forefinger. "You guys in or out?" he asked.

"Out," Keith said, closing the door and fixing Jill with a grimace.

The next room—this one impossibly pink and Disney-princess-themed—was empty. Jill was already backing out when Keith squealed, "Hungry Hippos. No way."

Upon a Lilliputian table with two equally itty-bitty chairs sat a board game consisting of four plastic hippos atop an orange base with a collection of white marbles in the center. Keith swung one long leg over a chair and plunked down onto its seat, his knees becoming level with his eyebrows.

"Uh. You know this game?" Jill asked.

"Know it. I'm invincible. I call blue," he said, spinning the board one turn to the right.

This left Jill with the pink hippo. Not necessarily her favorite color, but fitting given the Pepto-pink of the room. Slung over the footboard of the canopy bed, she spied a feather boa, for the creation of which a flamingo—or two—may have been plucked. She coiled it around her neck and lowered herself into the opposing seat that was too small even for her less-than-lanky limbs.

"Hey. No fair," Keith said. "There's no dress-up in Hungry Hippos."

"I thought you were invincible," Jill said. "If so, what difference could a few feathers make?"

Keith dipped his head and squinted. "Game on, then."

The *game*—the object of which was, by the random slamming of a lever, to cause the hippo's head to lunge and gobble marbles—took mere minutes to play. At the end of the *game*, which required neither timing nor skill, Jill's pink hippo had taken twelve of the twenty marbles.

Keith sat back, tugging at his hair. "No way. My first loss ever. It was that thing around your neck. It was a distraction."

Jill sighed. "What are you talking about? That was pure talent."

He crossed his arms. "So what don't you like about big parties?"

"Change of subject. I get it," she said, unwrapping the boa from her neck. "For starters, no one ever really talks to you. It's too loud and conversations are these half-shouted one-liners. And even if the other person could hear you, they're usually too busy checking out the scene to really listen."

"I hear you."

They both chuckled at his unintended pun. She noticed the little crinkled-papery lines that formed at the corners of his eyes. And his smile. He had perfect teeth.

"You don't sound like the college kids I knew," he continued.

"Is that a bad thing?"

"No, it's a good thing. I always wondered why they were there if they didn't take it seriously."

"I take it seriously," Jill said. "Maybe too seriously. I love school. I only wish . . ."

"What?"

"It's just a bad time right now for my family. I'm taking next semester off."

"Really? You're what? A sophomore?"

"Yes." Jill shrugged. "School will still be there in a few months." She stared out the black-as-coal window before turning back to look at Keith. "But my dad probably won't be."

Keith took a long time to respond, all the while holding her gaze. "On second thought," he said, "I think you're doing the right thing. Family takes care of family. Period."

"Is that why you're here with your dad?"

"Is that what you heard?"

"Yes."

He rubbed his jaw. "I'm worried about him." He stopped for a moment, as if deciding whether or not to continue. "He's in a bad place right now. Drinking too much. Out all hours. My mom left him pretty shattered. He really couldn't stand being in the same town with her and her . . . boyfriend." He fiddled with the game's marbles, moving them from his collection cup to the center starting position. "It got me thinking. Don't get too far down a path that doesn't make you happy. So I quit my job with the brokerage firm and showed up here. Thought I could keep an eye on my dad while I figure things out."

"So what are you gonna do?"

He smiled. "Still thinking that one through, and driving my aunt Hester crazy in the process." He smiled even wider. "I like the restaurant business. You never take it home with you at night. And every day, you start with a clean plate. Literally."

An outburst of voices and a thump against the wall sounded from the hallway.

"Should we keep looking for Jocelyn?" Keith asked, already stretching to a stand.

She was still nowhere to be found. They ended up back in the kitchen with two fresh beers.

"Do you think she left without us?" Jill asked.

"Why would she do that?"

"But how could we have missed her?"

Keith scratched his head. "You wanna play Ping-Pong till we find her? No one was using the table when we checked the basement. Double or nothing."

"I didn't realize there was anything on the hippo game."

"There's always something at stake."

"So what am I risking?"

"I'll tell you after I win."

Jill hadn't played in years, but found her game easily. Keith, on the other hand, swung too hard, the ball ricocheting off the walls, or took his eye off the ball, whiffing entirely, at times. With every miss, he looked at his paddle skeptically, as if for some flaw or defect. She beat him twenty-one to fifteen.

"Some night," he said, laying his paddle on the table. "Another epic loss."

"Let me guess," she said. "You'd been undefeated before this. An Olympic hopeful."

He smiled. "Olympics? That's for amateurs. I was going pro. About to embark on a world tour. This, however"—he gestured toward the table—"will kill my ranking."

"Tough break," she said.

There was a loud crash from a back room and a distinctive snorting laugh. Jill's stomach sank as she set her own paddle down. "I think I hear Jocelyn."

She and Keith walked across the room. A cloth curtain separated the finished part of the basement from an unfinished laundry and storage area. Jill pulled the panel to the side. At first, she didn't see anything, but then some movement in a pile of dirty clothing caught her eye. Jocelyn was tangled in the arms and legs of some guy. The fallen ironing board lay on the floor next to them. Jocelyn had presumably added her own dress to the pile of washing, as she was down to only her underwear and bra pulled down to her waist. She was on top and the guy's hands were inside her panties, cupping her butt.

"What the hell?" Keith said.

Jocelyn rolled off the guy, pulled up her bra, and began fumbling through the pile of clothes. "Where the heck is my dress?" she said in a boozy voice.

"Who the hell are they?" the guy asked.

Jocelyn found her dress and clutched it to her chest. "Silly, that's my sister and my boyfriend." She then leaned backward into the mound of laundry in a fit of laughter.

Keith's face clamped, a press of hard lines. "Happy fuckin' New Year to you, too." He took off, bounding up the stairs in four brisk steps.

"What the hell is wrong with you, Jocelyn?" Jill yelled. She, too, rushed up the stairs. Emerging into the kitchen, she heard the back door slam. She followed Keith out into the yard. He stood with his back to the house, shivering in the dark. She didn't know what to say, and as she hesitated the house behind her erupted into shouts. "Ten, nine, eight . . ."

"If you ask me," Jill said, "Jocelyn's an idiot."

"Five, four . . ."

"And drunk is no excuse," she said.

"One."

Keith whipped around. At first he seemed furious. Jill worried he would explode into some verbal, or even physical, tirade. She braced herself as the raucous chorus of "Happy New Year" pealed through the night air. Keith seized her by the shoulders and pulled her into a kiss. His right hand snaked itself up from her neck and deep into her curls while his left pressed her body into the contours of his own. His lips pressed hard on hers and his tongue explored her greedily. He let go, panting. "I'm sorry. You're going to think I did that to get back at Jocelyn."

Jill was still in shock. "Did you?"

He shook his head. "I'll admit I was pissed when I first saw them." He reached out and pulled Jill's pinkie and ring finger into his hand. "But the truth is, for about the last hour, I've been wishing I'd met you first."

CHAPTER FIVE

Fee

Tuesday Late Afternoon

"Drop me off here," Fee said.

"Good luck." Jill pulled the car up to the curb. "Break away—not a leg."

Fee sighed at her mom's humor attempt as she stormed across the field, backpack thwacking her butt while she dribbled the soccer ball left to right. She came to a tire-balding halt in front of the group of girls already passing balls back and forth. Crap. Marjory. Had she become even blonder and curvier in the two weeks since school let out? And why was she here, anyway? After making the ninth-grade cheerleading squad, Marjory had broadcast the news that she wouldn't have time for club soccer in the fall—an announcement that had been A-OK with Fee. Not only had it improved Fee's chances of moving from defense to offense, it meant an upcoming season without Marjory's inflated head blocking everything—the starting center position, Coach Wyatt's notice, and possibly even the sun itself. Marjory going out for the private—thus more competitive—fall club team meant she probably had her sights set on the spring high school team, too.

Fee, scowling at the prospect of going head-to-head with Marjory for another year, turned to her friend Cass. "What's she doing here?"

"Trying out like the rest of us," Cass said.

"Lucky us," Fee said, reaching into her bag and pulling out a LIVESTRONG band, which—speaking of luck—channeled hers.

"Uh-uh," Cass said with a shake of her head. "We make our own. Remember?"

With a sigh, Fee dropped the band back into her pack. The gesture was testament to Fee's trust in her SFAM—*sister from another mother.*

"Gather up," said an unfamiliar voice from behind. Fee turned to find an old guy in a tracksuit holding a clipboard.

"This is the U-16 tryouts," the guy said. Fee detected an accent similar to Magda and Borka's, but harsher, more clipped—something she hadn't thought possible.

A couple of girls continued their conversation.

"Ladies." He glared them into silence. "You give me your attention or you give me two laps." Clamped mouths indicated their preference of the two. "I am Coach Yuri and I will be replacing Coach Wyatt this season."

A ripple of surprise played over the small group. "Where's Coach Wyatt?" someone asked.

"Not here," was Coach Yuri's bark of a response.

No one dared asked for elaboration. Whereas Coach Liz Wyatt had considered soccer a game you *played* as in had fun, this Yuri character looked more the win-at-any-cost type—more KGB than BFF.

"Line up," Coach Yuri said.

Fee wondered what his experience was with that particular command. It'd be useful for—say—a firing squad.

"Two lines. We start with speed drills."

Coach Yuri tossed a ball about thirty yards and blew his whistle. Two girls raced to the ball. Whoever footed it first was offense; the other became, by default, a defender. They then battled it out to the goal at the other end of the field. It was no coincidence that Fee and Marjory lined up against each other. They'd been doing so for the past three seasons. It used to be a healthy rivalry between two close friends. Not so healthy anymore. Not since the Cedar Rapids tournament, where the team had lost in the finals: one to three. Postgame words had been exchanged. Fee had blamed Marjory for her two failed breakaways. Marjory had blamed Fee for letting three shots on goal get past her. Then Marjory had called Fee a loser, on and off the field. Fee may have, in response, called Marjory a stuck-up bitch. In truth, the disagreement had little to do with soccer. It was, rather, a hard boil of resentments left simmering for far too long.

Eighth grade had been a turning point in the once-tight trio of friends: Fee, Cass, and Marjory. For starters, Marjory had become the declared crush of half the boys in school, something Fee could have lived with had it not produced profound changes in Marjory's personality. She was becoming a hall-squealing, boy-crazy, popularity junkie: all the things she, Cass, and Marjory had once hated about the Godz—their own personal term for the arrogant better-thans, bigger-thans of the school. The term had originally been a shortened form of

Godzilla, but worked just as well as a reference to false idols. And it wasn't that Marjory was just emulating the Godz, she was becoming one—an almighty gargantuan of self-worship. As the school year came to an end and the move to a new building—the high school—had been contemplated, Marjory had pitched her strategy for success: she was to make cheerleading; Cass was to quit band and acquire a flatiron; Fee was to abandon her interest in the Geography Club, an organization Marjory had described as "Future Roadkill of America;" and they all three were to make the right friends. The last three weeks of school, Marjory had sat with "the right friends" at a separate table, leaving still-curly-haired Cass and wanderlust Fee with half-eaten sandwiches, an empty chair next to Cass, and glum faces. Cass, the peacemaker of the three, had predicted Marjory would tire of the phonies. It hadn't happened yet, but Cass's big black eyes were ever hopeful. Fee, on the other hand, was ready to offer next year's chair to someone else.

Fee and Marjory were up. Coach Yuri lobbed the ball and blew his whistle. Fee could feel every muscle in her legs grind as she raced down the field. She'd always had the height advantage, but somehow those twiggy uprights of Marjory's had traditionally pumped harder and faster. Joy burst from Fee's air-strapped lungs as she, a full step ahead, got to the ball first. There was no time to celebrate; Marjory elbowed her hard from behind. Fee knew all too well that possession was a disadvantage at this point. The dribbler had to time strides in relation to the ball, whereas the pursuer had no encumbrances, just an opponent in sight and a kick to block. Marjory gained the lead and rounded on Fee's right flank ten feet from the goal. Lefty Fee faked right, waited for Marjory's falter, and shot. Her kick bounced off the post, missing its mark.

"Clutch out again on that shot of yours?" Marjory asked.

Fee hung her head and braced her arms on her knees, a twofold out-of-air and in-frustration momentary collapse. She jogged back to the starting line.

"Your name?" a pen-in-hand Coach Yuri asked.

"Fee McCloud."

With the cap of his ballpoint, he scanned the roster. "Ah. Here. Felicity McCloud," he said, as if correcting her.

Fee noticed his *F*s sounded like *V*s.

"Was fast. Good." He looked up, scrutinizing her with squinty eyes of the palest gray blue Fee had ever seen. "Maybe I call you Velocity McCloud." He scraped his hand through the gray fringe skirting his bald dome.

Fee inhaled a big gulp of sweet confidence-filled air. Marjory crossed her arms over her heaving chest. It was either a new figure-enhancing bra, or Marjory, like carbon emissions, was a growing concern.

Fee thought back to last semester's dreaded science class, a third-period torture chamber in which she sat behind Marjory. The teacher, Mr. Gomez, had described a theory of evolution that believed attraction—i.e., species continuation—was based on brain chemistry. With all-too-bright eyes, he'd described scientific tests involving college-age male subjects, photos of random females, and increased brain activity and a flood of feel-good chemicals when the images depicted curvaceous women. Mr. Gomez had described the male subjects as snapping "to attention." Some smart mouth from the back of the room had called out, "Marjory has my attention." Marjory had swiveled in her seat to identify her admirer. Before turning back, she had whispered to Fee, "I guess that puts you at an attention deficit."

Fee looked down at her long, sturdy legs, boyish waist, and in-no-hurry breasts. Eat my dust, Mr. Gomez—and Marjory— she almost said out loud. Fee, no question the better student of the two, figured her type and Marjory's type had been going head-to-head since the days of loincloths and woolly mammoths. As Fee saw it, the advantage was hers. Smarter in situations—outmaneuvering a saber-tooth for instance—where cunning was required; and finally, yes finally, reaping the faster-than advantage her build predestined. Should one lone apple dangle across the clearing, Fee was sure her postpuberty Cro-Magnon counterpart would have reached it first—no bouncing pre-jog-bra boobs to slow her down. And Fee would choose survival over *attention* any day.

The rest of day one's tryouts went as expected. Fee and Marjory were the stars, locking eyes and going at it whenever they could. Never once cracking a smile, Coach Yuri wrapped up the session with "See everyone day two."

As they often did, Fee and Cass walked over to Dairy Queen after soccer. They were just sliding into a booth, dipped cones in hand, when the door opened and Marjory walked in with Logan Jones, the to-die-young-for hottie of Fee's grade. Practice over, Marjory had transformed herself. Her hair was pony-free and brushed out; she'd cinched her jersey into a hip-hugging knot; she'd slipped a denim miniskirt over her shorts; and had traded her cleats for wedged sandals. Fee—whose closet was way more Adidas than Abercrombie and who hadn't even removed her shin guards—watched as Logan dropped an arm over Marjory's shoulder and she, in turn, nestled into the crook of his neck. So they were an item. Since when? And as much as Fee didn't get all the fuss over Logan, a big ox of a boy—there was one thing she did get: the day's punch line.

Paleolithic Logan didn't give a rat's ass about Fee's smarts or stash of apples.

Fee watched them holding hands in line. He stepped away from the counter with a large sundae; she had a pop. Logan called over to a group of boys at a table near the back. Marjory, to Fee's complete surprise, slid into their booth next to Cass.

"Good tryouts," Marjory said.

Fee was too wary to respond.

"Thanks. You, too," Cass replied, practically panting with her readiness to forgive and forget.

A fat kid—around eleven or twelve with thick glasses and knock-knees—passed in front of their booth, tripping and spilling his shake down the front of his shirt.

"Must have his retard shoes on," Marjory said in a loud-on-purpose voice. She had the kind of vocals that carried, the way germs do.

"Marjory," Fee whispered pleadingly. She looked down at the table, not wanting to know if the boy—or his family only two tables over—had overheard.

"Why so touchy?" Marjory asked, her tone lowered now. "Do handicap parking permits run in your family?"

Glaring at Marjory, Fee thought *not mine*, but remembered walking into a basketball game behind Logan and his family and holding the door open for his younger sister.

"What'd you think of Coach Yuri?" Cass asked, changing the subject.

The question was obviously directed at Marjory as Fee and Cass had already declared him a Soviet defector in the witness protection program.

"Tough, but fair." Marjory took a big slurp of her pop,

probably diet. She was becoming the type of girl who didn't ingest calories in the presence of boys. For weeks, and from three tables over, Fee had watched Marjory's diminishing lunch tray.

Fee lapped a big tongueful of soft serve into her mouth. No way on God's great green soccer field did Marjory think Coach Yuri was fair. Something was up.

"Did you guys hear about that old lady who died, Hester Fraser?" Marjory placed her cup on the table. "You hear about that, Fee?"

"Yep." Fee cracked the last bite of her cone.

"My grandma knew her really well," Marjory said.

Neither Fee nor Cass responded.

"How about the nephew, Keith? You hear about him?" Marjory looked at Fee as she spoke.

"I met him," Fee said, fiddling with the tabletop saltshaker.

Marjory crossed her arms and sat back against the padded vinyl booth. She held Fee's stare for a long time, then turned to Cass. "Did your dad have a good Father's Day, Cass?"

As random a question as the girls had ever exchanged. Cass's dad was an insurance agent. Besides answering the door or providing the occasional ride, he rarely factored into their lives, never mind conversations.

"I guess," Cass said.

"Anything new with your family, Fee?" Marjory asked.

Though Fee was following Marjory's dropped hints— Hester, Keith, Father's Day, Fee's family—she was confused. When she asked her mom, just hours ago, the response that she'd met Keith "just after" had been end-of-story emphatic. She passed the shaker from hand to hand; salt granules skittered across the table.

"Why?"

"Not knowing anything about your dad must make Father's Day rough."

Fee hated the way Marjory was watching her with little piggy eyes for some sort of crack. And she was definitely steering the conversation. With her right hand, Fee brushed the spilled salt into her cupped left hand and quickly tossed it over her shoulder. Ever-practical Cass gave her a luck-is-dumb look.

"It's true I don't know my dad, but it's not true that I don't know anything about him. It's just . . . I'm not supposed to talk about it." It was a bold-faced lie, but Marjory deserved the detour.

"What's so top secret about deadbeat?" Marjory said, rolling her eyes.

Fee knew what kids whispered behind cupped hands. Poor Fee. No dad. No picture. No nothing. "He's not deadbeat; he's missing," Fee snapped, surprising even herself.

"What's the difference?" Marjory asked.

"As in a missing person," Fee said.

"Oh my gosh," Cass said, "you never told me."

Regret colored Fee's face. It was one thing deceiving Marjory, but there sat Cass: her dark eyes flared with concern.

"Sounds like the kind of thing people would know about," Marjory said.

"Know what?" Fee held her ground. "There was so little to go on that there really was no story." If Marjory hadn't been glaring at her with her eyebrows pinched together, Fee might have backed down, reined the story in. Instead, she unfurled it with a snap. "He was a foreign exchange student from Turkey"—the type of sandwich she'd had for lunch. "They met at Iowa. He went home for Christmas break, was expected to come back, finish the year, but he never did."

"Where's the mystery?" Marjory asked.

"He never made it back to Turkey either. He never boarded his connecting flight in Paris"—the topic of Fee's world cities report for social studies last semester. Her mind careened from a list of monuments to images from a made-for-TV movie where a guy had been shoved roughly into the back of an awaiting van. "Witnesses say he was with two men. That they were arguing."

"It's just like that show my mom used to watch," Cass said, "*Unsolved Mysteries*. The ghost stories and Bigfoot sightings were crap, but the missing persons' reports were the real deal."

"It happens more than you'd think," Fee said with an authority she never knew she had.

"So then how did you even know?" Marjory asked.

"The guy's parents have money. They hired investigators who talked to my mom, but they never found anything, ever."

"So if there are grandparents, how come you never talk about them?" Marjory asked.

"My mom never told them she was pregnant."

"Why not?" Marjory asked.

"The two guys he argued with were reported drug smugglers. My mom was scared. That's why she changed his name to something American and totally common." Fee never should have stayed up so late last weekend watching that movie. It had stuck with her, enough even to add an unnecessary layer to an already complicated story. Behind her navel, a burn of remorse began. "You guys have to promise you won't say anything. My mom would kill me." The first true thing she'd said for quite some time.

"Not to mention there'd be drug smugglers after your family," Marjory said.

"I knew I shouldn't have told you," Fee said.

"So what's up with that Keith guy, then?" Marjory scooted forward, lacing her fingers around the perspiring cup.

Something Fee was asking herself. "Nothing."

Marjory got up from the booth. "Crazy stuff. I hardly know what to think. So many stories."

"I've trusted you with a secret," Fee said, lowering her voice. "Do you promise not to tell?"

Marjory left behind a promise—and her empty cup.

CHAPTER SIX

Jill

Tuesday Late Afternoon

Jill spied a cozy threesome sitting in the Adirondacks at the edge of the pond. She smiled and was about to leave them to their repose, when a flash of red scarf caught her eye. Jill slipped into her garden clogs and skipped down the flagstone pavers, through the roses, and over the expansive lawn, noting Ruby's abandoned easel.

"Good morning," she said as she approached the trio.

A middle-aged man, whom Jill now recognized—with dread—as the fusspot from 202, brushed back a lock of stiff hair. "Good morning. My wife and I have been enjoying your lovely view back here." With a sweeping motion, he gestured to the dense woods that bordered the pond on the far side. "And your mother has been such charming company." Jill thought a chrome top, or even a greasy comb-over, would be better than the Ken-doll toupee. The wife, at least, was reserved, if a tad bland.

Ruby, for her part, smiled at Jill with the panache of a movie star. In fact, her large sunglasses and head scarf, tied under her chin, were vintage Grace Kelly. Jill was instantly alarmed. "Do tell, Mother, how have you been entertaining our guests?"

"I had heard this was once a home for wayward girls, but I hadn't known it was built as a commune," 202 said. "Your mother was just about to tell me more." With his thumb, he pushed thick plastic glasses up his nose.

Again with the home's history. Jill had always bristled at the word *commune*, the seventies having altered the conception of a goal-oriented community. "As my mother probably explained, my great-grandfather Angus McCloud was a Unitarian minister who devoted himself, and his own father's fortune, to the Transcendentalist movement. He built this house in 1898 as the cornerstone of a plain-living society. At the time, they owned over four hundred acres with eight small farmsteads operating toward a common goal." Jill had repeated the family's history so many times she had the speech memorized. Moreover, she had found it best to highlight this aspect of the home's past.

"Fascinating," 202 said. "What did they believe?"

This particular guest had Jill on edge. For starters, he was constantly underfoot, inspecting family antiques, examining paintings, and surveying the home. Even the appraiser who had corroborated in the loan transaction hadn't been as thorough.

"In pacifism," Jill said, "and in equality of the sexes, and even racial equality." There was also something false about him, though Jill couldn't quite figure out what. Probably the airs and pretensions, she thought, the guy likely grew up on Spam and Little Debbies. "No one held any personal wealth or derived any type of wage or salary. Everything was held for the glory of God and the community good."

"Ah," the man said. "Utopia."

And the final thing about the guy, the thing that made Jill's teeth grind, was that he was a big, fat, gotta-have-the-last-word, pain in the ass.

Ruby shrugged. "Sure, if you like backbreaking labor from sunup to sundown—six days a week, twelve religious services a week, and the overbearing scrutiny of the most pious, uptight, sexless, Scottish prick to cross the Atlantic." She snorted loudly. "Sex for procreation only. What a load of crap."

"Yes, well, by all reports, he was a character. And certainly committed to his ideals. He died at the ripe old age of ninety-one. Still, my mother never had the chance to actually meet him."

"I've heard the horror stories," Ruby barked. "He was a tyrant, a damned tyrant. It was my dear husband, Daniel, who finally pulled this family out of its black hole of religious fervor."

Jill knew it was too good to be true. Her mother regaling a guest with the historic significance of the home, exuding charm and grace. At least, Jill thought, this Ruby, riled-up and indignant Ruby, might slough off the news of Hester's death with all the import of last night's potato peels. "Mom, I wonder if I might have a private word with you."

Ruby heaved herself out of the chair with an agitated "Fine, but it better be good."

Jill wished 202 and his wife a pleasant day and steered her mother across the lawn. She waited until they were in the house and seated in their private quarters before she began. "I have some news," she said. "Hester died. The funeral's Thursday afternoon. And I've agreed to have the wake here Thursday evening."

Ruby clasped her hands together and brought them up close to her lips. She mumbled incoherently at first, and then managed an audible "The bitch is finally dead."

"Come on, Mom. It's all over now. Just let it go."

Ruby turned on Jill. "And why would you have that woman's wake in our home?"

"Mom, she's dead. What harm can it do?"

"What harm?" Ruby said, her voice shrill and agitated. "Well, she'll be bothering your father now, won't she? She'll get to him. I know she will."

"Please, Mom. It doesn't work like that. She's dead. It's over."

"You don't know her like I do," Ruby said.

CHAPTER SEVEN

Ruby

June 1965

"It will finish with a simple RSVP." Ruby enunciated the words with a ping of exasperation in her voice. "Yes, RSVP, the shortened form of 'respondez silver plate,'" she clipped, pulling the receiver back slightly and rolling her eyes in annoyance. "That's right." She couldn't decide if the printer was hard of hearing, a little slow, or intentionally goading her. As the deadline was tight, it had been his idea that she dictate copy over the phone. She suspected that he, like everyone else in town, had yet to warm to the notion of Ruby's new duties at the home.

Ruby heard a small rap at the door followed by a high-arching pip of a cough. Hester's long horsey nose appeared through the crack of the door and Ruby waved her in. "I will drop the hard copy by your shop later today." She hung up the phone and smiled wanly at Hester. "How were the roses?" she asked.

Hester had been waiting on Daniel for over thirty minutes. She'd amused herself with an inspection of the kitchen and a tour of the garden, but was getting impatient.

"Lovely as ever." Hester stepped across the room and leaned against the edge of Ruby's desk. A strand of her sleek bay-brown hair fell forward and she tucked it behind an ear. "Daniel says you're a very fast learner." She ran her finger across the large desktop calendar and let it trail to the top of the page, tracing the five, in 1965, with a loop of her index finger. "But you couldn't have even finished school," Hester said. "How old are you?"

"Nineteen."

"And with all your . . . personal difficulties . . . how far did you get?"

"Tenth grade. Plus half of eleventh."

"Well, then, you do incredibly well."

Ruby resented Hester's tone. It wasn't like Hester was that much older, four years tops. And who was Hester to talk? What did she *do*? What good was a fancy degree if all you did was prattle on about art, play tennis, and wait around for a marriage proposal like some spineless Victorian maiden. "I plan on finishing," Ruby said. "I always liked school, but they wouldn't let me stay."

Ruby had been an excellent student. A front-row, hand-in-the-air, shining example of diligence and determination. By second grade, her library card was tattered and worn. The town librarian had taken a shine to Ruby, likely realizing she was left unchaperoned after school. There wasn't much choice. Ruby's single mother, Esther, worked the counter at the Chelsey Diner from ten to six, five days a week, plus cleaned houses on the weekend. Poor thing. All those long hours probably contributed to her early death. She was certainly bone tired that night she stepped off a curb at two in the morning outside Jake's Bar, not paying attention and in a rush to get home to her unattended nine-year-old. Once under the roof of Aunt Mabel, Ruby had realized she'd have to hide her books and take care not to get too showy with her learning. Aunt Mabel complained Ruby was like her mother, a pretty blond head full of useless nonsense, and according to Aunt Mabel, "A fat lot of good it had done Esther. No husband, a kid to support, and slinging hash and mopping floors." Even throughout those pain-filled years bearing the derision of Aunt Mabel, Ruby had always been top in her class, until that morning when the school principal had called her into his office to discuss "her future." Aunt Mabel was there with her lips pulled so thin you could see the outline of her chipped front tooth. A counselor had hovered with such a compassionate show of pity and sympathy that Ruby thought the poor thing might sprout wings, and maybe even a halo. Two days later, Ruby found herself on a Greyhound bus headed north and clutching a pamphlet for the McCloud Home for Wayward Girls.

Hester crossed her long legs with an affectation that nettled Ruby's concentration. Hester was thin, painfully thin. Her clavicle looked like the wishbone Ruby had snapped on Thanksgiving Day. She wore silk stockings, black pointy pumps, and a teal-blue silk dress that darted in and around her skinny frame at impossible angles. Ruby stood. Her sweater was too tight and pulled across her breasts, making her feel large and exposed. She tapped the morning's files into an orderly group and turned to the file cabinet behind her desk, aware of Hester's pea-green gaze as she bent down. Hester made her feel all wrong, too busty, too curvy, common, pale, and colorless. As Ruby turned around, she found Hester holding a paper.

"Is this the invitation to the tea?" Hester asked.

Ruby had worked all morning checking—and rechecking—her spelling, grammar, and layout for the invitation to the home's annual fund-raiser. She felt a stab of mama-bear protectiveness at her labor in Hester's hands. "Yes."

"Should I have a look?" Hester asked. "I was a double major at Drake, you know, English and art history. I could proofread it for you."

Reaching over the desk, Ruby took the paper from Hester. All her life, she'd never liked help from anyone, even when her future looked bleak as tar. "Thank you, but it's not necessary. It's been checked. And besides, I've already dictated it to the printer over the phone. I just need to give him this copy later today as a formality." Ruby liked the word *formality*. It had an air of importance to it.

Hester gave Ruby a long, lingering look. "Suit yourself," she said. "Just thought you might like a second pair of eyes." Hester consulted her watch and sighed. "Oh, bother. We won't have time to stop at Merman's and look at the new canvases from Chicago." She stood and paced in front of the window. "I am determined to cultivate a collector's eye in Daniel, you know." Ruby wondered how much of an art collector anyone around here could be, but remained expressionless. "Do me a favor, Ruby. Remind him I'm waiting."

Ruby turned slowly. She was not Hester's employee, after all. "Of course," she said.

Daniel was making rounds with Dr. Perry. There were ten girls in the house. Six were in their last trimester and Glenda was on complete bed rest: pale, sickly, and in constant pain.

Daniel never liked to be disturbed during Dr. Perry's weekly visit, certainly not while the ward was so busy. Still, it was Hester. Her family was the home's largest benefactor, and she was Daniel's fiancée, no less.

Bounding up the wide front staircase, Ruby found Daniel and Dr. Perry in the corridor, their heads bent in consultation. She resented the position Hester was placing her in. She'd already told Daniel Hester was waiting, and he'd shaken her off with a firm not-now shrug of his head. But Dr. Perry had been here for ages already. Just as her mother had taught her, Ruby straightened her shoulders and advanced toward the two men. She wished she hadn't worn this old red sweater. It was tighter than some of her others and Dr. Perry's gaze always strayed. His eyes grew wet and bright when he talked to her, and he had an annoying habit of smacking and slurping his excess saliva.

"Miss Ruby," Dr. Perry said. "Always my favorite reason for visiting."

She nodded, avoiding his eyes. "Good afternoon, Dr. Perry."

"What can we do for you, Ruby?" Daniel asked.

"I'm sorry to bother you, but Hester wanted me to mention she's still waiting." Ruby saw a wave of annoyance play across Daniel's brow.

"Tell her we'll be done soon," Daniel replied.

Ruby found Hester on the sofa in the parlor, thumbing through a *Better Homes and Gardens* magazine. "They'll be down shortly," Ruby said, bending to straighten the stack of wholesome, family-oriented periodicals set out for the girls. "Can I interest you in something? Coffee, or tea?"

"You can interest me in something." Ruby was startled by the male voice. She looked up to find Dr. Perry. Daniel was just behind him.

Ruby straightened, blushing and hoping she hadn't exposed cleavage. She was never going to wear this red sweater again. Though it was as much Hester's once-over as Dr. Perry's that had crimson coloring her cheeks. "Of course, Dr. Perry. What would you like?"

"Now, there's a question with an easy answer." Dr. Perry rubbed his hands together. "I'll take whatever you're willing to give." He jabbed his elbow backward, nudging Daniel.

Daniel stepped forward, his face pulled in an awkward frown. "How about I have Cook rustle you up a cup of tea, Dr. Perry." Daniel, his back now to Dr. Perry, gave Ruby a quick nod, kind and apologetic. "Ruby needs to run to the printers for me." He looked at his watch. "In fact, you'd better not delay, Ruby." He encouraged her on her way with an almost imperceptible tilt of his head. "And, Hester, I'm sorry, but I'm going to have to meet you at your parents' later. I don't have time this afternoon for the gallery. Dr. Perry, I'll just pop into the kitchen and let Cook know about tea."

Ruby excused herself and walked back to the office. A moment later, Daniel entered the room. "Ruby, I'm sorry," he said. He took a step toward her. "He was inappropriate."

The office window looked out onto the petunia-lined flag-stone pathway and white entrance gate. It was, by far, the prettiest home Ruby had ever inhabited. It even smelled nice with honeysuckle climbing the trellises on either side of the front porch. From her tiny office, wafts of perfumed air folded her into a sense of calm and security. "It's nothing," she said.

He moved alongside her and turned her to face him by gently fingering the inside of her wrist. It was a touch so crushingly tender that her eyes welled.

"I want to know," he said, "has he ever . . ."

Daniel had never, in the two years since she'd come to his home, been in such close proximity to her person. Not even that tragic night he helped deliver Janine, when Dr. Perry's nurse had been held up by car trouble. Daniel's distance, his sense of propriety and decorum, was an enigma to Ruby. She'd grown up poked and prodded by the grubby pinching fingers of her uncle since she could first remember filling out her simple cotton dresses. Daniel confused her. For starters, he seemed older than twenty-eight. He carried his tall, thin frame with the hunch of a much older man. Also, he seemed above the caprices of a man in his twenties. This aloof manner had been a delightful novelty. Lately, though, she daydreamed of a happenstance that would throw them together in a confusion of time, space, and conduct. A tumble down the steps, a sprained ankle requiring his shoulder for support, or even a lift into his arms.

"You can tell me," he said. His gaze was intense, fiery even, and this was the first time Ruby allowed that they could, in fact, be on some sort of a collision course.

"No," she said quickly. "Please, it's nothing." In truth, Ruby had been wary of Dr. Perry for some time. He was forward with many of the girls at the home, the pretty ones anyway. But lately, since she'd become a permanent member of the staff, and no longer a charity case, he'd become more and more of a pest. It had begun following the death of baby Janine, whose cord-wrapped neck had fractured Ruby so completely that for a time a part of her had followed the tiny lifeless body into that black hole. She had no other way to cope with this void than to pull out her hair by the handful, until her eyes pooled with diversionary tears and clumps of blond fell to the ground. Daniel, and the others at the home, had been so worried by Ruby's strange melancholy that Dr. Perry had been called in regularly. The whole episode seemed to have allowed him some sort of familiarity with Ruby. And now he seemed to be escalating his advances and she feared he saw her as damaged or "as is" goods. And who was she to quibble over an impropriety?

There was a rustle at the door and Ruby looked up to see Hester's eyes narrowed onto the scene. Her voice was, however, calm and practiced. "Daniel, Cook wants to know if you'll be joining us for tea?"

Daniel let go of Ruby's arm.

Hester looked at Daniel, then at Ruby, and again at Daniel. "What should I tell Cook?"

Daniel's voice was gruff. "No tea. Thank you. As I said, I'm busy this afternoon."

Hester straightened her dress. "What a shame. And you force me to go to the gallery on my own." She stepped into the office and her eyes fell to the invitation left prominently at the center of Ruby's small desk. "The printer is, as you know, just a block away from Merman's. I can drop the invitation on my way." She smiled beatifically. "It's no bother. And this way Ruby doesn't have to go." Hester leaned over and carefully lifted the white paper. "It makes sense all the way around. Daniel can get back to work and Ruby can repay Dr. Perry for all his generous, unremunerated hours of community service by joining us for a nice cup of tea and a bit of pleasant company."

A week later, Ruby was called into Daniel's office. Hester sat in the chair opposite his desk with her long legs crossed at the ankle and her hands clasped primly in her lap. One step into the room and Ruby knew something was wrong. Daniel's face was the color of boiled rhubarb and he had pulled his normally crisp side part into a shaggy tumble of reed-brown hair. He motioned toward a stack of crisp white envelopes and square white cards on his desk.

"They're all ruined," he said.

"Ruined. How?" Ruby asked.

Daniel lifted a single card from the stack and read with irritation, " 'Respondez silver plate.' Silver plate! Is this some kind of a joke? It's *s'il vous plaît*. French for 'if you please.' "

Ruby gulped and took the card from Daniel. Her eyes scanned the bottom of the card in disbelief. "I never wrote 'silver plate.' I only wrote the abbreviation, 'RSVP.' The printer will tell you."

"I've checked with him," Daniel said. "He claims you stated 'silver plate' on the phone, and that it was written on the hard copy."

Ruby stammered. "I may have said it to him on the phone. I'm sorry, I guess I did think the phrase was silver plate, but I swear I didn't write it out. I only wrote the abbreviation."

Daniel scowled. "There are a hundred invitations here, Ruby. And they're all useless. We don't have the time or money to reprint."

Ruby's tummy felt a nagging pitch of shame and hurt, the way it had during the first four months she hid Janine under her apron. She had to think fast. Speed and tenacity had gotten her a good ways down the road from that miserable little gas station. She prided herself on escaping one jam after another, pressing a sweet pail of cider out of what another would consider slops and scraps. Ruby fanned the card to her face. Closing her eyes, she relived her labors over every detail of the invitation. She hadn't written the words out. She knew she hadn't. And why wouldn't an experienced printer have caught the error? She remembered their phone conversation and regretted the irritated tone she'd taken with him. She also remembered the way he'd made her repeat the phrase. Still, she simply hadn't written out 'silver plate.' Upon opening her eyes, she found Hester studying her.

"If only you had let me check the invitation like I offered," Hester said. She turned to Daniel. "All of this could have been avoided."

Ruby met Hester's expression of smug pity with an icy resolve. Ruby Jolene Renard might let someone get a head start, but they better watch their tail after that.

Ruby stepped toward the desk and scooped the invitations, envelopes and all, into her arms. "Don't worry," she said, "I'll fix them."

"Honestly, Ruby," Hester said with a scold. "There's nothing you can do . . ."

Ruby turned to Daniel. "I have an idea. If you'll just trust me . . ."

"Daniel," Hester said, "you'll just waste more time. Why don't you let me . . ."

"Please," Ruby said, "I can fix this."

Daniel looked from one to the other. "Hester, why don't we let Ruby get back to work?"

"But, Daniel . . ." Hester said.

"Everyone deserves a second chance," he said, and nodded to Ruby as she backed away with her arms full of cards and envelopes. "By God, it's the very foundation of this place."

Hester crossed her arms. "Well, then, technically this would be her third."

Ruby hurried back to her desk, stowed the misprinted invitations in her bottom drawer, retrieved her wallet from the top drawer, and hurried out the door. Winchester's Stationers closed at five, and Miller's Hardware at six.

At nine the next morning, Ruby nervously handed Daniel a revised version of the invitation. He took a long time reviewing it, turning the card front to back, and lifting the foil medallion with his finger to test its affixation. She had cut and glued into the corner of each invitation a three-layer decal of aluminum foil, lace doily, and white parchment. Within the parchment disk, she'd scrolled in a handsome script:

> *Open your calendar,*
> *and mark the date.*
> *We'll serve you from*
> *a Silver Plate.*

In a curve along the bottom of the affixed silver medallion, Ruby had penned "Inaugural Silver Plate Foundation Tea." And at the bottom of the invitation, she'd inked quotation marks around the infamous "Silver Plate" to make it seem a play on words. She hadn't matched the ornate brush script perfectly, but she had done a pretty good job, considering hers was handwritten.

Daniel looked up with a curious regard. "A silver-plate theme?"

"Yes. Well, the guests won't actually eat off the silver plates, there'll be a decorative holder under our traditional white plate. Jimmy, down at Miller's, has offered to cut and bevel the disks out of scrap plywood. He's even going to help me paint them silver. Reverend Havilland has already agreed to let us borrow the large silver offering plates for the scones and tea sand-wiches. I'll line them with white cloths. And I'm going to put little silver doilies between each saucer and cup." Ruby was talking so fast that she had to exhale with a great final gasp.

Daniel placed the invitation in the center of his leather desk tray. He propped his elbows on the desk and clasped his hands together, bringing his fists to his chin. "All right, Ruby. You've redeemed yourself." He smiled. "Funny enough, I was think-ing the event was getting a little stale. Maybe your theme will spark a little renewed interest this year."

Ruby held her ground. There was a remainder to the solu-tion that could prove messy. "What about Hester?"

"What about her?"

"If she tells her circle of friends it was a botch-and-patch job, then it will fail."

Daniel nodded. "I see what you mean. But don't worry, I'll talk to her. She knows how important this is to me, to the home."

The next two weeks were so busy that Ruby fell into bed every evening with aching legs, tired eyes, and a sense of purpose and industry she'd never felt before. Mrs. Harris, the head housekeeper, and Cook had been more than happy to hand over the annual chore of coordinating food, drinks, guest lists, florals, seating, and more to the industrious young secretary.

The two stalwart women had been slow to warm to Ruby. Daniel had not previously required a secretary, nor had any girl ever made the leap from home resident to staff member.

Their initial reserve was nothing new to Ruby. She'd been suffering the mincing disdain of adult women ever since she'd had to, humiliatingly, ask her aunt Mabel for a brassiere on her thirteenth birthday. Even Aunt Mabel, Ruby's dead mother's own sister, had acted as if Ruby had pushed and pulled the damn things into some sort of freakish swollen mounds. Regrettably, it would only be a few years later that Mabel's own no-good drunk of a husband would pinch and poke Ruby with a manic insistence and persistence that would eventually precipitate Ruby's departure. Ruby had learned the hard way that other women would hold her accountable for a pretty face and curves, because it sure wasn't Mabel's rooting swine of a husband who was sent away.

If nothing else, the tragedy surrounding poor baby Janine had at least smoothed Ruby's transition from ward to staff. Open hostility would have clouded the consciences of Mrs. Harris and Cook, good churchgoing women that they were. Distant and reproving, however, were perfectly justifiable to their way of thinking. Ruby had felt a pump of pride when Mrs. Harris had commented that Ruby hadn't "ruined things, yet." And even Daniel, who never rushed or wasted words, had already proclaimed it would be their best fund-raising tea ever. They'd presold more tickets, at a hundred dollars apiece, than any other year. Ruby couldn't wait for the event itself. Daniel would be beholden, positively beholden.

Ruby sat at the side entrance to the rear garden checking that the seating cards were in alphabetical order and neatly aligned. Guests would arrive shortly.

"How do I look?" Daniel asked.

Ruby, startled, looked up to see Daniel in a black tuxedo with tails, a top hat, and a silver cummerbund. "What?" she stammered. "What are you wearing?"

"Hester dropped it off this morning. A surprise. She left a note insisting I wear it and that I'll understand once our guests arrive." He smoothed the satin trim of the lapel nervously. "To tell the truth, I feel like a bit of a fool."

Ruby's mouth was dry. Her instincts told her Hester was up to something. "You look very handsome," she said. Indeed, he looked striking. His tall, thin frame suited the long cut of the coat. Wisps of his hair were combed back neatly and his doe-brown eyes sparkled against the crisp white shirt. Ruby stepped out from behind the table. When she'd dressed that morning, knowing she'd be on her feet all day, setting tables and carrying trays of food and drink, she'd opted for her old brown skirt, simple blue cotton blouse, and scuffed loafers. Moreover, Ruby had been working in the heat of the June day for hours. Her hair, pulled back into a simple ponytail, was lank and her bangs clung to her forehead in sweaty, oily clumps. Her underarms were damp and she was conscious of her musky odor.

Ruby heard a familiar ballyhoo and looked up to confirm her suspicions. Hester was walking across the flagstone path in a long silver satin gown that simply dazzled in the glow of the late afternoon. Her hair was swept up in an elaborate twist that must have cost her many dollars and many hours in the chair. She had tucked her beaded silver clutch between the flesh of her skinny forearm and bony chest. Years later, Ruby would catch but a glimpse of a woman stowing a book or tennis racquet or anything in this manner and be instantly transported back to the garden tea.

Ruby heard Daniel whistle low in a frank reaction of awe and appreciation. A roll of pain tumbled from Ruby's chest and exited her groin with a pinch and a prick. Hester stopped a few paces from them and, holding the evening bag away from her body, twirled with the grace and poise of a runway model.

"You look stunning," Daniel said.

"Why thank you," Hester replied. "You look very handsome yourself."

Daniel straightened his tie nervously. "What are you up to?"

Hester approached the table with two confident steps. "I've done what you asked. I have given this event my complete support. And I've taken Ruby's silver-plate theme to the next level. You wait and see. This will be the social event of the year."

Withering under Hester's smug look, Ruby tugged at her blouse, prying it away from her clammy skin.

Hester took Daniel by the arm. "May I have a word with you in private?"

A moment later he returned to the table where Ruby sat, expecting to welcome guests and hand them their place cards. "Ruby, Hester has offered to handle the welcome table." Daniel spoke softly. "Maybe it's a good idea. She knows everyone, and apparently there are quite a few newcomers this year." He picked at some small trace of lint on his cuff, averting his eyes from Ruby. "This way you can better manage the kitchen staff and the girls."

"But," Ruby said, "that's all under control."

"Hester really has gone out of her way," he said. "I didn't realize she was responsible for the increased attendance. She rattled off at least twenty of her acquaintances she's convinced to attend today. She'd like to be the official greeter." Daniel looked down at Ruby. His eyes registered regret, yet resolve. "I think it's a good idea."

Ruby shrugged and nodded. "Of course, whatever you

think is best." She pushed back her chair and stood. "I'll check on things in the kitchen."

As she walked across the grass, she saw Hester and Daniel, the illustrious host and hostess of the event, hovering at the welcome table. She kicked at a small weed at the edge of the flower border. Ten minutes ago she would have bent down to remove its offending presence among the bed of peonies and foxgloves. She entered the kitchen in a sour mood. The five girls who had been assigned the first half hour of serving sat around the kitchen table looking worn and weary. There had been a surge in pregnancy-related ailments that morning: cramps and backaches and fatigue. Granted, nobody liked to be put on display as the consequence of promiscuity and immorality, but, still, Ruby had thought they'd understood the importance of the event. If they had, they sure didn't show it.

"Come on, girls," Ruby said. "Smile, chins up, bellies out, and it will be done before you know it." She held the back door for them and walked them to the edge of the party, where the first guests were starting to gather. As she had suspected, they were dressed formally with glints of silver everywhere. Her seam-busting, every-day-garbed servers looked out of place, unseemly even, and she looked down at her own attire with irritation. Had it been last year's event, or the year before, she could have slipped in and out of the group without much differentiation. Guests had attended in light summer dresses, skirts, and pantsuits: simple and on the slightly casual side. Which, after all, made much more sense for an outdoor afternoon tea. There were still a few of the old guard who were dressed in such a manner, but the majority of the crowd, the younger ones—Hester's flock—dazzled in their silver finery. The men in waistcoats and jackets with fussy vests and bow

ties. The women in long flowy dresses of high sheen and stylish cuts that accentuated their bony backs and long necks.
Ruby chided herself for the ambush. She had thought of every
other detail. Why hadn't she treated herself to a new dress,
something bright and flashy? She would have gladly parted
with some of the savings she'd been hoarding for a rainy day.
She knew, now, that inclement weather came in many forms
and vowed to be better prepared next time.

Mrs. Harris brushed past her, stopped, and looked at her
watch. "What are you doing? You should be up front."

When Ruby had announced, two days earlier, that she
would be greeting the guests herself, Mrs. Harris had objected.
"We always have one of the girls at the entrance, not staff."

Ruby had waved this away with a simple directive: "Daniel
has allowed me to make some changes this year." Ruby had
been to the event twice now, once as a house member and
once as a staff member. As a house member, she had been the
one chosen to welcome the guests. She had bounced through
pregnancy easily and, at seven months, still wore her burden
high and fairly flat. She knew, herself, that she'd made an
impression on many of the guests. She'd been quiet, respectful, and a clean, bright example of the caliber of girl supported
by their generous donations. Last year, as a new staff member,
she'd been kept in the kitchen making sandwiches and arranging trays of pastries for the girls to pass. She'd watched from
the window over the kitchen sink as the area's social elite had
sipped and nibbled and mixed and mingled.

"There's been a change of plans," Ruby said to Mrs. Harris
with every bit of matter-of-factness she could lace through her
voice. "Hester has offered to greet the guests. It's very nice of
her, actually. It frees me up for other things."

Mrs. Harris tilted her head down and looked at Ruby over her eyeglasses. She then took them off for a proper look out to the garden. "Well, la-di-da," she said. "What is everyone wearing?"

"Isn't Hester sneaky? She must have been planning this for some time. And isn't it a wonderful idea?"

"If you say so," Mrs. Harris said. "And as long as you're not busy, could you keep an eye on the lavatory?" She wiped her hands down the front of her apron. "They may look like royalty, but they're no better than a pen of filthy pigs, the lot of them." Mrs. Harris bustled off muttering to herself.

Ruby kept to the house and perimeter of the party. She oversaw the girls rotating through their shifts, answered phones, and, from time to time, kept an eye on the lavatory: wiping down the sinks and keeping discarded hand towels off the floor. Toward the end of the party, she lingered at the low stone wall fiddling with the fragrant sweet-pea blossoms that had recently bloomed. She watched the flit of guests as they moved from one small circle to another. There seemed to be a cadence and rhythm that moved them in accord, so that one took the place vacated by another. It reminded her of a hoe-down she'd attended once with Aunt Mabel and her lump of a husband. Ruby had never been much of a dancer. To be fair, no one had ever taken the time to teach her. She'd been pushed and pulled and spun and swung by one partner after another over that dirty barn floor until she'd felt like a rag mop. Just once she wanted to feel a part of the machinery of something. She spied Hester and Daniel gliding across the lawn. He had his hand pressed gently against the small of her back and she dipped her head toward him as he spoke into her ear. Ruby scowled and headed back to the kitchen.

CHAPTER EIGHT

Fee

Wednesday Afternoon

Fee sat at the kitchen table and picked little green balls out of her egg salad. She hated it when her mom went all Martha on them and added capers.

Ruby walked in; closed the door behind her; and scanned the room as if looking for something, or someone. She wore a silk dress so shiny and purple it pulsated, and a nubby boiled wool sweater of marigold yellow. Fee thought her grandma was clutching her tummy in pain until she realized Booboo had something tucked under her sweater. Ruby then pulled out an empty wine bottle and stashed it under the sink with the other recyclables. Fee's eyes widened as she watched her wobble unsteadily across the floor and almost miss the chair she dropped into.

"Booboo, are you okay?"

Ruby looked around, a childlike innocence redrawing the lines of her face. "Why wouldn't I be?"

Fee craned her neck under the table to get another look. "That's some outfit you got on. What's the occasion?" Ruby, dedicated to her post at the check-in desk, favored dresses, but they were usually standard-issue, old-lady garb in dusty pastels.

Ruby adjusted her position, sitting higher in the ladder-back chair. "A woman does not need an occasion to take pride in her appearance."

Fee wasn't so sure that any woman accessorizing a Barney-purple dress with a Big Bird–yellow cardigan could talk about pride—even allowing for the fact that Fee had a bizarre aversion to yellow in all its bile-tinged shades.

"But are you celebrating something?"

"No."

"So what's up with the bottle?"

Ruby cleared her throat. "That wasn't mine. One of the guests left that lying around."

"Hmm." Even from across the table, Fee could smell the wine on Ruby's breath. She looked at her grandma and twitched her mouth side to side. Booboo was either a closet guzzler, cracking with old age, or the best damned acting talent never to be discovered. She had been the kind of blond beauty who could have easily gotten out of their little sinkhole of a town. She could have headed east to Broadway, or west to Hollywood. Instead, she got her pretty little tail trapped by a husband, two kids, and the conventions of the day. "Mom's not gonna like it if she finds out."

"Then our guests should dispose of their own empties, shouldn't they?" Ruby stood and straightened the pleats of her rumpled dress. "Well, have a nice evening, Janine. I'm turning in."

"Booboo, it's the middle of the day. And I'm Fee. Remember?"

Ruby stopped and braced her thick arms on the rungs of the chair. "No, no, no. All my girls start with a *J*. Janine, Jocelyn, and Jillian."

"Janine's dead, Booboo. She died at birth. I'm Fee."

Ruby shuffled off, muttering, "What the hell kind of name is Fee? It doesn't even start with a *J*."

Fee dropped a napkin over her sandwich and inflated her cheeks with a big puff of frustration. *What the?* Booboo had always been more partner-in-crime than parental unit, and always up for a good time, but what Fee had just witnessed was downright weird. And this wasn't the first time Fee had caught her drinking and hiding it. But she was an adult, right? And it wasn't like she was hurting anyone.

Thank God Aunt Jocelyn was on her way. It would be someone else, besides her busy mom, to keep an eye on Booboo. Fee checked the clock. Aunt Jocelyn was an hour late. Due at noon and it was already ten past one. And she wouldn't even have a good excuse. You gotta love that. Aunt Jocelyn was one of Fee's favorite people. She was proof to the notion you didn't have to grow up if you didn't want to. She lived in L.A. and—finding it paid way more than hair—did massage and color therapy for the rich and famous. Only someone as fly as Aunt Jocelyn could make a career out of back rubs and color wheels. She was three years older than Fee's mom, but looked and acted years younger. Her haircut and color were always killer. She kept her legs tight by kickboxing and her arms cut by rock climbing. And she never dressed for comfort like her mom. According to Aunt Jocelyn, she didn't dress to impress, she dressed to impale. She would say this while doing a knife-to-the-heart routine. Fee would never forget the time she actually saw a guy clutch his chest in reaction to Jocelyn in a tube top. Aunt Jocelyn didn't have a wardrobe, she had weaponry.

Fee got up from the table and opened the fridge. Of course there was no pop; her mom acted like it was a vice on par with cocaine or heroin. Fee exhaled in frustration at the selection of juices, green teas, and flavored waters. Aunt Jocelyn practically lived on Diet Mountain Dew. Fee loved the way she called it soda, never pop, she was so totally West Coast in that way. And she always drank from a straw, so as not to stain the porcelain veneers that cost her two thousand dollars apiece. Everything about Aunt Jocelyn and her life was cool, especially the distance she'd put between herself and Iowa. Fee got that decision of Jocelyn's. Fee's mom wasn't as impressed with Jocelyn's lifestyle. She didn't like California and speculated that Jocelyn was lonely and isolated amid the users, climbers, and wannabes of L.A. Though Fee knew her mom loved Iowa, loved their small town, and loved their historic home, she wondered about the left-out, sideline feeling of staying put your whole life. Fee got a little tired of her summer breaks being spent catering to others on vacation. For her part, Fee planned on being the one with a suitcase and a camera.

A horn tooted outside. She closed the fridge and hurried out the back door.

Jocelyn stepped out of a huge monster of a car, shutting the door with a back tap of her right foot. Her hair was long and blond with a couple of wispy flips framing her face and a few perfectly spaced big chunky orange highlights. She wore pencil-thin jeans and shoes so pointy they could pick ice. Though Fee's style was way more sporty, she admired her aunt's cool factor.

"Aunt Jocelyn!" Fee ran to her aunt and threw her arms around her neck. "What are you driving?"

Jocelyn gave a backward glance at the car. "It's a Hummer, the H3. What do you think?"

"Awesome," Fee said.

"It's perfect," Jill said, joining them in the driveway. She stood with her arms crossed, looking at the rental car and shaking her head in disapproval. "We can lead a small incursion into Canada while you're here."

"Why not?" Jocelyn winked at Fee. "Unlimited mileage." She took a few steps toward Jill. They hugged with a quick, shallow pull.

"So how much was this thing?" Jill asked.

"Who cares?" Jocelyn said. "It will be worth every penny if there's a funeral procession."

"Will you drive me to soccer in it?" Fee said, hopping up and down. "Please, please."

"We have to leave in just a few minutes, honey," Jill said. "Jocelyn probably wants to relax and settle in."

"Are you kidding?" Jocelyn jangled the key fob. "This hulk was built for making an entrance. So let's make it a good one."

"Thank you. Thank you. Thank you." Fee ran inside to grab her bag and cleats.

Fee's emotions progressed from surprise to shock to glee as Jocelyn pulled up over the curb and onto the grass, delivering Fee within inches of the painted white lines. It was definitely a no-driving, no-parking area, but Jocelyn didn't care. She wrestled the beast into park and climbed out the driver's side. Every girl on the field stopped their warm-up routine to gape. And it wasn't just the girls; Jocelyn had the full attention of both Coach Yuri and Logan, who had been nose to nose with Marjory.

"You can't park there," Coach Yuri said.

Jocelyn smoothed her hair and took a step forward—away from the car. "I'm not staying. Just dropping off."

"You can't drop off here either."

Jocelyn smiled and looked around. "Now, what happened to that road? It was there a minute ago." She brushed some imaginary dust from shoes red enough to make noise even on the streets of New York, but on a soccer field in the middle of the corn belt, they screamed volumes—and Jocelyn had everyone listening.

Fee could tell Coach Yuri was trying to suppress a smile, but he couldn't. Jocelyn got him. "Everybody gather up," Coach Yuri said. "We get started."

"Kick some ass," Jocelyn called through her megaphone hands, and then turned and scrambled back into the Hummer.

Fee dropped her backpack into the pile of scattered belongings. Logan came up behind her. "Nice ride."

She pulled her hair back and quickly looped it into a scrunchie. "Thanks."

"Who was that?" he asked.

"My aunt."

"Wow" was all Logan could manage before Fee jogged the dozen steps separating her from the huddled team.

Marjory, having observed Logan and Fee talking, scowled with open hostility. *Not a bad start to things,* Fee thought to herself. She'd pulled Marjory's head out of the game and diverted Logan with a look at the wider gene pool Fee represented. And Fee couldn't help but think of Marjory's fat-faced mother—not much DNA promise there.

Tryouts, day two, was a scrimmage. To no one's surprise, Fee and Marjory landed on opposite teams. The shocker was that Fee played offense while Marjory was given the task of defending her. Fee was warming to Coach Yuri, despite his brusque manner. The most satisfying turn of the day's events was not Fee's three goals; it was, rather, Cass's two goals for the other team. She had been chosen—over Marjory—as center and had stepped up. Her performance was worth a high five and big grizzly of a hug from Fee.

Logan—who'd watched the tryouts sitting among the jumble of backpacks, soccer balls, and water bottles—stood as Fee and Cass had collected their things. "Impressive," he said.

Cass's dark eyes flared in both size and luster. Her breath went raspy and even her black curls seemed to plump in reaction. "Thanks," she said in a voice so uncharacteristically high that Fee cast a wary eye for flying glass.

Marjory approached, shooting a suspicious glance from Fee to Logan to Cass. "Nice work, girls. I guess every dog has his day," she said airily as if a flip of hair and a show of teeth magicked nasty into nice.

Fee noticed Logan's head snap to the side.

Careful, Marjory, Fee thought, *or we'll all get a flash of just what's under that candy coating.*

Fee walked over to a nearby picnic table, threw her bag across its top, dug out her flip-flops, and collapsed onto the bench. She looked up and was surprised to see that Marjory had followed her. Logan and Cass remained some distance away.

"Rematch soon," Marjory said through clenched teeth.

"Looking forward to it," Fee replied, slipping off one cleat and then the other.

"By the way." Marjory stopped and kicked at a spiky weed with the toe of her Nike. "I think you should know, what you told us yesterday had me so worried"—she clutched at her chest, not even trying to make her act believable—"well, my mom could tell I was upset about something. I may have told her."

"May have?" Fee asked, yanking off a sock with an angry snap.

"Did," Marjory corrected.

Shit. Marjory's mother was one of those mombot types, a know-all, know-everyone busybody.

"And?" Fee asked.

"I think my mom will be calling your mom."

"Why?" Fee was too terrorized to link words together.

"Out of concern," Marjory said before jogging off.

A few moments later, Cass dropped next to her onto the bench. Fee slid her toes into her sandals.

"What was that all about?" Cass asked.

"Marjory blabbed everything to her mommy," Fee said with a snarl, "and wanted me to know."

"I didn't tell anyone," the ever-loyal Cass said.

Cass deserved to know the truth. Besides, that would make it seem like a conspiracy against Marjory, instead of an outrageous fraud. Hopefully.

"Hey, Cass . . ."

"Is that one with either of you?" Fee was startled by Coach Yuri's approach and looked up to view Borka storming across the grass.

"Yeah. My ride." Fee had hoped for a return trip in the Hummer.

Borka approached with her lips thin and tight. "You keep me waiting," she said.

Fee noticed Coach Yuri's head bob in curiosity, presumably in reaction to Borka's accent.

"I'll call you later," Fee said to Cass. She'd tell Cass it was all a joke that got out of hand, or a test to see if Marjory really was trying to be their friend again. Or she could text. Or maybe Marjory was bluffing. Fee knew sure as hell that there were plenty of things Marjory didn't tell her mom. She probably should have reminded Marjory of that yesterday. Fee trudged after Borka with tight calves and a twist in her gut.

CHAPTER NINE

Jill

Wednesday Late Afternoon

On duty at the reception desk for an AWOL Ruby, Jill heard the porch boards creak and looked up to see Keith filling the frame of the original carved walnut door. She smiled, although she felt a worming in her belly. At least this go-around she was the home team and had pulled together both a uniform and a game plan. She wore gray linen pants, a white eyelet cotton blouse, and her favorite black wedge sandals. Earlier, Jocelyn had inspected her and proclaimed a wardrobe absent of color exposed one's chi. Jill figured she'd worn these pants for at least a dozen business meetings and hadn't felt she flashed her chi at anyone yet. Regardless, this was going to be a no-nonsense appointment; a typed contract specified the menu, prices, hours of service, staff details, and payment terms.

Keith strode up to the antique check-in table and dropped

three tattered books on top of the contract that was to be her script.

"Good afternoon," he said. He wore a red short-sleeved cotton shirt and Levi's. He'd always worn Levi's. The car's seat belt had left a diagonal crush of wrinkles from his left shoulder to his right hip.

"Good afternoon," she said with his same almost formal tone. "What are these?"

Keith patted the top book with his hand. She noticed, and remembered, the surprisingly golden hairs that feathered his forearms, extending far down onto the backs of his hands.

"These were the only personal effects my aunt kept in her room at the nursing home. They obviously meant a great deal to her."

He leaned over to her side of the desk and flipped open the top book's cover. He smelled the same. All these years later, the guy still lathered up with Irish Spring.

"Here." He pointed with his index finger. "They're signed 'To H. With all my love, D.' *H* is obviously Hester, but I figured the *D* must be Daniel." He closed the book and rapped it with his knuckle. "I thought you'd like to have them, since they were originally your father's."

Jill stood and stacked the books on their side, quickly browsing the titles: *The Good Earth*, *The Grapes of Wrath*, and *The Confessions of Nat Turner*. "Thank you." Somehow this small distraction flustered her. "I do remember he liked Steinbeck," she said, fluffing her hair and regaining composure.

"I hope you don't think it's odd, given their broken engagement. Anyway, I figured they belonged here on your shelves. I would have just given them to charity."

"No. Not odd if they were signed by my father. Thank you." She gestured with her hand toward the back of the house. "Would you like me to walk you through the arrangements?"

"If it isn't the prodigal son returned," Jocelyn said, coming from behind Jill and barreling into Keith's chest for a full-contact, boob-squashing hug, one, Jill noticed, he seemed surprised by. "Like they say, lost socks, stray dogs, and all toes turn up eventually."

"I thought it was bad pennies," Keith said, straightening his shirt.

"Them, too," Jocelyn said, jutting her molten-chocolate-colored skirt against the desk. Her flamingo-pink blouse had a frilly collar that she fingered with her left hand.

Had she changed? Jill wondered. She'd been in jeans and an Aéropostale T-shirt, hadn't she? As she fiddled with the books, Jill's eye was drawn to the large, desktop calendar. In Jocelyn's handwriting, under her own "Keith, 4 p.m." notation, an all-caps "BREATHE" was scribbled. Jill huffed at a piece of advice she considered on par with other ridiculous expressions like "relax" and "loosen up." As if the intake of oxygen were voluntary, and bones, muscles, and sinew lightened on command. She lifted the small stack of books and placed them over today's box on the calendar.

"So what's the game plan?" Jocelyn continued.

"I was just about to go over tomorrow's arrangements with Keith."

"Sounds boring," Jocelyn said.

"It's a wake," Jill said. "There's no game plan because there are no games."

"Pity," Jocelyn said. "I'll leave you two to it, then." She

sauntered off toward the kitchen, her heels clacking across the hardwood floors.

"Sorry about that," Jill said. "She should have been more respectful."

"It's okay," he said. "I've had plenty of doom and gloom this week." He dipped his head to the side. "Besides, we played a few games in our day."

Jill's heart hammered up and down. "You sucked at Hungry Hippos."

"My greatest defeat to date. But I did manage a game or two of Monopoly on you. And Life—I owned you at Life."

Jill was thankful for the easy banter—a relief given the awkwardness of their previous run-ins and so unlike the way they'd originally parted—still, his choice of words left her with a hollow in the area where her heart had so recently pounded. *His* greatest defeat? *He* owned *her* at Life? On that one, she had to begrudgingly concede, though he had once peopled one of those tiny cars with a couple and four little blue and pink "brood" pegs and called it "their future."

"Should we start in the dining room?" she asked.

Though the plans were straightforward, Jill's tummy was jumpy as if she were in front of a crowd, not one all-smiles individual who was fully engaged, asking sensible questions, and wobbling his head in approval of every aspect of the event. She'd forgotten—or suppressed—the uncanny way his eyes followed her, focused on her, so clearly relegating all else to the periphery. She wished he would stop.

They ended up in the lounge at the window overlooking the brick terrace and view of the pond.

"I always loved this house." Keith walked to the floor-to-ceiling fieldstone fireplace and rubbed his hand along the rocked front. "I forgot how massive this thing was." He gave it a good tap with the flat of his palm.

"The home was built before central heating," she said.

"This would have done the trick."

"Plus the other six original fireplaces upstairs."

"Six?"

"Twelve now," Jill said. "When I remodeled two years ago, I added six more and converted them all to gas."

"The place looks great."

"It did bump the property up to four stars." She failed to mention that it had also bumped her monthly expenditures beyond what she could afford.

She wondered if he had to think about anything as crass as money. Hester's estate had long been the subject of gossip, but no one knew for sure how much, if anything, remained. The business end of their meeting had concluded so quickly, too quickly.

"Can I get you some coffee or tea?"

"No, thank you."

Too bad they weren't arranging a wedding. There would have been a lot more to discuss. And even possibly a rehearsal dinner to coordinate as well. They might have spent the better part of the day together planning a wedding.

Jill was so paralyzed by the inanity of these thoughts, her feet froze. She braced herself against a club chair.

"Are you okay?" he asked.

"Yes. Fine."

A wedding for which he was the planner could only be his. He clasped his hands. "I enjoyed meeting Fee."

A comment that did nothing to improve things.

"She's very pretty," he continued.

Worse still.

"And you." He held his palms open. "Look at you. You haven't changed a bit."

"Libations," Jocelyn said, stepping into the room with a tray of drinks balanced on her right palm. "Dirty-tinis, my specialty." She held the tray up to Jill and Keith.

"I shouldn't," Jill said, checking her watch. "I have to set out the nightly wine and cheese for the guests."

"Fee's got it under control," Jocelyn said. "She's putting it out on the patio. It's going to be a gorgeous evening." She waved the tray back and forth, causing the drinks to lap against the sides of the wide-rimmed glasses. "Help me out here; these things are getting heavy."

Keith relieved her of a drink. Jill did the same.

"I do like a good dirty martini now and then," Keith said, lifting the glass in a toasting gesture.

"Here's to it," Jocelyn said, raising her own. "The dirtier the better."

Keith spluttered and coughed either in reaction to the drink's potency or to Jocelyn's obvious innuendo.

Wary of both, Jill sipped at the brackish liquid. She'd never been much of a gin fan, but the salty olive juice did much to improve the Pine-Sol-ish aftertaste. She took a bigger swallow, and then another.

"Let's have a seat and relax," Jocelyn said, plopping herself smack-dab in the middle of one of the two face-to-face sofas. Keith settled against one of the arms of the opposing couch. Given Jocelyn's squatter's sprawl, Jill had no choice but to sit next to Keith.

"This is nice, isn't it?" Jocelyn said, crossing her legs and unfurling her non-drink-holding arm across the back of the sofa.

Jill took another swig of her drink. It was nice, she had to admit. Very nice. An unexpected cocktail so early in the day: a luxury she rarely enjoyed given she was usually waiting on others. With another slurp, she felt an overall sense of cheer slide down her throat, ripple over her tummy, and continue down to her toes with a small fizz. She deserved this; she vowed to do it more often.

As if this small pledge had angered one of the more spiteful of fates, Fee appeared in the doorway. "Mom, one of the guests spilled. What gets red wine out?"

Jill stretched to set her empty drink on the coffee table. Before she could react, Jocelyn was halfway to the kitchen. "I'll take care of it."

Jill called through cupped hands, "Dish soap and hydrogen peroxide. Both are under the kitchen sink. And blot, don't scrub."

"I thought it was club soda," Keith said.

"Doesn't work nearly as well. Even white wine works better."

"White wine?"

"Yes."

"On top of the red?"

"Yep."

"So, should one of your guests spill red wine down their front, one of your remedies is to spray 'em with white. It sounds like fun, anyway. How do you get out ketchup stains?"

"I guess I should try mayo," she said, beating him to his own joke. "Although, I've got one underfoot right now that I wouldn't mind hosing down with mustard—*gas*."

He laughed, shaking the sofa. She covered her smile with

her hand. It was wrong, deliciously wrong, to disparage a guest. She then placed her hands at either side of her, intending to get up and check on Jocelyn and Fee.

"A light moment is just what I needed," he said, fidgeting and dropping one of his fists over her flattened, palms-down hand. "I knew I was looking forward to today's meeting."

She froze, the ball of his hand still resting on hers. It was an innocent gesture—one clenched mitt resting atop the back of another's hand—nothing like the way their fingers had once intertwined seemingly of their own accord. From the dining room, Jill saw Jocelyn advancing with two more drinks in her hands.

"Refreshers," she said, eyes zeroing in on their point of contact.

Keith pulled his hand away, lifting both in a shieldlike front. "Not for me."

"Jill!" Ruby's voice croaked from the hallway.

By her mother's plaintive tone, Jill could tell she had some sort of grievance or ailment. A moment later, Ruby pushed around the door frame. Again, she wore a head scarf and dark sunglasses, but this time with a frilly sleeveless nightgown. She held her fingers to her forehead as if it were in danger of detaching, the effort of which caused both her forearms and pendulous breasts to jiggle. "I have a splitting headache and can't find any Tylenol."

"Did you check my bathroom?" Jill asked.

"Empty bottle," Ruby said.

Jill shot a quick look at Keith, who had graciously walked back to the window for another look out onto the property. "I've got some in my purse. I'll bring them to your room in a minute." Ruby shuffled off with a wobbly gait and Jill was instantly alarmed. Bleary-eyed and in her pajamas at five p.m.? She wasn't just drinking, she was drunk. It wasn't the first time Jill had had suspicions about Ruby overindulging, which Ruby categorically denied—but this was obvious. And what must Keith think? The whole damn household, guests included—Fee the only exception—was on some kind of bender. Jocelyn, to fan the flames, stood holding one of the drinks she had offered to Jill and Keith, while knocking back the other.

"I'm sorry," Jill said to Keith. "I should check on my mom."

Keith batted her apology away with a swipe of his hand. "I need to be going anyway. Visitation hours. And Hester never did like to be kept waiting."

CHAPTER TEN

Jill

Wednesday Night

Patio tidied, Jill headed for the kitchen. Though she was already to-the-bone tired, she knew a head start on some of the next day's preparations would lighten the load of an already stressful day.

"So what are you wearing to the funeral tomorrow?" Jocelyn had arranged two kitchen chairs face-to-face. She had her butt on one and feet propped up on the other. Her toes were splayed wide in a foam separator and she was painting her toenails with careful strokes of hot-pink polish. Dinner dishes littered the table and darkness pressed in from the window above the sink.

"I'm wearing my red dress," Ruby said, appearing in the doorway. "And I'm sitting in the front row."

Jocelyn raised her eyebrows and smiled at Jill. "I was asking Jill, Mom, but gotta give you props for an interesting choice."

"Glad you're feeling better, Mom," Jill said, suspecting again—despite her mom's denial—that the headache had been hangover induced.

"Tylenol kicked in," Ruby replied.

"And we've discussed this already," Jill said. "It's probably best if you stay here. In case one of the guests needs something." She placed clean white mugs onto a painted black tray, prepping for the next day.

"Bull." Ruby smacked her open palm on the kitchen counter. "She ruined my wedding day. It's only fair I ruin her funeral."

"I'll tell you this much, Mom," Jill said. "Unless you wear something black and respectable, and promise to behave, we're not taking you. You have no car and no license, remember?"

Ruby rolled her eyes and shrugged. "I'll call a cab."

"They won't come," Jill said. "You're blacklisted." The result of an incident involving Ruby, a spontaneous casino junket to Meskwaki, a $287 cab fare, and a new friend named Artie.

Jocelyn snorted with laughter, bringing her hand to her mouth. "Blacklisted by the local taxis. You couldn't make this shit up." She dipped the tip of the brush into the tiny bottle. "Maybe I'm the one you should be worried about. No one's asked me what I'm wearing."

"Why?" Jill asked, wariness implied in her tone. "What are you wearing?"

"The most heavenly little black dress on earth," Jocelyn replied. "It's a Ralph Lauren halter made of crepe de chine."

"It's a funeral," Jill said, "not the Academy Awards."

"Yeah, well, even if I ever scored a ticket to the Oscars, it's not like it would be an occasion where I'd be in attendance with my sister, an ex-boyfriend of both of ours, my mother, and her sworn enemy and rival."

"Why do I have to keep reminding everyone that Hester is dead?" Jill stood holding the tray of mugs, inching toward the door to the dining room. "You all act like she's still a force to be reckoned with."

"If the casket's open, then she'll be dressed, and then she counts," Jocelyn said. "I plan on outdoing every woman in the room, including the dead one."

"She's like seventy. She'll probably be laid out in some old froufrou dress." Jill pushed the swinging door open with her foot and was surprised to find Fee on the other side.

"Jesus, Fee, you're the second person this week to startle me in here."

"Who was the first?" Fee plucked an apple from the fruit bowl on the sideboard. "Did the ghost of Hester pay you a visit?"

"Not you, too?"

"Booboo says she'll be the haunting kind of ghost."

"That's crazy talk."

"Was what Aunt Jocelyn just said crazy? About that Keith guy being an ex of both of yours."

"You heard that?"

"Yes."

Jill set the mugs down. "Not crazy. Just old news."

"So what's the story?"

Jill put her hands on her hips. "Boy meets Jocelyn. They date. Boy meets me. We date. Boy leaves town. End of story."

"I think you left something out," Fee said.

"Like what?"

"Like the part where you get from the boy dating Jocelyn to the boy dating you."

"It was casual between Jocelyn and Keith. You can ask her yourself."

"Ask me what?" Jocelyn said, swinging open the kitchen door. The white foam separator still splaying her painted toes.

"Fee overheard what you said about Keith. I clarified that you and he were finished. After which Keith and I dated for a few months before he left town."

"All true," Jocelyn said. "Missing a few details, but accurate."

"What details?" Fee asked, eyes brightening.

Jill's breath caught. She had hoped they'd finished this conversation at the farmers' market. She'd been bracing herself for this line of questioning since the moment she'd known Keith was coming back. All her life, Fee had no choice but to accept Jill's explanation that her father wasn't in the picture. Period. Still, it was only natural that she wanted more. *What did he look like? Where was he from? What did he do? What was his ancestry?* Jill had been providing the bare minimum of information since Fee was old enough to wonder why God made lima beans, and why she had no daddy. The last thing she needed was Jocelyn chiming in with her version of events.

"Nothing of importance," Jill said, locking eyes with Jocelyn.

Jocelyn snorted. "Keith didn't think it was nothing when I cheated on him."

"You cheated on him?" Fee asked, her mouth agape.

Jill shot Jocelyn a stop-now glare.

"My bad," Jocelyn said. "Your mother, on the other hand, would never behave that way. Not to anyone, never mind the love of her life."

"He was the love of her life?" Fee asked, her chin pulling back.

Jill flared her eyes and bobbed her head forward at Jocelyn.

"It wasn't unrequited or anything tragic like that," Jocelyn said. "He was just as gaga for your mama as she was for him."

"Then I don't get it," Fee said. "What really happened? And if I have the timing straight, it means that Mom would have been . . ."

"Coming, Mother," spill-the-beans Jocelyn said in response to a silent kitchen. She then disappeared back through the doorway, leaving Jill to the mess.

"Mom? What was that all about?"

Jill shook her head. For one who claimed extrasensory abilities and ultrasensitive intuitions, Jocelyn had just been the equivalent of a *blind* bull in a china shop.

"Jocelyn, as usual, said too much, but—trust me—it doesn't change anything."

"But—"

"Honey," Jill interrupted, "when Keith left town, he had every right. Do you understand me?"

"Yes. I think so, anyway."

"Good. Because it's old news and wouldn't change anything." Jill pushed open the kitchen door. Jocelyn had decamped; Ruby was gone, too. "It's late. Time for bed."

"But . . ."

"No buts. See you tomorrow," Jill said, holding the door open for the cement-shoed Fee. "Sweet dreams."

Watching Fee slump her way through to their private quarters, Jill mused that her own dreams had been soured years ago.

CHAPTER ELEVEN

Fee

Thursday

Fee and Ruby were in the kitchen rolling silverware into napkins for the evening's event—a dead-lady party, as Ruby called it—when the phone rang.

Fee stood and answered it. "Hello."

"Is that you, Fee? It's Mrs. Miller. Is your mom home?"

Crap. Marjory's mom. "No. She's out." She wasn't. She was upstairs.

"Who is it?" Ruby asked.

"Who was that?" Mrs. Miller asked.

"My grandma."

"Can I talk to her?" Mrs. Miller asked.

"What?"

"Can I talk to Ruby?"

"Oh. Sure." Fee passed the suddenly-leaden handset to Booboo. "It's my friend Marjory's mom. I'm not sure what she wants."

"Hello," Booboo said. Booboo was silent for a long time, listening.

A jagged edge of Fee's thumb's cuticle had been bothering her all day. She dug at it with the nail of her middle finger.

"A Turkish exchange student," Ruby said.

Shit. Fee scraped her thumb against the rough denim of her cutoffs.

"Could you repeat that?" Ruby asked, after which she was, again, quiet for a long time.

Fee brought her thumb to her mouth and bit down along the side, removing both nail and skin.

"Drug smugglers!" Ruby said. Her voice was high and thin.

Acid began trickling through Fee's veins. Everything hurt: her head, her stomach, and the darn gash she'd ripped in the side of her thumb.

"I can't tell you how distressing this is," Ruby finally said.

Fee pressed her eyes shut. She was about to be outed to Marjory. An outing she deserved, but would still hurt like a friggin' cannonball to the head. And what would Cass say? She hadn't called or texted her like she meant to. She'd been too chicken.

"None of this should have been revealed to her friends," Ruby said.

Huh? Fee opened her eyes.

"My daughter has never chosen to go public with this story. I'm sure you can appreciate her concerns and, therefore, respect her privacy."

There was another long pause.

"I'll tell her you called," Ruby said, setting the phone on the table.

"Thank you," Fee said in a small voice.

"For what?"

"For covering for me with Mrs. Miller."

"Who's Mrs. Miller?" Ruby's mouth was set in a pucker and her brows lifted with mischief.

Fee could think of only one reason for such a conspiratorial look. "Booboo, did we just make some kind of deal? You know, because of the wine thing yesterday?"

"What wine? I don't know anything about any wine."

Fee sat staring at Booboo. She honestly didn't know if she was negotiating with a shark or a flounder. Once again, she wondered if she should talk to her mom, but really didn't want the conversation with Mrs. Miller divulged as a consequence. Not like her mom would have time today, anyway. She was a wheels-up, burning-rubber taskmaster, one Fee knew to get out of the way of.

Later that day, Fee stood in a corner balancing a tray of hors d'oeuvres on her flattened palm. She felt like an idiot. She was supposed to be circulating and passing the Gorgonzola puffs. *To hell with that,* she thought as she popped one into her mouth, and then made a face of disgust. Blech. She scanned the room for her mom and saw her talking to Aunt Jocelyn and that Keith guy. Her mom had the day off; she hadn't been forced to act like some hired hand at one of the biggest turnouts this town had seen since they'd thrown a parade in honor of Joe Hodder's state wrestling title. Two old guys passed behind Fee. One of them said, "Must be the sister from California."

Fee looked again at the trio. A shaft of light streamed through the floor-to-ceiling floral drapery panel, spilling a wash of pastels over the three of them. Aunt Jocelyn threw her head back and laughed. *At least someone is having a good time.*

Fee's breath caught in a tangle when she observed Mrs. Miller come into view and pass uncomfortably close to where her mother stood chatting. Mrs. Miller even seemed to pause, contemplating a break into the conversation, but then was called over by another group of women. Fee exhaled an anxious breath. She set the tray down on the sideboard, untied her white apron, and stuffed it into one of the drawers. She straightened the skirt of the dress Aunt Jocelyn had lent her. Leave it to Jocelyn to bring no less than three black dresses. Jocelyn was wearing the killer halter, but she'd let Fee have her pick of the other two. She'd chosen the nubby silk one with a satin off-the-shoulder band. Though it was loose through the butt and hips, Fee felt great in it, incredibly grown up.

Two antiques approached the tray she'd just set down. Fee didn't recognize them, but there were a lot of people she didn't know. She shook her long brown hair into her face. Hopefully, they wouldn't remember her as staff and ask her for a fresh drink or clean towels for the toilet. Fee backed toward the window, pretending to need its small shaft of the clammy afternoon's pitiful breeze. The fat one reached out with thick fingers and popped a roll into her mouth. She chewed with her eyes shut and there were tiny flakes of crust stuck to the waxy lumps of her burnt-orange lipstick. She reopened her eyes, which were bright with piggishness. "Well, now, isn't that a cozy trio." The woman tilted her head toward the far corner of the room, where Fee's mom was still talking with Aunt Jocelyn and Keith. "What do you think will come out of it this time? Another mystery child?" She shook with a low, conspiring chuckle.

The other one, with blue cotton-candy hair, shooshed her. "Really, Maude. Behave. I hear she's a nice girl, and pretty by all accounts."

"It's a wonder he dares show his face around here," Maude said. "Poor Hester, having to endure the gossip and innuendo he left in his wake."

"I don't know, I'd put my money on her running him off. Any whiff of a mess and Hester cleaned house. Her brother, for instance."

"Like father like son," Maude said.

"I always liked William," Blue Hair said. "I had a thing for him myself, once upon a time."

Maude snorted. "Ruby ruined him. It wasn't enough to have Daniel, she had to have William, too."

"Now stop it. Who knows what really happened there?"

"A lot of good it did her, anyway," Maude said. "Just look at her."

Fee snuck a glance backward. Her grandmother was posed provocatively on the rolled arm of a sofa. She had a glass of red wine in one hand and the other on the arm of an old man.

"I need to find the ladies'," Blue Hair said. "Too much decaf."

"I'll come with you," Maude said. "I want to see what they've done with the rest of the place. I hear it's not bad."

Fee watched the two old ladies walk away, and then she glared at the threesome of her mom, Aunt Jocelyn, and Keith. Her mother's he-had-every-right-to-leave denial had seemed pretty rock-solid. But what did that really mean? And if she couldn't trust her mom, then who could she trust? In frustration, she groaned Marge Simpson style and then headed for her room. As she passed Ruby, she overheard her say to her gentleman friend, "Once upon a time I might have."

CHAPTER TWELVE

Ruby

July 1965

Ruby sat on the front porch sipping lemonade. Daniel and Hester had just left for church, Hester departing with one of her smug "I'll pray for you" exit lines. If there was a God, Ruby figured He wouldn't need the likes of Hester to do His recruiting. She really had some nerve. Ever since the disastrous fundraising tea, Hester had been parading around like the Dairy Princess at the state fair. And worse still, she and Daniel had set a wedding date for October, only three months away. Before the tea, Hester had been carrying on about how June weddings were a Fraser family tradition. Now she seemed to be in some great rush to the altar. Ruby knew it wasn't for the reason that sent many a young couple dashing down the aisle while the bride's dress still fit. No, Ruby knew it'd take a solemn vow—and possibly a crowbar—to pry Hester's bony knees apart. It was, rather, Hester's primal reaction to a territorial challenge.

Ruby heard the rumble of an engine and the crunch of gravel and looked up to see a car pulling into the driveway. Not just any old car, a convertible, tar black with cream panels, and chrome so radiant that Ruby had to fight the urge to fan herself. The driver pulled to a stop, climbed out of the car, and took a few loping strides to the porch steps. He paused with one foot on the second stair, one hand on his waist, and another stroking his chin.

"Would you happen to know where I might find Daniel and Hester?" He smiled pleasantly and had such a relaxed and unhurried air about him that Ruby didn't mind one bit that he hadn't bothered to introduce himself. He was tall with sleek brown hair and had the build of an athlete. The sleeves of his crisp white shirt were rolled to his elbows, exposing tanned and muscled forearms.

"They just left for church."

"Bother," he said. "Late again and now I've missed them." He bent to rub a small scuff from the point of his wingtip. "At least I can rest assured ol' Hissy will pray for my lost soul."

Ruby had always found a certain charm in playful irreverence. "Hissy?" she asked with a small smile.

"Sorry," he said. "Just a nickname I have for Hester." He took two steps, mounting the porch steps, and extended his right hand to Ruby. "And here I haven't even introduced myself. William Fraser, Hester's brother."

Ruby shook hands, but was so surprised by this announcement she could think of nothing to say. And then all of a sudden it made perfect sense. The features, which were so horsey and mannish on Hester, had somehow reworked and reassembled themselves on her brother so as to be pleasant, handsome even.

"And you must be Ruby. My sister has mentioned you." He pulled his hand from hers and she instantly missed its dry warmth. "Of course she failed to mention you were the kind of pretty that turns angels green." He winked at her. "Then again, I wouldn't expect her to have much appreciation in that department." He rolled his eyes. "An art major, no less."

Ruby nervously brushed her pale blond hair back behind her shoulder. It was getting long and had a tendency to plump and coil in the humidity. "You could wait for them. They usually come straight back here. Would you like a lemonade or iced tea?"

He looked at his watch. "They won't come straight back today. We've got a reservation at the Fairview for lunch. I suppose they'll expect me, even if I missed church."

"Oh." Ruby was vexed. As Sunday was Cook's day off, Ruby had, herself, assembled two cold plates of fried chicken, sliced tomatoes, and corn muffins. They were wrapped in wax paper and stacked neatly in the icebox. A small gesture she performed each Sunday above and beyond her stated areas of responsibility. Daniel could have at least let her know of his plans.

"Would you like to come?" he said.

"I beg your pardon?"

"To lunch. How would you like to come?"

Ruby colored. "Thank you, but I couldn't."

"Why not?"

She fingered the collar of her blue cotton blouse. "It wouldn't be right. I wouldn't be welcome."

The brown of William's eyes darkened to turf. "That's a load of muck. Wouldn't be welcome by whom?"

Ruby wished she hadn't said anything. "I didn't mean unwelcome really. It's just Daniel's my boss and—"

"So. I know he's a little stuffy and Hester's probably got him on a pretty short leash, but is he really all that strict?"

"No. He's not like that at all. It's probably me. I'd feel funny." She squirmed in her seat and made a small gesture toward her form. "I wouldn't even know what to wear."

"I think you look just fine right now." He dipped his head and pursed his lips. "Plus, I bet you could make an old dish-rag look good."

William fixed his eyes on the chair next to Ruby's and nod-ded in its direction. "Tell you what. I'll take that glass of iced tea you so politely offered and then I'll wait right here while you change." He lowered himself into the porch chair, stretch-ing his long legs out in front of him.

Ruby's breath got all tangled. She'd never been to the Fair-view. By all accounts, it was very classy. Still, she recoiled at the thought of Hester's face when . . . Then again, Hester's face. Ruby's mouth tilted up playfully. "What should I wear?"

William sat back and stroked his chin with long fingers. "Do you have a red dress, by any chance?"

She didn't, but she had one of such a deep, fleshy coral that Sophia, one of the new girls, had once referred to it as "titty pink." She cleared her throat. "Will something in the pink family do?"

He grinned. "It certainly will."

Ruby rushed to her room and dressed in a flurry of nerves. She'd worn the dress to the home's Easter party, but that after-noon had been unseasonably cool and she'd kept the matching jacket on all day, buttoned tight. She'd boil in the jacket today, so left it hanging in her small wardrobe. She looped a strand of pearls, the only possession she had of her mother's, behind her neck and fiddled with the clasp. Checking the mirror, she was a little self-conscious of the fact that the dress, with its thin shoulder straps and heart-shaped bodice, accentuated her bust. From a drawer, she pulled an embroidered shawl of cream silk. It was frayed at the edge and some of the stitching was loose, but it would have to do. She wrapped the shawl around her tightly and hurried back to William.

He stood as she stepped onto the porch and then whistled low. "Well, hello again," he said in a voice so heavy and slow Ruby thought he might need a winch to get to the next sentence. He shook some imaginary heft from his shoulders and said, "Now, that's a dress."

At the Fairview, William ushered her into the lobby and held out his arm for her to grasp. "Shall we?"

From her seat at the table, Hester was the first to spot them. From across the room, Ruby could see her mouth fold into a bitter pull. Daniel, whose back had been turned to them, pivoted in his seat to see what had caught Hester in such an awkward haw.

William eased Ruby into a seat facing Daniel and said, "Look what I found." He bent to give Hester a cool peck on the cheek and then turned to shake hands with Daniel. "Sorry to have missed you at church," he said. "I thought we were supposed to meet at Daniel's place." He nodded toward Ruby. "And then I got distracted by this lovely young thing."

Ruby squirmed as she felt all three turn to regard her. She fingered her mother's pearls with one hand and held the knot to the shawl with the other.

"Daniel, you never mentioned what a gem you've got holed up out there." William took his seat and lifted the large black leather menu. "If I'd known, I'd have made more of an effort to get home for a visit."

"I should have thought of the introduction myself." Daniel's voice was calm and controlled, but Ruby noted it was thicker than usual, as if having passed through something sticky.

"Probably too busy with wedding plans," William said. "In any case, that would have taken all the fun out of today." He uprighted the tall menu so only his cap of thick hair was visible. "How about a bottle of Riesling?" he said. "It's early, but for some reason I feel like celebrating." He lowered the leather folder to just below his eye level. "Must be the company."

Lunch was wonderful. The room tinkled with excitement: the plink of wineglasses, the breathy murmur of important conversations, and the rich aroma of savory dishes. Ruby even loved the heft of the starched white linen napkin on her lap. She had been confused to find no prices on her menu and had at first cautiously ordered baked chicken with roast potatoes and asparagus. William balked at such simple fare and insisted, quite adamantly, that she have the lobster. Upon discovering she'd never tasted lobster, he had been as giddy as a carousel horse, standing over her, encircling her with his broad arms as he expertly demonstrated how to properly crack the tail and claws and quarry its succulent meat.

And as William's mirth and merriment increased, Daniel's seemed to diminish. William drank the bulk of the second bottle of wine, whereas Daniel was temperate, blocking William from refilling his glass by covering his hand over the goblet. For her part, it was only Ruby's second taste of alcohol. Last Christmas, one of the girls had snuck a bottle of cold duck into the house and they'd corralled in one of the upstairs bedrooms to pass the warm, sticky bottle around the small circle. The Riesling, by comparison, was crisp and cold, and

Ruby liked the tingly sensation it awakened in her. And William was such an attentive date that she felt perfectly at ease; indeed, his effusive compliments and encouragements buoyed her overall good cheer.

Hester, on the other hand, did her part to tamp down the mood. She found two occasions to insert into the conversation the fact that William was waiting to hear about admission to law school and what a shame it was his stay would be brief.

"How about dessert?" William's eyes locked onto Ruby. He had an impish quality to him that had kept her smiling throughout the meal.

"I'm stuffed," she declared.

"Oh, come on," he said. "We'll have the circus cone."

"Don't be ridiculous," Hester said. "That's on the children's menu."

"So what?" William said. "It's fun."

"They won't serve it to you," Hester said.

"Sure they will. I've had it before."

"When you were five," Hester snapped.

William affected a child's voice, "Don't worry, Mommy, I'll say please." Turning to Ruby, he winked and smiled so endearingly she had to giggle, which caused Hester's eyebrows to arch and converge in two angry gashes.

The circus cone was a bowl of ice cream with a scoop of vanilla as clown face, the upended cone as its hat, chocolate-chip eyes, a pecan nose, a maraschino-cherry mouth, and a ruffle of whipped cream at its neckline. Ruby ate the whole thing while Hester huffed over her cup of black coffee.

When they finally emerged into the heat of the late afternoon, Ruby was surprised to see it was still daylight.

Daniel stepped forward. "It makes the most sense for me to drive Ruby and you to drive Hester. No sense crossing paths just to double back."

Hester made a sharp caw, as if something scratched to be said. Her darkened eyes flitted between Daniel and Ruby and then Daniel again. Finally she said, "Of course, it only makes sense."

Daniel was quiet for the first few minutes of the ride, uncomfortably quiet. Ruby's mind kept looping over the events of the day to make sure she hadn't embarrassed him or compromised him in any way. She finally spoke first. "I really enjoyed myself. I'd never been anywhere so fancy before. The lobster was delicious. And William is so funny . . ."

Daniel cleared his throat. "Ruby, I want to talk to you about William."

"What about him?"

He gripped the steering wheel with both hands, and his body posture was rigid. "It's just . . . he has a bit of a reputation."

"What kind of reputation?"

"As a player, a ladies' man." He turned to regard her. "Do you know what I mean by that?"

She couldn't help the look of insolence that weighted her eyelids as she turned to look out toward her side of the road. It figured. Her most painful shards of memory had all begun as a sliver of hope. "Yes, of course I know what that means."

He extended his arm straight out the window to indicate a left turn. The broken turn signal was one of several recent failings of his old Ford. She had overheard Hester chiding him to get a new car, but he'd shaken her off saying he couldn't afford one. "He's also known for not sticking to anything for very long, schools, jobs, towns, or girls. I just wouldn't want to see you get hurt."

She thought about the way Daniel had been so protective over Dr. Perry's advances. Then she remembered Hester's sharp knuckle wearing Daniel's family diamond. Too late for Ruby not to get hurt. She tucked one end of her shawl into the other, retying its crisp knot. "We had lunch. That's all. It's not like I'm going to see him again."

But she did see him again, and again. It started the next day with a bouquet of deep purple and blazing yellow irises and a card that stated, "For a real gem." No one had ever given Ruby flowers before. She placed them front and center on her small desk and loved the way they spilled summertime all over her day. William stopped by later that evening in his shiny convertible to make sure she'd received the flowers and to invite her for a drive and picnic along the river the following day. Daniel hadn't asked about the flowers, but then again, he had been quiet and standoffish all day.

William proved to be an attentive suitor. They swam at the country club; he took her to a jazz concert; and he gave her private golf lessons. Ruby had never been treated to so many special outings in all her life. She never knew what to wear and it took all the girls in the house chipping in with bits and pieces: a swimsuit borrowed from Mira, seersucker shorts from Tammy, and a shimmery robin's-egg-blue scarf from Debbie. The entire house seemed to crackle with the news and gossip of Ruby's every adventure. The excitement seemed to soften dour old Cook, who once even offered to pack a picnic lunch and chocked it full of her specialties: fried chicken, buttermilk biscuits, corn pudding, and two fat slices of her three-decker chocolate cake. She went so far as to tuck in a bottle of hard cider, admonishing Ruby with a "don't tell" finger to her pursed lips.

No need to elaborate who wasn't to be told. Daniel's sour mood continued. He complained that two girls had skipped their appointments with the family services' counselor. There was all too much wastage going on, lights left on all hours, food taken from the pantry without permission. And he begrudged every moment of free time Ruby requested. Ruby stood her ground. She had been working as Daniel's secretary for almost two years and hadn't taken a formal vacation day in all that time. And so what if it was all so rushed and last minute, and if she never gave him proper notice? Besides, she liked the way William referred to it as spontaneous.

Things continued like this for three weeks. William gave her driving lessons, taught her how to distinguish a salad fork from a dessert fork and a soup spoon from a teaspoon, and bought her a tennis racquet, tennis shoes, and a white tennis dress. They took bike rides and car rides, and swam and golfed, and ate at restaurants, and sometimes just sat in his car sipping champagne—real champagne, from France—straight from the bottle and listening to the radio. Whenever the chart-topper "Satisfaction" by the Rolling Stones came on, William would sing along and insist that Ruby join in. William was fun, and she liked just about everything about him: the way he groaned with pleasure every time he saw her, the way he never made her feel out of place or less than anyone else, the way he asked about her hardships and then held her closely, calling her a "poor angel," and the way he reveled in her awakening to so many things. He told her, over and over, that he'd never met anyone like her and that he was sick to death of the vanity and vapidity of the girls he met at college or in his family's circle of acquaintances. He also said she was the most disarming combination of child and enchantress he had ever met. It was the second of those two which had Ruby a little worried.

For the first two weeks he had been a perfect gentleman, content with deep kisses and clothes-on caresses. Just the night before, though, he had begged her to let him unbutton her cotton sweater, and then unhook her bra. He'd been so gentle and so appreciative, cupping and mounding and kissing her breasts, and groaning and literally heaving with pleasure. As much as he was slow and considerate, she remembered the way her nasty uncle had slobbered all over her and she wanted no part of that. It took a few minutes for the wolf man to exit William, and for normal breathing to return, and still a few more for him to cobble together a few coherent words. She could tell he wasn't used to meeting with resistance, or persevering in the face of it, in any case. She remembered Daniel had called him a "player," which she supposed meant he'd been with plenty of girls. And it didn't look like it had done any of them much good.

She figured her only hope was to be different, completely different. Let people think and say what they like. God knows there were probably all sorts of rumors about her, especially since they'd been seen around town a lot. Now that Daniel and Hester had set a date, she was trying very hard to envision a future with William. She resolved to give him a fair chance, one free of contrasts and comparisons. Though she doubted his presence would ever untether her the way Daniel's did, she confessed for William a genuine fondness, one she hoped would mature.

Her suspicions about rumors were confirmed later that

week when one of the girls told Ruby that she'd heard from someone else that William's car had been rocking something fierce over at the Moonlight Drive-in Theater last Friday. And some passerby had supposedly seen more than just the neon sign flashing. Ruby didn't bother to deny it. She and William had been munching burgers and sipping Cokes at Joe's Diner on Friday, clear across town from the drive-in. Surprisingly, this newest rumor had two interesting side effects. Hester was so clip and curt she could barely bring herself to utter the most basic of civilities in Ruby's presence. Clearly, she felt William's low standards reflected on herself and, most likely, their entire family. Even more interesting was Daniel's flustered behavior around Ruby. He seemed jittery and could barely look her in the face. He also had dark owl-like circles around his eyes, and, indeed, she had heard him stirring late into the wee hours for several nights running. He had also taken to long walks around the pond. On more than one occasion it had seemed like he wanted to discuss something with her, something meaningful, but then he'd brushed her off with a "never mind" or "it wasn't important."

Ruby had always been a determined individual and willing to work on skills where she knew herself lacking. Swimming was no exception. She had been embarrassed at William's club, having no more confidence in the water than the splashing toddlers. The home's spring-fed pond offered an opportunity for practice. Its farthest edge, a finger-shaped inlet, had a sandy beach and was surrounded by dense trees providing privacy.

Ruby finished her work one unbearably warm evening and hurried to the pond. Knowing the sun would soon tumble behind the thick canopy of trees, she did not waste time running upstairs for a bathing suit. She stepped to the shoreline, already unbuttoning her dress. It fell to the grass. The water felt like smooth glass against her calves and she luxuriated in this before venturing farther, until the water lapped gently against her thighs. She looked down at her panties and bra. She'd need to walk back to the house after the swim. The pleated skirt of her dress probably wouldn't cling, but a wet bra would soak the thin bodice. She unhooked the eyelets at the back and, wadding the fabric into a ball, threw it onto the grass with her dress. Just as she was turning back to the water, a movement in the trees caught her eye. She and Daniel locked eyes for a moment before she covered her breasts with crossed hands. She then dipped down to her knees to conceal herself in the murky water.

Daniel did not mention the event after returning from his walk, or all the next day. Finally, a few days later, as Ruby was sitting on the porch swing listening to a transistor radio and waiting for William to pick her up, Daniel eased himself into a rocker. He sat with his hands hanging between his knees.

"What on earth are you listening to?" he asked.

"The Rolling Stones. They're William's favorite," Ruby said. "You don't like them?"

"They're interesting; I'll give you that much," Daniel said with a shake of his head. After a long pause, he asked, "Does he make you happy? If only I knew you were happy."

She hardly knew how to respond. What if she said he didn't? Was there a wrong way to answer this question? Daniel's sober tone had her confused.

"He makes me feel special." It was an honest reply.

Daniel stood abruptly. "Good. I'm glad to hear it. You deserve as much." He took a few short strides toward the front door. "Have a good evening, Ruby."

The next night, just as Ruby was pulling the last of the day's letters from the typewriter, Daniel came out of his office and leaned against her desk.

"How're you doing for a front crawl?" he asked.

"I beg your pardon?"

"Your swim stroke. Has anyone ever given you a proper lesson?"

"No." William had proclaimed her deficiencies in this area "distressing," but had capitalized on her weakness by dragging her into the deep end, where he knew she would cling to him, powerless and at his mercy.

"That won't do. You'll need a proper backstroke, too."

"I guess."

"Tell you what." He checked his watch. "Meet me at the pond in twenty minutes; we'll have you swimming in no time."

She was bashful at first, skittish to disclose the full extent of her inexperience. His initial demonstrations, the way he knifed through the water with speed and agility, did little to settle her nerves. But he was such a patient teacher that she soon relaxed. Instead of teasing—as William had with her tennis serve and golf swing—Daniel was encouraging, if a little sober. After a spate of "head down" and "kick" commands, she'd splashed him, willfully provoking his smile, and a return faceful of water.

Daniel's technique of teaching the backstroke—one of holding the small of her back as she flutter-kicked and windmilled her arms—made it difficult for Ruby to concentrate, never mind coordinate body parts. It must be, she thought, what floating on a cloud felt like, a weightless suspension of time and place. She found herself staring into his eyes, which were much brighter and more playful away from the responsibilities of work. It was better, at any rate, than staring at his bare chest. He wasn't burly like William, but for such a thin frame, he was surprisingly ropy.

She hated when tumbling darkness pulled them from the water. During the short walk back, Ruby had sensed him growing quieter, more aloof. When the house came into view, he straightened, as if yanked upward—and painfully—by some invisible force.

"Thank you for the lesson," she said as they walked up the flagged path.

"You were a natural."

"See you in the morning, then." She hesitated on the porch, hoping for an excuse to linger.

With Daniel holding the door open for her and girls' voices wafting from the staircase, Ruby knew that now was another time to heed that "head down" command. Its complement, "kick," was also on her mind. She wanted to. And scream. Instead, she reminded herself of the futility of such thoughts. Daniel was her boss. Her engaged boss. Anything more, anything familial, would be of the married-into-the-same-family variety.

When, a week later, William invited her to a family dinner in honor of his mother's birthday, Ruby sensed it was a corner turned. By his own admission, he hadn't introduced a girl to his parents "in ages" and crowed that she would "make their wait worth their while." She was aware, through Daniel, that they were great travelers, particularly since the father had retired. They had just returned from some grand trip and the gathering would also be the first formal assembly since Daniel and Hester had set a date. When Ruby had asked William what she should wear, he had cheekily responded, "Show 'em what you got." It had not been the reply she had anticipated.

Finding Hester, the following day, on the phone in Ruby's office was also unexpected. Hester always used Daniel's office. Ruby was, however, relieved to overhear Hester instructing someone, presumably a dry cleaner, that she simply had to have her red Christian Dior gown by Sunday. Hester recradled the phone and nodded to Ruby.

"Sorry. I hope you don't mind my intrusion. You were away from your desk at just the moment I remembered something which simply could not wait."

"No problem," Ruby said. She smiled to herself, grateful for the tip-off. Hester wouldn't leave her looking dowdy and underdressed a second time.

Ruby coaxed a stubborn curl into submission and stepped back from the mirror for a full-length view. She had slept all night with sponge curlers and had a head of springy coils to show for her efforts. One of the girls had loaned her a formal dress with a fitted strapless bodice in black taffeta and a full ballerina-style skirt of cream tulle that hooped over a tight taffeta underlayer. Dressed as she was, Ruby felt like she could spin right into a dance number with Fred Astaire. She hurried from her room to the foyer-pacing William.

"How do I look?" she asked, descending the last step.

He pulled at his lower lip. "Perfect."

"Not too much?" She adjusted her mother's pearls.

"Not for me."

The Frasers lived on High Street, known for its elegant homes. Ruby marveled at the manicured lawns, chiseled topiaries, lush flower beds, stately columns, commanding brick facades, and above all, the trees. A column of towering silver maples, some close to one hundred feet tall, lined the boulevard, creating a sentry both imposing and impressive. William parked behind a hunter-green Bentley.

"Are you ready?" he asked. "Not nervous?"

"Why? Should I be?" Something in his tone made the bottoms of her feet itch.

"Of course not," he said. "Just remember, being different is what makes you special."

He was out of his seat and around to her side of the car before she could ask what he meant. With urgency, he rushed her up the front steps and quickly dispatched her shawl and purse to a nameless maid. He then escorted her into a very large sitting room, one for which she was sure the family had a formal title, like the drawing room or grand hall. Her eye, which had first been pulled to an ornately carved marble fireplace, quickly found the two other women present. Everything in Ruby—her heart, courage, confidence, breakfast, and lunch—keeled and capsized. She felt she might have even let out a small gurgle. *Drab, dowdy*, and *demure* were the first three words that popped into Ruby's head, quickly followed by *damn*. William's mother and Hester looked like they had just returned from a librarians' convention, at which they'd been the ho-hums of honor.

William cleared his throat. "Mom, Pops, I'd like you to meet Ruby." His voice was high and clear. He was obviously enjoying himself. "Ruby, these are my parents, Harold and Regina Fraser."

They both stood, he from one of the wing chairs at the side of the fireplace, and she from an overstuffed chintz armchair. Regina wore a smoky-blue linen skirt and gray silk blouse buttoned high with a fussy little scarf further sealing things off. She was tall and thin with her gray hair screwed tightly into a bun at the nape of her neck. Harold wore tan corduroy pants and a crisp white shirt. They both shook Ruby's hand mechanically. When Regina's eyes wandered down to Ruby's dress, her face pinched in obvious discomfort.

Harold spoke first. "Very good to meet you, Ruby." He gestured toward an open spot on the sofa. "Please be seated, there next to Daniel and Hester."

Hester, who had clearly known the dress code, wore a long fitted pencil skirt in camel, a brackish-brown short-sleeved cotton sweater set, and flats.

Ruby wanted to turn and run. Feeling ridiculous and exposed, she took in a sharp, piercing gulp of air. "I'm overdressed." She looked imploringly at Hester. "I thought I heard you say you were wearing a ball gown."

Hester rolled her eyes. "You overheard me with the cleaners. I said I needed my dress by today. I packed for New York this morning."

Daniel's eyes flitted from one to the other. "You're not leaving for New York until Friday."

"Yes, but I packed today. You know how I hate to put things off." Hester gave a small snort of a laugh. "I didn't realize you were listening to my conversation." She shook her head. "Pity. If you'd only asked."

William cut in, "You look marvelous, Ruby. Puts a little instant sparkle into another one of these drab evenings."

Regina's eyes snapped like kindling. "Drab?"

"Don't start, William," Harold said.

William ignored them both. "What is it we're drinking?" He walked toward a bar cart. "Ah, sherry. I should have guessed. Oh well, it's better than tea and crumpets." He raised the bottle. "Ruby, can I pour you one?"

"No, thank you." The last thing she needed was to get tipsy, fall off her high heels, and spill out of the stupid strapless contraption. Ruby was beginning to pick up on the dynamics of the family. And William's fleece was darkening by the moment.

William proceeded to drink more than his share of the sherry and then the white wine served with dinner. He became loud and churlish and somewhat rude. In his defense, his parents made no effort to include Ruby in their conversation. They went on and on about their recent trip to "the Continent." Ruby figured there were enough of them that you should be specific. It was as if Asia and Africa and the others didn't count. Just as she, a little backwoods wayward, didn't count either. No one asked her anything about herself. Or her travels. Or her friendship with William. Though it wasn't like she had anything to offer regarding the divinity of the Sistine Chapel, or the serenade of a gondolier, or the majesty of the Vienna Symphony Orchestra. William, if he wasn't listing his own ports of call, was being inappropriate. When Regina had hailed the Eiffel Tower as a modern wonder, William had roughly clasped an arm around Ruby's shoulder and said, "You can keep your Eiffel, I got my own eyeful right here."

Hester was in high form. She had spent a college semester in Paris studying art history and could match her mother tit for tat on museums, cathedrals, and the best streets for shopping. She announced she would get Daniel "abroad" in the very near future, even if it killed her. Ruby liked the sound of that, Hester laid out in a coffin with her cold, bony fingers clutching two stampless passports. And whereas the parents made no effort to include Ruby in the conversation, Hester seemed to go out of her way—at just the wrong moment. When the topic turned to artists, Hester pointedly asked Ruby her favorite. When Ruby replied Norman Rockwell, Hester laughed out loud, proclaiming with that uppity clack of hers, "Of course he is." Ruby looked around at the family's collection of modern art. A donkey and its tail could do better, Ruby thought. As could she. And she would someday, *dammit*, without a fancy degree either.

When the topic turned to sports, Hester asked Ruby what she played. Hester knew full well Ruby didn't have time to "play" at anything. Ruby had replied, "Nothing," to which Hester clucked her disapproval.

"You really should take something up." Hester looked Ruby up and down appraisingly. "You have the type of figure that will go flabby."

At that moment Ruby thought she might like to "take up" a baseball bat, or a croquet mallet, but not in the name of good sportsmanship.

For his part, Daniel seemed to grow moody as Hester grew chatty and William drunk. Daniel was clearly irritated with Hester and had given her a sharp "Hester, really" after her comment about Ruby's figure. Hester had shrugged him off with a simple "It's true." Yet even before that, he had seemed out of sorts. Ruby had no idea what he was normally like around the family, but in her opinion he wasn't himself. His usual air of quiet and reserve, which she normally found calming, came across tonight as aloof and withdrawn.

After dinner they retired to the drawing room, as Ruby now knew it was referred to. In honor of Regina's birthday, Harold served champagne and Hester rolled in a towering birthday cake with enough candles to torch a small village. As soon as the dessert plates were reduced to crumbs, Ruby asked William to drive her home. Daniel overheard the request.

"I'll drive Ruby," Daniel said. He stood and rattled the keys in his pocket. "Tomorrow's a busy day. I'll need to be up early."

"No, no, I'll take her," William said. "She's my date after all."

"Don't be silly." Regina turned to William. "You're in no condition to drive. Let Daniel take her."

"I'm perfectly able to drive," William said.

"The hell you are," Harold said. "I bought the car. I pay the insurance. And I'll be damned if I'll see another one end up in a crumpled heap. Daniel will drive the girl home."

After an entire evening with the family, Ruby was nothing more than "the girl." All the more reason to go. And better with Daniel than William after his performance all night. Good-byes were perfunctory. William was angry and sullen. Only the maid who returned her shawl and purse gave Ruby anything resembling a *come back soon*.

The car ride home was quiet. They were almost there before Daniel finally spoke.

"Are you all right?"

At that moment it all clung to her like cold, wet clothing. She had made a colossal fool of herself. She wore the wrong thing, had nothing to say, and was obviously the dead mouse the family's rangy alley cat delighted in dropping at their feet. William would probably be done with her now, having played his prank. And Daniel had witnessed the whole thing. She began to cry softly until she could no longer contain herself and her body racked with loud sobs.

He pulled off the country road and put the car in park. "Ruby," he said with alarm. "What is it?"

"I feel like such a fool," she said through tears. "They hated me. I don't know what I was thinking. I will never be good enough for people like them."

Daniel's voice was firm and clear. "You have nothing to be ashamed of."

"I was an idiot," she said. "I dressed like one, and I sounded like one."

"Listen to me. You have nothing to be ashamed of. You were polite, and dignified, and the only one who I saw making an idiot of himself was William."

"They didn't like me."

"There aren't many they do."

"They like you," she said.

"They tolerate me. In truth, Hester could do better."

Ruby let out a small laugh. This was the Daniel she knew and liked. "I'm simple," she said. "A small-town country bumpkin compared to them. Not at all William's type."

"Hey." He reached his right index finger across the space between them, turning her chin toward him. "Don't ever let anyone make you question yourself like that. You are a catch, Ruby. An absolute catch. You're smart, and beautiful, and funny, and could have any guy you wanted."

"No, I couldn't." She looked at him squarely, tears clung to her lashes.

"Sure you could."

"I can't have you," she said.

It sounded as if something balled in Daniel's throat. He finally scratched out a barely audible "Oh, Ruby." She braced herself for his rejection. It would be kind and gentle, but still firm. She closed her eyes and steadied herself for more humiliation. He released her chin. His hand, warm and strong, cupped the nape of her neck and, then, his mouth was on hers. He kissed her softly, and with such tenderness she thought she might begin to cry all over again. His breath, a mixture of sweet and spicy, whispered over her until she opened her own mouth under his. Daniel moved closer to her side of the car's commodious bench seat. He nuzzled her chin and throat and she arched closer to him in response. When he took her face between his hands and gazed upon her with longing, her breath caught in her heaving chest.

"Ruby, I've been an idiot. Seeing you with William these past few weeks, it's been driving me out of my mind." He kissed her all along her neckline. "What you just said. It gave me hope you had feelings for me."

"I do," she said, ducking her head into another one of his kisses.

After a moment, he broke free again. "This isn't a game to me. You know I wouldn't do that to you."

"I know. You're not like that."

"Oh, Ruby," he groaned. "I can hardly believe what's happening." He pulled her into him and then lowered her onto her back. She lay beneath him, his kisses smothering her from her mouth, to her throat, to the flesh of her cleavage that spilled precariously from the strapless dress.

"I'll break things off with Hester tomorrow."

"I'll do the same with William."

He raised himself, gazing at her. "Hold fast," he said in a teasing tone.

"What? Why?"

"I don't know how she'll take it; we could be in for a real squall."

"I don't mind," she said, figuring she could withstand any storm with Daniel as her port.

CHAPTER THIRTEEN

Jill

Thursday Late Afternoon

In search of Fee, Jill ventured into the throng of black-clad guests.

"There you are," Jocelyn said, pulling Jill into her tête-à-tête with Keith. "Are your ears ringing? I was just complimenting you. Everything is perfect. Tasteful and subdued, but still enjoyable. And you agreed, right, Keith?"

"Absolutely."

Jill had been aware of their conversation for a while now. Jocelyn, in her halter dress, wasn't hard to miss. She wondered what else they'd found to discuss. She doubted Jocelyn would linger long on a "tasteful and subdued" topic.

As if in sync with her thoughts, Jocelyn said, "I was also telling Keith how you and I have been talking, for some time now, about a trip to Boston."

They hadn't. Ever.

"We could check out Keith's new restaurant," Jocelyn continued. "Indian-French fusion. It sounds fantastic."

"Thanks," Keith said. "It reflects my travels."

Jill became aware of the attention they were attracting. In particular, Karen Miller—mother of Marjory and blabber of gossip—seemed to be watching greedily. When etiquette allowed, Jill intended to excuse herself.

"How long did you live in Bombay?" Jocelyn asked.

"It's Mumbai now," Jill said.

"See." Jocelyn turned to Keith. "Still smart as ever."

"Two years," Keith said.

"Your travels sound fascinating—Tahiti, Australia, India, Paris, London," Jocelyn said, ticking the places off on her fingers. "What brought you back to the States?"

"When I left here I headed west. Seems like I just kept going until I came full circle."

Jill noticed Keith rounded his shoulders in the same way he had fifteen years ago.

"And what was your favorite place?" Jocelyn asked.

"Probably Sydney."

"Yet you didn't stay."

"Just kept moving."

"And now Beantown," she said.

"And now Beantown."

"So are you glad to be back?" Jocelyn asked.

"Very."

"I'll leave you two to catch up, then," Jocelyn said, pointing to an individual entering the room. "I think I see an old high school friend."

He wasn't. He was a handsome and new-to-town doctor, divorced and a bit of a tomcat, should rumors be correct. Jocelyn's radar was up and working, if not her subtlety.

Jill had already felt awkward in the conversation. It was bad enough that she had felt like a spectator to their conversation, her head bouncing back and forth, passively following their exchange. Worse still, their threesome had attracted stares and elicited whispers.

"I'd love to show you around Boston."

"Oh, you know Jocelyn, all talk. The truth is I don't get away much."

Jill and Fee had managed a few spring breaks to Florida and to California to visit Jocelyn, but the planning and preparation involved in leaving the inn to Ruby, Borka, and Magda's care left her too exhausted and nervous to enjoy the trips.

"It's not a long flight."

Jill supposed that all that separated Keith from what he wanted to do was sky. She, on the other hand, had obstacles. She scanned the room. *Where the hell is Fee?* Ruby, unfortunately, was easy to spot. Her wineglass was sloshing back and forth like a listing schooner. Even though Jill had practically stuffed her into an old Hefty bag of a black dress, she still managed to look inappropriate. And the wig. Jill had been unable to talk her out of it: a short, brunette blunt cut. Still more troubling, Ruby had a gentleman friend—one of their guests.

"My condolences," an older gentleman said, offering Keith his hand and providing Jill the escape hatch she required.

"If you'll excuse me," she said. "I should check on things."

"Mom, can I get you a cup of coffee?" Jill asked.

Ruby held her wineglass up high. It was half empty. She

then drank with great dramatic flair, raising her glass again when she had drained it. "No, but you can get me a refill."

"How many have you had?"

"One too few." Ruby coyly smiled at her new friend.

"I'll get you one, Ruby." The man shuffled away with a hand placed gingerly at his waist, the spot where his body crumpled forward like a dead branch.

"What are you up to?" Jill asked.

"None of your business."

"Mom, he's a guest."

Ruby reached under her wig and extracted a key. "Yes he is. Room 109."

"Where did you get that?"

"From Martin, of course."

Ruby had shown a renewed interest in men of late. It had seemed harmless enough, innocent flirtations, though some of the guests' wives had responded with a possessive tuck into the crook of their husband's arm. In this instance, Jill suspected Ruby's performance had more to do with an overall disdain for the event and payback resolve than any real interest in the bowed and buckling Martin. "This isn't the time or place. Have a little respect."

"Respect," Ruby said. "Don't start with me. Besides, I cooperated. I'm wearing a potato sack and I didn't say boo during that boring eulogy. This is my house, and I'll make a new acquaintance if I want to."

"Please, Mom." Jill looked around the room. Jocelyn and the doctor were chatting in a corner. Keith had attracted a wider circle of sympathy wishers, including one very attractive woman. "I've got enough to contend with today." A discarded tray of hors d'oeuvres caught Jill's eye. "Have you seen Fee?"

"No."

Martin came into view, padding across the room with two glasses of wine. Jill shook her head and left her mom with a final "Be good. And give the man his key back. Now."

Jill was waylaid by the ghoulish Jasper Cloris, who wanted to compliment her on the arrangements, and then by the president of the local historical society, Katherine Parks, who had always been fascinated by the home's "past lives." She asked about the new roof, new windows, plumbing overhaul, refinishing of wood floors, and landscaping. Jill wondered where she had obtained such a detailed list of projects. Did Katherine have an inside man at the bank? Did she already know that Jill's loan payments had increased by 20 percent a month? Jill's nerves had her inventing all kinds of ridiculous intrigues. Was that sliver of paper, visible from the outside pocket of Katherine's purse, a late notice from the Prairie State Bank to be hand-delivered? Did the historical society envision new digs? Were they sizing her place up as museum potential? Jill took a deep breath and replied to Katherine's inquiries with words such as *refreshing*, *reviving*, *modernizing*, and her snowcapper, "such a great investment."

Jill had finally escaped Katherine when she got caught in something akin to a reverse receiving line, wishing a stream of guests "good-bye" and "drive safely." By the time she was free, the party was over, and she couldn't locate anyone: not her mom or Fee or Jocelyn. She was in the kitchen dropping white mugs into the dishwasher when she heard a knock. The door swung open and Keith poked his head into the room.

"Jill, I'm sorry to bother you, but there's a problem out here."

Jill wiped her hands on a dishcloth. "What is it?"

"Come see."

She followed Keith into the lounge. She couldn't imagine

what the matter was, everything looked fine, a few wineglasses and dirty plates lying here and there, but nothing unexpected. She'd have it all tidied before lights-out. And then something caught her eye. Two legs, with thick nylon knee-highs bunched around the ankles, stuck out from behind the sofa. Jill recognized the black pumps she'd horned Ruby's callused toes into earlier that day. The scene reminded Jill of the Wicked Witch's predicament after she found herself flattened by Dorothy's twister-thrown house.

"What on earth?"

"She's okay," Keith said. "Snoring like a jackhammer."

Jill took a few steps to the couch. Ruby was laid out straighter than Hester had been, with her arms rigid at her sides and her toes pointing straight into the air. There was an upturned wineglass just a few inches away. "Have mercy."

"I can carry her for you. Where would you like to put her?"

"In a nursing home." Jill noticed Keith's head did a little surprised chicken peck at her remark. "Forget I said that," she said, blowing her bangs up off her forehead. "She's been a handful lately. And the funeral has unsettled her, stirring up old memories. Thanks for finding her. I can take it from here. I'll get Jocelyn to help me."

"She left. I saw her take off."

"Then I'll get Fee."

Keith tilted his head to the side. "Ruby's a full-size woman; you'll still need help."

Jill bit her bottom lip. She hated help from anyone, always had. Even in perfectly innocent predicaments, like a flat tire or asking for directions. But hauling her drunken mother to bed was the kind of mortification on par with a loan to post bail. "She'll wake up soon, and then I'll help her to her room."

Keith shook his head. "She should be on a bed. She'll wake up stiff and confused."

She'd forgotten about his voice, deep and persuasive when he wanted to be. She lifted her hands, a sign of forfeit. "You're right. She won't like waking up like this. Let's get her to her room."

"Show me the way." Keith leaned over Ruby and grunted as he strained to get ahold of her.

A sound came from the foyer.

"Shit," Jill said.

"Yoo-hoo, Jill. Are you in there?"

She recognized the voice of Darcy Pruitt, also known as the "preacher's strife," whose own pulpit-pounding husband couldn't measure up to her exacting standards. Jill took a few quick steps toward the hallway.

"There you are. I've been looking all over for you." Darcy stepped into the room.

Jill glanced back. Instead of spying Ruby's chubby ankles, she saw a magazine rack placed strategically in front of her and Keith perched on the arm of the sofa, thumbing through a copy of *Ladies' Home Journal*.

Jill breathed a sigh of relief, but her voice was still flustered. She nervously plumped her hair. "What can I do for you?"

Darcy seemed to sniff out Jill's disquiet. She glanced at Jill, then at Keith, and back at Jill with a smug look. "Have I interrupted something?"

"Of course not," Jill said.

Darcy raised her eyebrows. "I just wanted to compliment you on the arrangements, but I won't keep you. You're obviously busy. And Reverend Pruitt is waiting in the car."

Jill didn't know which was worse, Darcy knowing Ruby

was soaked to a briny pickle or speculating about her and Keith. She walked Darcy to the front door, trying as hard as she could to sound cool and casual. By the time she returned, Keith had managed to get Ruby into a sitting position. She was groggy and mumbling.

"Mom, do you think you can walk?"

"Of course I can walk," Ruby said. She lumbered to her feet, and then promptly tumbled sideways.

Keith managed to catch her, but was almost bowled over in the process. "Whoa, there."

"Mom, we're going to help you to your room," Jill said. She and Keith each took a side and slowly walked Ruby into the hallway and through the door to their private quarters.

They settled Ruby onto her bed, Keith discreetly stepping out while Jill—revering nursing-home workers and sheep-shearers worldwide—got Ruby out of her dress and into a nightgown.

When Jill tiptoed past her ball-curled, gargle-mouthed mother and pulled the door closed behind her, it was more than the gloom of the empty family room sandbagging her chest. Keith was nowhere to be seen. What had she expected? It was late. He'd had a long, sobering day. His part in settling Ruby long done. There was nothing to keep him. *An involvement long forgotten.*

By some ancestral nocturnal instinct, she padfooted across the family room, into the kitchen, and then out onto the patio. Her mindless perambulation was halted at the low rock wall separating the patio from the lawn rolling down to the pond. She posted her arms at wide angles upon the knobby stone surface and looked out at the moonlit pond and its beetling forest backdrop.

She had also had a long, sobering day. In addition to a heat in her thighs already registering the physical toll, imprinted moments washed over her. The minister's eloquent eulogy accepting and exalting, even, life's vagaries. His celebration of fellowship, the kind that brought friends and family in wondrous acknowledgment of all of life's passages. Passages. His theme. One she now let roll over her with a tidal pull.

Behind her, the slow plod of hesitant steps stirred her from her meditation.

"I . . . I couldn't leave," Keith said, coming to stand at her side, brushing her even in passing. The warmth of his body so tangible and lingering she felt she could gather it, throw it over her shoulder like a fur stole. "Am I disturbing you?"

"No."

"How's Ruby?"

"Sleeping."

"I couldn't if I tried," he said. "Too keyed up from the day. But I'm probably keeping you up."

"I'm not too sure sleep will come easily for me, either."

She turned, facing the house and perching upon the wall. He did, too, scooching closer to her in the process. Her sensory circuits had already been firing; his proximity was yet another breaker thrown. Summer nights had always undone her. The gentlest of breezes ruffled her dress, lifting its hem like the playful tug of a lover's first entreaty. A heady ribbon of jasmine tickled her nose until she wanted to plunge it into even more delights: the triangle of flesh exposed by Keith's unbuttoned shirt and loosened tie, for instance. And the buzz of cicadas grew louder, more incessant, shrieking with their command: *kiss him already, kiss him already.*

As if he were quickened by the same lures, Keith's head

dipped into the hollow of Jill's neck, where he nuzzled under her jawline. His splayed fingers trailed up her shoulders and neck and into her scalp while his mouth rose to meet hers with greed and urgency. Another hand clamped the silky overlay of her dress just under her buttocks and began crimping and gathering until her thigh was exposed and his fingers found skin and rubbed with ascending strokes. She was at once torn between two fervid and opposing wills. One, impetuous and too long denied, was reciprocating, escalating even, the passion of his kiss. The other was pummeled by doubt and distrust. Panting, she broke free of his grasp, tears already springing to her eyes.

"I can't," she said.

"I'm sorry." He jumped to a stand. "I shouldn't have . . ."

"It's just that . . . you'll be leaving . . ."

"You don't have to explain," he said, distancing himself with a backward step.

"It wouldn't be—"

"Please, don't," he said, holding his hand up. "Maybe it's easiest not to . . ."

"Yes. Easiest not to," she repeated numbly.

"I should go," he said, backing another three paces. "It's late. I've overstayed my welcome. You're probably exhausted. I . . . I hope . . . How about good night for now?"

"Yes. Good night."

With a turn and a dozen strides he was on the path and had disappeared into the night. For many moments she watched the corner of the house he had rounded with eager eyes. Instead of his return, the thing she hated herself for wanting, she saw the flash of a face ducking from a window and a flutter of curtains in its wake. Fee's window. Fee's curtains. Fee's face.

With barely the energy to drag one leaden foot in front of another, she headed for the haven of bed. She'd deal with Fee—and everything else—tomorrow, because how much worse could it get by then, anyway?

CHAPTER FOURTEEN

Jill

Friday Morning

Hours later, never having entirely surrendered to sleep, Jill swung her legs to the side of her bed and slowly unfolded to a stand. She shuffled across worn floorboards, pausing at the window to witness dawn crowning behind the line of pines and remembering another day that had begun with a view onto the same stand of trees.

Parting the curtains into a curled shave of light, Jill—on hiatus from university—peeked out at the flocked trees and a fresh six inches that had fallen overnight.

"Open them," her dad called from his sickbed. In the ten weeks since the New Year, he had deteriorated rapidly. He hadn't taken food in days and could barely manage a few sips of water. A rolling hospital-style bed had been set up in the dining room so they could keep any eye on him continuously. A hospice nurse visited daily to tend to his IV drip of morphine. His doctor had wanted to admit him, but he'd refused. He wanted to die in the house his grandfather had built, surrounded by his family and life's work.

Jill pulled the heavy drapes slowly, revealing a yard covered in snow. It lay in windswept ridges resembling a baked meringue topping.

"The crocuses?" her dad asked.

"Buried. Poor things," she said, instantly regretting her choice of words.

"The vagaries of life," he said, wincing as a spasm of pain crimped him into a small, hard knot.

"Do you need anything?" she asked, knowing he never did. He endured the pain with such fortitude that she was humbled, daily, by his tenacity.

She was shocked, therefore, at his "I do, in fact" response. "What?"

"Your mother will need help," he said in a voice splintering with emotion. "She got hurt, badly hurt, at a very young age." His mouth was dry; his cracked lips smacked back and forth, fishlike, in an effort to work up a little saliva. "For all the spunk and spirit she musters, there are times when the old wounds reopen, leaving her sad and vulnerable. I'm worried. She's already showing signs." He became restless, using precious energy to grasp at Jill with shaky hands. "We McClouds, we take care of one another. We hold fast. Promise me that you'll take care of her, that you'll take care of *everything*."

"I will."

"Say it out loud."

"I promise."

"There's my girl," he said, collapsing backward, spent.

She was his girl. For as long as she could remember, Jocelyn—blond and bubbly—had been proclaimed "all Ruby," whereas Jill's McCloud clan coloring and earnestness had long earned her the title of "Daddy's girl." She was more than happy to live up to the title, spending long, lazy winter days with him, their two heads bent over a cribbage or chess board. She also shared his love of books and old movies, *Philadelphia Story* the declared favorite of them both. And she had always shown an interest in their Highland heritage, going so far as to develop a taste for colcannon, smoked salmon, bitter marmalade, and—later in life—a good scotch whisky. Though she never had warmed to the melancholy wail of bagpipes.

After their chat, he'd settled, almost comfortably, gazing out onto the wintry scene.

Hours later, Jocelyn dropped onto the skirted chair facing the small vanity in Jill's bedroom. "I feel sick," she said, fiddling listlessly with a knockoff bottle of Chanel. A small spray of scent, illuminated by the weak afternoon light, floated like dust particles. Jocelyn winced. "Gag me. Even this makes me want to wretch."

"We all feel the same," Jill said. An undeniable pall had lingered over the home for weeks. Jill was quiet. Ruby was fretful, and Jocelyn, for her part, was mad at everything. She broke up with John Foley, moaned and complained about her customers, hated winter, hated Iowa, and anything else that had the misfortune to cross her path or her mind.

"It's not just that," Jocelyn said. "I mean I really feel sick. I think I'm coming down with something."

"Is it one of your migraines?"

Jocelyn corked her ears with her index fingers. "No, no, no, no, no. Don't even say the word."

Migraines were the unmentionable black hole into which Jocelyn fell for days at a time.

"Sorry."

Jocelyn lowered her hands. "This is different."

There *was* something greenish to Jocelyn's complexion. Jill took a seat on the bed, leaned against the headboard, and stretched her legs in front of her. "Dr. Bradley said there's a lot of flu going around. Mom's not looking too good either. She went to lie down right after lunch."

Jocelyn stood slowly, bracing herself against the vanity top. "I think I'm gonna do the same. But first I think I'll go hang my head inside the toilet bowl. I know it's my turn, but can you give Dad his meds?"

"Yeah. Sure."

Jill watched as her sister shuffled out of the room. There was a rap at the window and she turned to see Keith with his face pressed against the dirty pane. She grasped the double-hung and, with effort, lifted the heavy frame.

He scrambled into the room and turned to muscle the window shut. "I thought Jocelyn would never leave."

"What are you doing? How long have you been out there?"

He rubbed his hands together. "Too long. I thought I might have to build a shelter out of pine boughs and that stack of newspapers around the side of the house."

"Why didn't you ring the front door, for goodness' sake? You're always welcome here, no reason to be sneaking around." Keith had, in fact, been using the window to Jill's room as a portal for some time now, but only for shadow visits, those falling between midnight and sunup.

"I didn't want to deal with Jocelyn. She's just so . . . moody."

"It's not you. Anger is her way of dealing, I guess."

I didn't want to disturb your father either. The last time I came by he had that bad spell and needed medication."

"That's pretty common. It had nothing to do with you. He likes you. He told me so. Said you had a good head on your shoulders."

"I wish I got to know him when he was well."

"I wish you had, too." Jill looked at her Timex. "I have to give him his medicine in a few minutes. You can't stay long."

He pulled her into an embrace. "I won't, but I needed to see you." He kissed the top of her head and then pulled her chin up with the tip of his index finger, kissing her full on the mouth. "I missed you. I thought you'd call last night."

She wrapped her arms around his waist and pressed even closer into him. Keith had been the only bright spot in a very bleak winter. She wouldn't have believed her heart had room for both grief and rapture, yet his presence managed, without fail, to snap her into some sort of heightened awareness of every little thing: the good, the bad, life at its essence. He'd been empathetic to her family's situation, giving her plenty of rant room in their conversations and a flannel shoulder to cry on. And he'd been incredibly patient, waiting for the late-night phone call with her cryptic message that she still hadn't fixed the broken latch on her window, their code for "It's safe to come visit now."

"I was exhausted. Dad was in a lot of pain, more than ever. And he was having trouble breathing. I was on the phone with the doctor twice. We almost rushed him to emergency, but then decided to honor his wishes and ride it out here."

"Sorry. I didn't know." He rocked her back and forth in his arms. "You'll get through this. I'm not saying you won't miss him, but at least you can get back to some degree of normalcy."

"I don't know if I even remember normal."

"Maybe there is no normal," Keith said. "My dad checked himself out of that rehab clinic my aunt is footing the bill for. He made it four weeks and then just up and walked. He's down in Florida somewhere, and Hester's furious. Says he isn't welcome back, ever, unless he's sober."

He pulled away and looked her in the eyes, his own painted with concern. "Sorry. I can't believe I'm talking about my screwed-up family with everything you're going through."

"It's all right. Kind of a relief to focus on something else."

"Has your mom decided what she's going to do with the house?"

There were only two girls left, one of whom had already delivered and the other due within a few weeks. One had decided to adopt out. The other had a job and apartment waiting in Des Moines, an arrangement Jill had worked out with a church they'd kept close ties with over the years. Even without their personal crisis, other factors had contributed to a steady waning of girls. A growing acceptance of pregnant teens remaining with their families—progress, certainly, in the eyes of her father—meant the type of girl they took in was changing. Theirs were the hard-luck, runaway cases requiring stacks of public assistance applications, cooperation with social workers and, at times, local law enforcement.

"It's pretty scary. She refuses to talk about it. And Jocelyn's leaving for California on the first wagon train out of here."

"And you're going back to school in the fall."

"That's the plan."

"Your mom should sell."

"What?" Jill stepped away from him. "How could you say that? My great-grandfather built this house."

"It's immense." Keith gestured with his hands. "What would she do with all this space?"

Jill bit her lip. Not only had she, her mother, and her sister been avoiding this conversation, but she'd even managed to bury it deep in her subconscious, avoiding the worry and panic. Dealing with her dad's immediate concerns was crisis enough. "It's not worth thinking about yet."

"I've been doing some thinking." Keith reached out and held Jill's hand. "About what I want to do." He pumped her arm back and forth, as if working a jump rope. "And there's only one common thread in each scenario."

"What's that?"

"You. Each and every one of them seems torture without you."

No guy had ever factored her into his future. Jill felt tingly and warm and happier than she had in weeks. "What does that mean?"

"It means hurry up and finish school so we can escape."

"Escape?"

"Let's head west and keep on going," he said. "San Francisco for starters, and then somewhere in the Pacific. I'm thinking Fiji."

"You mean live there?"

"Why not?"

"What would we do?"

"Travel, take odd jobs, like in restaurants and bars, meet characters, eat crazy things, collect memories and exotic recipes. For a while, at least. A couple years maybe." He plied her hand nervously. "My dad never liked being a lawyer. His parents pressured him into it. He claims he never got to explore his own interests. He says he blinked and he was fifty. He wishes he'd had more adventures. Well, I gave the corporate world a shot; it wasn't for me. I'm ready for a little travel."

"I don't know." Jill pulled her hand away and ran it through her hair. "Travel's one thing. But living overseas? Even just for a few years. I guess I always pictured myself here somehow." She gestured out the window to the winter cloaked landscape. "In Iowa at the very least."

"That's not how I picture you." He pulled her back into an embrace. "I picture you on a beach somewhere with tan legs and a wet bikini."

She felt his warm breath tickle the hairs on her neck.

"Or in some mountain cabin, your bare butt on a bearskin rug in front of a roaring fire." He kissed her again hungrily.

She wiggled free. "You're messing with my mind. All I want to think about right now is my dad and my family and home. It's all so sad. At his request, we've brought all the family photos and memorabilia into his sickroom. The other day I found him staring at that old kilt of his and crying."

"I'd cry, too, if I had to wear a skirt."

She elbowed him. "It's not a skirt. It's a kilt."

"A type of skirt."

"A man-skirt, though."

"No such thing."

She rolled her eyes. "The point is he never got to wear it. It didn't arrive in time. Besides, their wedding ended up being a very small affair."

"But the marriage was long. Maybe they were tears of joy."

"I hardly think joy."

"Relief, then."

"Relief?"

"That he never had to wear the skirt."

"The *kilt*," she corrected.

"I don't care what you call it, a guy's gotta be pretty darn confident of his manhood to pull that off. Not to mention his legs."

"Maybe he had nice legs."

"Let's hope."

Jill shook her head side to side and then shoved Keith. "And anyway, stop it."

"What?"

"Stop lightening the mood."

"I'm sorry. I just wanted to see a smile, even a tiny one. It's been a while." He put his hands at her waist and pulled her close, kissing her softly at first, and then deeply.

"Damn you." She groaned and pulled away. "I have to give my dad his meds."

"I can be very quick," he whispered. He unbuttoned and unzipped her jeans. They fell to her ankles, and she stepped out of them. His fingers tugged at the lace of her panties. She unbuttoned his jeans and he shrugged his sweatshirt over his head. She stood before him, kissing his chest, when the door flung open and Jocelyn stood there wild-eyed.

"Jesus!" Jocelyn said.

Jill stepped away from Keith and returned the angry tone. "You don't knock."

Jocelyn glowered and looked from Jill to Keith and back to Jill. "Dad's dead. Thought you might like to know."

The weeks following the funeral were, without equal, the roughest Jill had ever endured. The stress of it had her head feeling like it had been cleaved in two with an ax, and her stomach like it was digesting nails and razors. Her mother, as her father had predicted, was overcome with sorrow, barely taking care of herself. And still-mad-at-the-world Jocelyn was in manic preparation mode for her upcoming move to California. Her way of dealing with grief, besides a fighter's stance and balled fists, was to move on. She was working overtime, trying frantically to save enough for the cross-country trek. Jill had gone almost two weeks without having any real contact with Jocelyn and was startled, one night, to come across her in the dining room with a large ceramic dish of lasagna and a fork. Jocelyn stood guiltily as Jill sat down across from her; Jill was surprised to notice Jocelyn had put on a few pounds. Jocelyn had always had a Ruby-like voluptuousness to her, but she was usually diligent about her weight.

"What's going on?" Jill asked.

"Getting rid of the last of the pity food. I found this in the freezer next to Mrs. Kirchner's raspberry cobbler." Jocelyn started to clear the dish from the table. "I guess I'm like Mom. I eat my way through stress." It had always been a family joke that Ruby washed troubles away with a tall glass of milk and a big slice of cake.

"Wait a minute," Jill said. "I thought we could talk."

"About what?"

"About the stack of insurance papers and bank statements I've been sorting through for starters. I spoke to the lawyer again today."

Jocelyn sat back down, but still clutched the dirty dish. "Really, Jill, can't you and Mom just handle all of that? Do I really need to be involved?"

"I could do with the help." Jill remembered her promise to her father to take care of it all, but she was only just beginning to comprehend the enormity of the task.

"How much help could I be? I am leaving, after all."

"We can't just dump this on Mom."

"You have a head for all that stuff. I trust you."

"I just thought we should discuss it. Keith thinks we should—"

"Please," Jocelyn cut in, "can you, for once, finish a sentence without Keith's name cropping up. It's really annoying."

Jill sat in shocked silence. Granted, Jocelyn was mad at everyone and everything, but her resentment at Jill and Keith's relationship seemed to be growing. Jill had hoped their father's illness and death would put it all in perspective. Life is short, so forgive and forget. Jocelyn, however, seemed determined to remain in begrudge-and-fester mode. "Seeing as you find my relationship with Keith so annoying, it will probably make your day to hear that he's leaving town on Saturday for three months."

"Three months? Where's he going?"

"His mom, impatient for him to get another real job, finally gave in to his interest in a culinary career. She got him a job as a sous-chef on a private yacht. She's happy because he'll be rubbing elbows with the boating set or getting back to—as she calls it—civilization. He agreed because he'll be working under a really great chef."

"So, did he break up with you?" Jocelyn sounded almost gleeful.

"No." Jill hated the way Jocelyn looked at her with a mixture of pity and triumph. "As a matter of fact, he almost didn't take the job because of me. But his mom went to a lot of trouble. And it's only three months and a great opportunity. Anyway, he told me he loved me. He said he's never, in all his life, met anyone like me. And he's coming back. He's definitely coming back." Jill, cringing at the doubt and defensiveness in her voice, tucked a clump of hair behind her ear.

Jocelyn laughed. "Of course he is."

"He promised."

Jocelyn stood and took a step away from the table. "The house and everything goes to Mom. It's her decision, not mine and not yours, so on second thought, stay out of it." Jocelyn's face went all red and puffy. "And tell Keith to stay out of it, too. The last person Mom needs sticking his nose into all her personal information is Hester Fraser's nephew."

Jocelyn marched out of the room, leaving Jill to brood. What Jocelyn said was true. The will had left the estate to their mother. This was no surprise; Jill had discussed as much with her dad. The surprise was Ruby's abdication of all involvement, which was what Jill had wanted to discuss with Jocelyn. Ruby showed no interest, nor offered any assistance, in sorting through the tangle of family finances. She acted listless and detached, manic in spurts, and then feeble and sickly. Even her hair was thinning. The other morning, Jill found an entire clump of it on her mom's pillow. It was just as well that the McCloud Home for Girls was officially closed. Jill had already mailed a letter to the long list of donors and benefactors advising them and thanking them for their years of support.

Even without the care and upkeep of young girls, Jill was becoming convinced her mother was unable to handle the responsibility of such a large home.

Her concerns grew the next morning when she found Ruby in the kitchen rummaging through the pantry. She wore Daniel's old brown terrycloth robe. It was faded and frayed and much too big for Ruby.

"What are you looking for?" Jill asked.

"Olives."

"What do you need olives for?"

"Meat loaf." A large can of kidney beans fell onto the checked linoleum floor with a *thwack*, and Ruby kicked it out of her way.

"You're making meat loaf now?" It was ten in the morning. Ruby had obviously just woken up. Her hair looked unusually thin and was matted on one side. Her eyes were red and swollen. "What about those checks I left you to sign? Did you get to them?"

"I'm hungry. And there's some ground sirloin in the fridge."

Jill knew there was ground sirloin, because she had bought it yesterday and intended to fry burgers for that night's dinner. "I don't know if we have olives."

"Then I'll make pancakes." Ruby sounded frantic. She pulled at her bangs.

Jill shook her head. "Mom, we need to talk about the house."

"What about it?"

"How are you going to manage? Jocelyn's leaving for California as soon as she pulls enough money together." Jill crossed her arms and leaned against the kitchen counter. "And I'm going back to school in the fall."

Ruby paused for a moment, looking at Jill as if this were new information. Something shadowy passed over her eyes. "Janine will need new school shoes in the fall." Ruby had found a box of Aunt Jemima and was dumping an unmeasured quantity into a mixing bowl. Flour dust lifted into the air and then settled in a ring around the outside of the large bowl. "Her favorite color is red."

Jill's eyes flashed back and forth, and she held her breath, not believing what she was hearing. It was an acknowledged fact that Ruby had suffered some sort of exhaustion or breakdown after the death of baby Janine. And again following the pre-Jocelyn miscarriage, but those incidents were years ago. And stories were one thing, but to observe such behavior firsthand was something else entirely. Jill now understood her father's deathbed concerns and the signs he claimed to have observed.

"Josh should take her to buy them. Little Janine loves to drive in his convertible." Ruby stirred the dry mix with a frantic pump of her arm, the wooden spoon clicking against the side of the bowl.

"Mom, you need eggs and milk." Jill hoped directions to a simple task would bring her back. She opened the fridge, pulled out eggs and a gallon of milk, and set them on the counter next to Ruby's mixing bowl. "We were talking about the house. What you want to do with it."

Ruby sloshed milk into the bowl. "Daniel will know what to do." Ruby cracked one egg, and then another, on top of the mix. She started stirring again, whipping the batter violently. Clumps of white paste splattered onto the counter.

Jill stepped in. "Why don't you let me do that for you. You go rest. I'll call you when I'm done."

Ruby allowed Jill to take the spoon from her. She shuffled toward the kitchen door, then stopped. "Janine likes blueberries in hers," she called over her shoulder. "Josh likes his rolled with lemon juice and butter."

"Got it." Jill turned to hide the tears pooling in the corners of her eyes. There had been, over the years, the occasional mention of Ruby's first sweetheart and baby Janine's father, Josh, who had died in a car accident. And Janine's name was part and parcel of the family. Jill had, however, never heard them discussed as if they were living, breathing entities with an appetite for pancakes.

CHAPTER FIFTEEN

Jill

Friday Morning

From the kitchen, a clatter and garbled voices—as if sifting through the neck of an hourglass—startled Jill, the yesteryear plaint of Ruby morphing into the stilted accents of Borka and Magda in response to some small commotion. Following the briefest of showers, Jill, wet-headed and puffy-eyed, fell into step with them. While refilling 202's coffee, she was more than a little surprised to look up and find Ruby pressing a map of local antiques shops into the hands of a guest.

Pot in hand, Jill followed her mother through the hallway and back to her post at the front desk.

"Good morning, Mom. You're up earlier than I expected."

Seated at the check-in desk, Ruby dovetailed her fingers in front of her. "What are you talking about? I always start at seven."

"It's just, after last night, I thought you wouldn't feel up to it."

"I feel fine."

And she looked it, too. Her knee-length navy skirt was pressed, her lilac blouse was tasteful and summery, and she appeared rested and composed.

Confused, but reluctant to break whatever mood or caprice Ruby was enjoying, Jill backed away. "Three checkouts, if I'm remembering correctly."

"A breeze," Ruby said, her hands still clasped.

A breeze, Jill thought, walking away, could be heat's welcome respite or a storm's harbinger. She hoped for the former.

Late into the breakfast service, Jocelyn shambled into the kitchen and dropped her boxer-clad butt into a chair. Within moments, Borka, practically genuflecting, placed a steaming mug of black coffee in front of her. Jill had to stop and firmly plant her feet to support her openmouthed gape. Borka had been known to grumble at a paying guest's request for a fork to go with their eggs.

"Thanks, Borka," Jocelyn said, drafting the piping hot aroma toward her flared nostrils with a fanning motion.

"Anything else we can get you this morning?" Jill asked, finishing with a chiding glance at Borka. "Foot rub, bowl of grapes?"

Borka slunk off to join Magda clearing dishes from the dining room.

"If you're offering, I'll take the lowdown on last night," Jocelyn said.

"You mean Mom getting drunk?"

"She got a little tipsy. So what? Hester's death had her stressed out."

"I don't know . . . I have a weird feeling. I think we should keep an eye on her."

"I saw her a minute ago. She looks okay to me. Anyway, I was asking about you and Keith. How did the reunion go?"

"It was a wake," Jill said, refilling her own mug of coffee.

"Not between you and Keith, it wasn't." Jocelyn drew her knees up to her chest and wrapped her arms around them, perched on the chair as if bracing for something interesting.

Jill poured a healthy measure of heavy cream—the real stuff, locally produced—into her cup. Jocelyn's antics of the previous night weren't too subtle, nor was this morning's probe. Dr. Jocelyn—the pheromone-sniffing relationship savant—had her shingle out and was open for business. "You'll be disappointed."

"Why?"

Jill took a seat at the table across from Jocelyn. "Because it's pointless."

"Pointless how?"

"For many reasons. The first thousand are the miles between here and Boston. Then there are the responsibilities keeping us on our sides of that divide. He has a restaurant and I have an inn, not to mention a daughter and, at times, a drunken mother who needs putting to bed."

"Minor details," Jocelyn said, swatting at the air.

"Hardly. More like major roadblocks. And kiss or no kiss, I'm not trekking out onto a minefield."

"You kissed?"

"Yes." Jill groaned the word. "But don't read anything into it. I stopped it, thank goodness, except . . ."

"Except what?"

"I'm pretty sure Fee saw us through the window." Jill rubbed at her forehead. "God knows what she thinks. Normally I'd have woken her up by now, but today I'm in no hurry."

"So are you going to see him again?"

"No. Definitely not. I told you, it's hopeless."

Jocelyn lowered her legs to the ground. "You're something else. So damn stubborn."

"I'm not stubborn; I'm realistic."

"You're an ass is what you are," Jocelyn said, scrambling to a stand. With annoyance, she wrenched open the refrigerator. "So, tell me, are last night's leftovers up for grabs?" There was a bite to her tone.

"Help yourself." Jill was only slightly reassured when Jocelyn lifted the corner off a Tupperware container and fished out a cream-cheese-stuffed roll of salami.

"And for the record," Jocelyn said, her body half hidden behind the industrial-size, stainless-steel panel, "I think you're making another karma buster of a mistake."

Jocelyn's posture was a coincidence. Her choice of words, however, were not. They were a deliberate reminder of that fateful summer.

Jill poked her head around the door, hiding her body from view. It was Keith. He was obviously fed up with leaving messages on the answering machine.

"Jill. Thank God. I've been so worried. No one answers your phone." He was tan from his three months at sea and his brown curls had taken on a few golden highlights. "Didn't you get my messages?" His eyes were bright and his tone urgent. "I've been back for almost a week now. What's going on?"

Jill had been dreading this encounter. "I'm really sorry, but I can't talk right now."

Keith pushed his foot into the small opening that she'd allowed. "Jill, you're acting strange. You've got me worried."

It took half Jill's strength to keep him from pushing into the foyer, and the other half from throwing the door wide open and rushing into his arms. "Please don't worry. We're fine. We're just dealing with some things right now. Still deciding what to do with the place now that Dad's not here." She heard a rustling in the hallway behind her. "Sorry, but I have to go."

"I don't understand." Keith's eyes were wild. "Jill, it's me. Why won't you let me in?"

"We're just . . . We're just not taking any visitors right now."

"Visitors? Visitors? Is that what I am? A visitor?"

"I can't explain other than it's not a good time."

"I think you should try. I think you owe me that much." Keith's tone had drifted from concerned to offended.

"It's just . . ." Jill knew she was being rude. Keith deserved better. He would never have treated her like this. She also knew there wasn't anything she could do, at the moment, to remedy the situation.

"Is there someone else? Did you meet someone while I was gone?"

"No." She answered quickly, hoping to dispel any concerns in that area.

"Did I do something wrong?"

"No."

"Then what is it? Help me out here."

"I really can't say other than it's not a good time." She tried desperately to sound firm. "I really have to go." Jill would never forget the look on Keith's face as she kicked his foot from the door. A withering look so dry, she knew in that instant she'd done irreparable damage. She swallowed hard, thinking there'd be worse to come.

Jill shut the door and turned to find Jocelyn sitting on the stairs, just a few feet away.

"We're making a huge mistake," Jocelyn said.

"No. We're not."

"Yes. We are. A karma-busting mistake. And hurting someone in the process." Jocelyn stood and blocked Jill's attempt to ascend the stairs. "He really cares for you. And there's some weird, tangible, destiny-filled magnetism between you two. I'm sorry I was so mean and green with envy about it, but it's true."

Jill heaved and felt her shoulders sag. "It doesn't change anything."

"It should."

"So then are you going to stay?"

Jocelyn's face flushed pink. "No."

"We're back where we started, then, aren't we? I'm doing this. I've made up my mind. So just stick to the plan, will you?"

"And what if I don't?"

"Then you'll ruin everything." Jill felt a thread of panic dragging through her voice. "And I really can't handle any more at this point."

"I'm sick of being stuck here day in and day out." Jocelyn kicked the banister with her foot. "It's not normal. I need to go out, get some air. If I can't work, then let me at least go on the next shopping run. You've done the last two."

Jill hesitated. Even though Jocelyn had agreed to the plan, Jill really had no right to keep her under lockdown. It was, however, important that neither one of them be seen in town for the next few months. Twice now, Jill had driven an hour each way to a grocery store so as not to run into anyone she knew. Even sporting a ball cap and sunglasses, she had been a nervous ninny that someone would recognize her. She wasn't so sure Jocelyn would head quite so far out of town, or take the same pains not to call attention to herself.

"Fine," Jill said, "but we'll go together. And it's an hour each way, so no complaining."

"Earth to Jill," Jocelyn said, stabbing her finger at a Post-it note stuck to the surface of the table. "Mom just walked this in. It's a message from the bank."

"Thanks. I'll call them in a bit."

"Any problems?" Jocelyn asked.

"No," Jill said. "Routine business. Why do you ask?"

"Oh, I don't know." Jocelyn tilted her head. "Mom said he didn't seem too cheery."

"He's a banker, not a game-show host."

Jocelyn eagle-eyed Jill before turning and declaring, "Good enough. I'm off to shower."

Jill stood, peeling the baby-pink note from the table, and looked out the window of the home that had defined four generations of her family. Most of the time, the very bones of the house filled her with conviction that she was preserving the honor and history of her family, that she had done the right thing. Her recent actions, however, had put the entire property in jeopardy. The new roof and plumbing were necessary, but she should have waited on the floors, windows, and room decor. How had she let that weasel of a mortgage broker talk her into such a stupid loan? He had sat at her kitchen table and assured her, repeatedly, that should interest rates spike, she could simply refinance. He made it sound about as easy as converting water to ice, or water to steam, neglecting to mention that a long, punishing drought was on its way. And with the increased monthly payments, she'd had to cut back drastically on advertising. She still owed *Midwest Touring* magazine for four months of print ads. When she'd spoken with them a month ago, they had given her a deadline of two weeks before they turned the debt over to a collection agency.

And what would Jocelyn, Fee, and her mother's response be to this financial mess? It wasn't like the house was hers to do with as she pleased. It technically belonged to Ruby, who, when cosigning the loan documents, was reassured by Jill that it was just "boring paperwork." Ruby's current will left everything shared equally among Jill, Jocelyn, and Fee. Fee: who had yet to make an appearance that morning. Jill pocketed the message and went in search of sleeping beauty.

CHAPTER SIXTEEN

Fee

Friday

"Knock, knock." Fee heard her mother's voice calling out her actions. An "up and at 'em" was followed by a creak of the door.

Flopping to a backside presentation, Fee taste-tested her mother's tone of voice: hesitant with a smatch of apology. *Crap.* Her mother *had* seen her at the window.

"I think we should talk about last night," Jill said.

"So talk."

"First, sit up and look at me."

Fee lugged her sheet-tangled body to an upright position.

"If you have questions about last night, I'll answer them."

Leading with trump, Fee asked, "What was everyone whispering about last night? About you and Aunt Jocelyn and that Keith guy?" She watched a slide show of emotions scroll across her mother's face: surprise, confusion, and a glint of annoyance.

"Why? What did you hear?"

"I heard you guys called a cozy trio, and me a mystery child."

"Who said that?"

"Does it matter?"

By the look on her mother's face, Fee knew it did, despite her "not really" reply.

"What were they talking about?" Fee asked.

"Old gossip. People love rumors. No matter how ancient, or misinformed, or hurtful."

"And are you so sure he had every right to leave?"

"Yes."

"It wasn't him, not some guy named Al Thomas, who got you pregnant?"

"No."

"You wouldn't lie to me?"

"Not about that."

Which Fee, mentally tallied, left all kinds of wiggle room. "So what's up with you two now? There's definitely something going on, given what I saw last night out on the patio."

"What you saw was a . . . mistake. A moment of craziness. But he doesn't live around here, and will be gone soon. Could be gone already for all I know. So don't read too much into it."

Judging by the way she lowered her eyes, avoiding Fee's stare, Fee did read something into it, but just what, and how much, she wasn't sure.

"Get up and get dressed. You can give Borka and Magda a hand with the rooms," her mom said, turning and leaving.

Fee scrunched her nose. Her mother's hasty, breeze-generating exit did nothing to clear the fishy smell she left in her place.

Hours later, Fee was outside, waiting for her ride, when she spied Aunt Jocelyn heading out to her car.

"Where ya going?" Fee asked.

"Meeting an old friend," Jocelyn said.

"Must be some friend," Fee said, ballooning her eyes in awe at Aunt Jocelyn's fused-on jeans and low-cut lime-and-white striped top. "You look amazing."

"What this?" Jocelyn said, swiping her hand down the contours of her body. "Business wear. Technically, *un*finished business wear."

A part of Fee wanted to ask her aunt to explain; another part—coming in with the majority rule—was pretty sure she didn't want to know or wouldn't understand, anyway. What kind of business would Aunt Jocelyn have here? Plus, even for her line of work, it hardly looked like business attire. But that was the beauty of Aunt Jocelyn. She didn't let others define her. She was—in her own words—a free agent. Except, Fee knew Jocelyn wasn't entirely opposed to settling down. Theirs had always been a special relationship. Just last summer Jocelyn had told Fee that she wanted to break off a section of white picket fence for herself, that she sometimes thought about dognapping a golden retriever and snatching a stroller. She had been kidding about the means, but the underlying wish for her own happy ending was there.

"And how about you?" Jocelyn asked, circling Fee and

sniffing with flared nostrils like some sort of freakin' airport dog. "Hmm. I can't get a read on it. Something's up, though."

Fee knew all about her aunt's high-def sensory abilities: colors, smells, hormones, and other organic matter that Aunt Jocelyn claimed to pick up like some kind of radio tower. But what could she possibly be sniffing on Fee?

"Where are you headed off to?"

"A sleepover with my friend, Cass."

"You don't both like the same guy, do you?"

"No."

Jocelyn lifted her eyebrows. "Weird. I'm definitely picking up some sort of betrayal signal."

An old Jeep Cherokee pulled down the long driveway. Cass's sister was driving and Cass sat next to her. One of the great things about Cass was her licensed seventeen-year-old sister, Mel. It was way cooler to be chauffeured by an older sibling than a parent.

"That's my ride. Gotta go." Fee took a few steps distancing herself from Jocelyn and her superhuman sensories.

"Be careful," Jocelyn called out.

"What? Why?"

"Your aura colors are all over the place." Jocelyn pushed her sunglasses up onto her head, fixing Fee with a forthright gaze. "You're vulnerable."

Fee walked to the car. She hadn't expected Aunt Jocelyn to go all hard-core hippie on her. As if she didn't have enough to think about. The conversation between the two old ladies at the wake already had her head spinning. "Cozy trio" made it sound like there was some kind of love triangle or rivalry over that Keith guy, the guy her mom had mashed with last night. And why would they use the words *mystery child*? As if the mystery of her own making—a drug-smuggling Turkish student—wasn't enough. Fee scrambled into the backseat of Cass's family's car with her head about ready to blow a lobe.

"Where to?" Mel asked.

"The Bijou," Cass said.

Mel dropped the girls off at the Bijou, the only downtown movie theater. The seats weren't cushy or roomy; there were only two screens; it didn't always have the latest releases; and it smelled like wet dog—but it was close, cheap, and something to do. They bought tickets at the outdoor kiosk. Once inside, they got snacks. While pumping butter onto her tub of popcorn, Fee saw Marjory and two of her "right friends" come through the door. *Crap*. It was hardly a coincidence given the Bijou was *the* place to hang on a Friday—still, Fee cursed the fates. Not that she'd admit belief in fates or destiny to cause-and-effect Cass.

"Hey, guys," Marjory said, breaking into her best yearbook smile. "I was wondering if we'd run into you tonight."

"Hi," Cass said. At least when *she* smiled it was genuine.

"You guys didn't happen to see my yellow soccer ball, did you?" Marjory asked.

"No," Fee said. The falsetto lift to Marjory's voice buzzed Fee to attention.

"It's the weirdest thing." Marjory tapped at her bubblegum-pink-glossed lips. "It just went *missing* after practice."

Marjory's friends giggled. Fee supposed these friends—one mini, the other a big maxi type—offered the sort of feminine protection that a girl like Marjory needed.

"Look," Mini said, opening her purse for Fee and Cass.

"We're *smuggling* our own snacks into the movie." Three sticks of jerky lay atop a jumble of girl crap—*turkey* jerky.

"Are you on *drugs?*" Marjory forced Mini's purse closed. "Do you want to get us kicked out?"

Seeing as Will Peters had once Frisbee'd one of the theater's seat cushions from the front row to the back and had enjoyed his moviegoing experience from trailers to credits, Fee hardly thought that three strips of leathery meat were going to attract much notice. Of course, Fee knew their performance had nothing to do with lost balls or contraband snacks.

"Enjoy the movie," Maxi said, pulling Mini and Marjory away. They didn't even wait until they were out of earshot for the hysteria to begin.

So much for leak-guard technology, Fee thought in a rush of anger that quickly expanded to embarrassment and regret.

"Bitch," Cass said rather uncharacteristically.

"Big, bad bitch," Fee said.

"And so insensitive to your situation. It has to be hard enough."

Of all the things for realist Cass to believe in, she just had to pick Fee. Shame added its tug to Fee's nagging insides. The hard part, Fee thought, was finding the right way to fess up to Cass. The lobby of the Bijou was definitely not the place, but tonight during their sleepover she just had to come clean. Cass would understand. She was, after all, Fee's SFAM.

CHAPTER SEVENTEEN

Jill

Friday

Jill was in her element. Six couples, all sipping wine and nibbling appetizers, encircled her. This would be a good crowd. They were chatty and pleasant. She just hoped old 202 didn't poke a hole in the evening.

"We'll start with a game called *Two Truths and a Lie.*" They listened with eager faces, and Jill plumped with satisfaction. "Each of you will introduce yourself and where you're from, and then state three things about yourself: two things that are true and one that's a lie. We'll go around the circle and everyone, except your spouse or companion, will guess which of the three was your lie. When someone guesses correctly, they earn a point. Whoever has the most points after everyone has had a turn wins a bottle of wine."

She pointed to a bottle of Cabernet wrapped in cellophane

and tied with raffia. Everyone seemed on board, and they were all still smiling.

"I'll go first, just as an example, but it won't count." She stood and faced the group. "My name is Jill McCloud and I'm from Scotch Derry, born and raised." She held up her index finger. "Number one, at age ten I won a blue ribbon at the state fair for the longest pigtails." Her middle finger joined the index. "Number two, I collect salt and pepper shakers." She gestured a number three. "And finally, I have a tattoo of a nimbus on my left hip."

"The tattoo is the lie," a male voice called from the doorway.

Jill looked up to find Keith and Jocelyn striding across the room.

"Are we too late to join in?" Jocelyn asked. "This is my favorite of your games."

Pink slapped to Jill's cheeks. Where had they come from? Why were they together? And what were they doing here? Especially now, of all moments, when she stood in front of a group talking about pigtails and tattoos. She pushed at her dangling beaded bracelets until they clamped snugly around her freckled forearm.

"Everyone. This is my sister, Jocelyn, and her . . . friend Keith."

All eyes lifted to the newcomers. They did make an attractive pair.

"If no one objects, then I guess we can make room for two more." Though she'd never say so, she herself objected, inwardly reliving a lifetime of memories where Jocelyn had found Jill's loose thread and tugged. Jill was crushed to think, after all these years, that some kind of rivalry persisted.

"So are we going to play this one out?" asked a middle-aged man with a Fu Manchu mustache, muscled biceps, and a tight white T-shirt.

"Yes. As an example." Jill could still feel the sting in her cheeks. "We'd now go around the room and everyone would state which they think is the lie, except, of course, for my sister."

"I think it's the tattoo," Fu Man said.

As the rounds were made, ten out of the twelve guests guessed, correctly, that the tattoo was the lie. Jill was confounded. Normally the fact most people didn't know—with any real certainty—what a nimbus was or looked like quite ironically rendered it more plausible. She couldn't help but feel Keith's comment had come across as insider knowledge, all the more embarrassing considering the two Parsons chairs which Jocelyn had dragged to the circle were so intimately positioned that the blue of Jocelyn's denim melded into the faded black of Keith's cargoes.

Fu Man, whose name was Victor and who was from Minneapolis, offered to go first. His truths were he kept a ten-foot python and was a volunteer firefighter; his lie that he was afraid of clowns. It wasn't a bad lie, but Jill knew immediately—as did most of the guests—that this guy wouldn't easily admit to many fears.

His companion did better. No one suspected that the full-figured bohemian with her long gray hair and ankle-length skirt was a member of Mensa.

202 was still an enigma to Jill. All three of his statements seemed like fabrications, and Jill had an odd feeling he didn't enjoy the spotlight. Possibly, he was discomfited by the fact that one of his wife's statements, that today was her birthday, was not the lie. Jill noticed him lift his eyes to the ceiling in self-reproach.

Last were Jocelyn and Keith. Jocelyn played the shock card with her three statements: one, she had implants; two, she could ask "Which way is the bar?" in five languages; and three, Hugh Grant asked for her phone number after she gave him a hot and heavy massage. The way her boobs jiggled when she reenacted the neck rub was a dead giveaway. Everyone knew they were real.

Keith started by stating he had helped build a school in Thailand. In this game, Jill reminded herself, altruism was rarely the lie. He also claimed to have climbed Mount Fuji. Jill recollected that he was not a driven athlete. He played high school football to please his father and could serve himself out of trouble on a tennis court, but had himself claimed it more recreation than sport. Mountain climbing. She just couldn't picture it. Finally, he said he'd contracted malaria in Kenya and had lain on a cot in a small village clinic with dirt floors and flapping canvas walls for ten days. The school turned out to be the lie, which Jill couldn't help but admit as clever. She also noticed his travels got a lot of oohs and aahs from the group, which ironically made him slouch and Jocelyn preen.

After the game, the guests drifted away, most of them to walk in the garden. Jill hurried to her room and grabbed a wrapped gift off her dresser. It was a birthday present for her friend Hen, whom she'd be seeing on Sunday. She bustled down to the patio where 202 was engaged in conversation with another guest while their wives walked through the roses. Jill tapped him lightly on the shoulder and he turned. She briefly displayed the small square box and then slipped it into his jacket pocket.

"A silver bracelet, simple but elegant. Should you not require it, you can return it to me tomorrow. Should it be of some use to you, we can settle up later." Judging by his reaction, he'd be visiting her, checkbook in hand.

Upon returning to the parlor, she found Jocelyn and Keith still in their seats. Jill poured herself a glass of wine and sat opposite them.

"When did Victor and his sister check in?" Jocelyn asked.

"This afternoon. And why do you think she's his sister?"

"It was obvious. I knew they weren't a couple the moment I laid eyes on them."

"How could you know that immediately?" Jill asked.

"It's a gift. I don't know why you always question it." Jocelyn crossed her legs. "Let me guess, separate rooms."

"Yes," Jill said with reluctance. She herself hadn't given much thought to their arrangements. Separate rooms were not unheard of for new couples.

"Anyway, the sister gives off some serious spoken-for vibes, while Victor's on-the-market signal could blow you to Nebraska."

"How do you know he's not just looking for a little side action?" Keith asked.

"Nothing alike," Jocelyn said with a slash of her hand. "When free and clear, a guy puts out something earthy and green. If cheating, it's musky and brown."

If eligible had a scent and a spoke on the color wheel, as did monogamy, as did infidelity—Jill wondered how her own brand of loneliness would register. Was she off the chart, as in negligible, undetectable? It wasn't as if she had lived an entirely chaste and cloistered existence. There had been several brief affairs, and she and David Skovel had dated for five years. He wanted to marry her, help raise Fee, and have one or two of their own. Her reluctance had been annoying, even to her-self. He had been sweet with Fee, having known her from age four to nine, and had repeatedly offered to make legal Skovels of both of them. Ruby had salivated at the very idea of a wed-ding in the family. Her own slapped-together affair and then two never-the-bride daughters were the great regrets of her life. Knowing she'd never marry him, Jill had finally broken it off. But that had been years ago; before yesterday, she hadn't been kissed by a guy since . . . she didn't even know.

"Like I said, Victor's green is interesting, and it went from mossy to grassy. I think he fancied someone in the room," Jocelyn said with a lift of her eyebrows.

Jill snapped to, realizing she'd missed a portion of what Jocelyn had said. "What?"

"Have I mentioned how pretty you look tonight?" Jocelyn asked.

"What? Me?" Jill asked. "Forget it. I don't go for the biker type."

"I don't know about any of Jocelyn's extrasensory stuff, but did you notice?" Keith moved forward in his chair, address-ing Jill. "He was the winner. *Victor* was the winner."

"So?" Jocelyn asked.

Keith continued to look directly at Jill. "And Peter, he got off to a pretty good start, but then he fizzled out."

"I don't get it," Jocelyn said.

Keith sat back in his seat. "Just a little philosophy I have about names and destiny. You haven't forgotten, have you, Jill?"

Of course she hadn't forgotten. And, yes, she had noticed; Victor anyway. The Peter one got past her.

"How cute. You two still have your own language." Jocelyn

stood. "If you're ready to go, Keith, I'll drive you home." She gazed out the large picture window to the gardens. "Oh, look, Jill, your winner's coming up the path. And he's all alone."

Jill had enough. She stood and lifted two dirty wineglasses and a stack of cheese plates from the coffee table. "Time for me to call it a night, anyway. See you in the morning, Jocelyn." The good night exchanged with Keith was far more awkward. Neither bringing up the fact that it could be good-bye for who knew how long, forever a real possibility.

Sucking in air so thin she felt light-headed, she hurried to the kitchen, where she found Ruby staring out the kitchen window toward the garage.

"Dear God in heaven," Ruby said. "That's William with Jocelyn."

Jill set the dishes down and came to stand behind her mother.

"That's not William, Mom."

Ruby's hand shook as she raised it to the side of her face. "He seems fine, doesn't he?"

Jill looked out to where her mother was looking. "Mom, that's Keith. You know Keith. Jocelyn's driving him home." Jill spoke calmly, feeling her own breathing grow steadier. "William was Keith's father. There was a family resemblance, but William is dead. He died a couple years ago."

"I know. I killed him."

"No, Mom. He died in Florida. Of a heart attack."

Ruby nodded her head up and down. "Like I said. I killed him."

CHAPTER EIGHTEEN

Ruby

October 1965

Ruby held a check and a typed letter in her hand and stared down Clive Jones, catering manager of the Beaulieu Hotel. "What do you mean our reception has been canceled?"

Clive sat behind a massive oak desk and clutched a large black leather reservations log to his chest. "There was a clerical error. It seems another party had already booked the ballroom for Saturday the twenty-seventh of November. My assistant should never have written you a contract."

Ruby frowned. "But this is our wedding. The invitations have been mailed. You can't just cancel the reservation."

Clive exhaled loudly. "The reservation is not confirmed until the deposit has cleared. You will find wording to that effect in the contract."

Ruby waved the check in his face. "But I sent you the payment a month ago. On time. And now you send it back to me with a cancellation notice!"

Clive tugged at his collar. "We never deposited the check. We were looking into the misunderstanding." He fiddled with a cuff link. "We deeply regret the mix-up. Perhaps we could look at another date?" Clive set the book on his desk and opened it. He thumbed past one page, and then another. His pale eyes darted back and forth while his long white fingers scanned columns of cramped ink notations. "It won't be until January. What with all the holiday parties."

"January?"

"Yes. Both the twelfth and the twenty-sixth are open. Or would you like me to look in February?"

Ruby raised her voice. "We can't wait until January or February."

Clive lifted his eyebrows.

"Nobody gets married in the dead of winter."

Clive continued to thumb through his book. "Of course there is April or May. And most couples prefer a springtime wedding."

Ruby panted as if she had just climbed stairs, or ran for miles, or whacked an incompetent clerk over the head with a heavy book. She took a long moment to calm herself and process the information. "Can you tell me who has booked the room that evening?" There was a new lift to Ruby's voice.

He cleared his throat with a gutless cough. "The Garden Society."

Ruby laughed out loud. "The Garden Society. In November!" Ruby ripped first the letter, and then the check, into strips of meaningless scrap. "Tell me," she said, fixing Clive with cadaver-cold eyes, "is Hester Fraser, as president of the Garden Society, the contact name on that event?"

Though he made no reply, Clive's ratlike twitches confirmed her suspicions.

Back at the house, she received a call from the florist. They would, regrettably, be unable to service the wedding due to a prior commitment. The photographer called with a similar excuse, as did the bakery. Within the next few days, they began to receive the invitation response cards. They all came back with regrets.

Daniel found Ruby facedown on the bed and with her head buried in a pillow, which did little to muffle the sobs. He patted her gently on the back. "We knew we'd make an enemy."

"She's evil," Ruby said into the down feathers, "and has no soul."

"She's hurt and incredibly angry."

Ruby lifted her head. "How can you defend her?"

"I'm not defending her. Nor am I surprised at her reaction." Daniel pulled Ruby's hand into his own. "I told you she threw a fit. I've never seen her like that before. I knew there would be hell to pay."

"Hell to pay, because she's Satan."

Daniel had described the breakup to Ruby months ago. He proclaimed it the worst confrontation of his life. Hester had been apoplectic with rage. She called him a lech and a degenerate, and wanted to know how many of the girls in the home he had availed himself of over the years. He actually feared she might strike him.

Daniel helped Ruby to a sitting position. "Personally, I never wanted a big wedding. Is it really so important to you?"

Ruby took a deep breath. She had always wanted a formal wedding with a whole sea of onlookers. She wanted to wear a white dress, drink champagne, and slice into an iced tower of at least six layers. It would have legitimized everything. Daniel had chosen her and was willing to stand up in front of the entire community to say so. Peering into the deep pools of Daniel's eyes, she knew, then, how little any of that mattered. "I thought it was."

"If we postpone, she wins. Is that what you want?"

"I don't want her to win," Ruby said with childlike defiance.

Daniel laughed. "She can't. Not in the end, anyway." He pulled Ruby's hand to his lips. "We will be married."

"What should we do?"

"We marry here. Today. No matter if there are only the servants and girls in the house as witnesses. We'll have a service in the parlor and dinner in the dining room. I'll call Reverend Murray right now."

"Today!"

"Why not?"

"Because we're not ready. I don't have a dress or flowers. What will we serve for dinner? And your kilt. You've sent away to Scotland for the clan tartan. You were going to wear formal Highland dress."

"I don't care about that. Any of it. All I care is that we declare our love and commitment."

"What about the bagpipes? You wanted bagpipes."

"Ruby, all I want is you."

"You're right," she said. "It's not the wedding that matters. It's the marriage."

"You see." Daniel pulled her into his arms. "We're already starting to think alike."

Several days later, Ruby fingered her new gold band absentmindedly as she walked out of the library and straight into the path of William.

"William," she said. "What a surprise." He wore the same glum expression she'd left him with all those weeks ago.

"Ruby. I'm glad I ran into you." His voice was sad and his eyes were red. "I wanted to say good-bye."

It was only four in the afternoon, but Ruby thought she smelled whisky on his breath. "You're leaving?"

"I'm going to clerk for a law office in Boston until school starts in January." He jammed his fists deep into his pockets. "I either cut the mustard, or they cut the cord."

Something churned in her tummy. The breakup had not rendered William angry or mean. It had, however, cuffed him sharply. That day, in his car, he had turned from her, needing a moment to compose himself. His eyes had been runny and his voice had wavered, but still he'd been a perfect gentleman.

"I hear congratulations are in order," he said after a pause.

"Thank you. And I really do wish you the best," Ruby said.

"I know."

"Good luck at school."

"Good luck to you." He took a step back, hesitating, and then leaned forward. "And don't let her get to you. She's out for blood, you know."

Ruby was startled by his warning. "I'll watch my back."

"And just so you know," he said. "Your man, Daniel, he really wasn't her type." William lifted his eyebrows. "Still, she'll never forgive. I want you to know, I had a long discussion with my parents. Hester had them talked into pulling their financial support from the home. I think I've convinced them it would reflect poorly on them, make them look petty and vindictive." He shifted from one foot to the other. "People of character don't take their anger out on charities, now, do they?"

Ruby was cut by his kindness. "Why would you do such a thing?"

William brushed a lock of hair off his forehead. "Because it made Hester madder than a gored bull." He crossed his arms over his crisp white shirt. "Plus, you're still the best girl I ever met. Even if you did break my heart."

CHAPTER NINETEEN

Fee

Friday–Saturday

After the movie, Fee and Cass went back to Cass's house for a sleepover. As usual, they hung out in the basement, where a pool table and game systems provided entertainment as well as an excuse to seclude themselves. Despite good intentions and poured-concrete soundproofing, Fee still couldn't bring herself to confess her LeBron-on-steroids-size tale. When Cass suggested chocolate-chip cookies, Fee eagerly consented, not realizing it would entail a postmidnight bake fest. Cass's house was small. Granted, her parents were in bed, but Fee had no idea how much noise carried to the first-floor master. And Fee's confession required the kind of privacy only a separate, preferably subterranean, level could provide.

Shortly before one, as they sat at the island debating if the cookies tasted better dunked in root beer or Gatorade, Cass cleared her throat. "I want you to know something," she said.

"What?"

"There's a rumor going around about your aunt Jocelyn."

"What kind of rumor?"

Cass strummed her fingernails on the island top, making a *tip-tap, tip-tap* sound. "About Jocelyn and that Keith guy."

"What did you hear?"

"You're not going to like it."

"Just tell me." Fee shouldn't have had that big scoop of cookie dough. The raw egg wasn't settling well.

"I guess it's what Marjory was hinting at before. My sister heard from one of her teammates that Keith used to go with both your mom and Jocelyn."

"I already knew that."

"And that he dumped Jocelyn, dumped your mom, and left town because he didn't want to be a dad." Cass dipped her head nervously. "But the weird thing is they're saying it was Jocelyn he left pregnant."

Fee forgot to breathe. Her trapped swell of air came out as a huff. This was what the two women at the dead-lady party were talking about: why they used the term *mystery child*. And how exactly had she asked her mom? How had her mom phrased her denial? Was her mom's dismissal of Keith only correct on a technicality—a loophole. One where Keith hadn't left *her* pregnant? Cass was looking at Fee with big, bugged-out eyes. *Now what?* Fee thought. Her goal for the night, to deny the drug-smuggling Turk, would give credibility to this new version of events. Fee's mind was bucking that notion with a fury that left her hurt and angrier than she'd been in a long time.

"That's nuts," Fee snapped. "I hope you stuck up for me. I hope you told Mel to tell whoever is spreading that shit to shut up."

"I did," Cass said. "Except I couldn't very well tell Mel the truth."

The truth. What the hell was it? Fee hurt in a place she couldn't name, couldn't find on an anatomy chart, couldn't even point to. And it was too crazy to think about. No way Aunt Jocelyn would leave her baby. And why would one sister raise the other's child?

"I don't feel so good," Fee said. "I ate too much batter. I need to crash."

For the rest of the night, Fee lay on the old sofa in the basement listening to Cass's nearby purr of blocked nasals and convinced herself that rumors were usually just that.

CHAPTER TWENTY

Jill

Saturday

Jill was dragged from sleep by a pounding at her door. 202 stood in the hallway.

"Is something wrong?" she asked.

"I'm afraid I have a small emergency."

Jill looked out into the hallway, expecting water soaking the carpets or flames licking up the walls. "What is it?"

"My laptop crashed."

Jill looked back out to the hallway. For his sake, there'd better be something more to the emergency. A dead body at the very least. "What?"

"I apologize. You have every right to think I'm crazy." Indeed, he stood at her door in the middle of the night carrying a brief-case and wearing striped pajamas rolled to the knee and brown, sockless loafers. "But I wonder if I might use a computer?"

"I don't have a business center."

"How about your personal computer?"

"You want to use my private office?" Jill rubbed the face of her watch. "At two a.m.?"

"Like I said, it's an emergency. Business. I really can't say any more."

This guy was something else. Her computer was her lifeline. It contained everything—her business files, bank accounts, personal correspondence, medical records—everything. She'd be crazy to let a stranger use it. Moreover, he was stranger than most. Something about this guy gave her goose bumps in places she didn't even know she had skin.

"How long would it take?" she asked.

"A couple of hours."

"A couple of hours?" Plenty of time to steal someone's identity, charge to the high heavens, and open accounts to banks of countries she'd never even heard of. Fog rolled through Jill's brain. Had she been dreaming she lost all her teeth on a tennis court, but Keith played on, calling out a score of forty–love? "Is it really that urgent?"

"Yes."

"And I can trust you?" Because, she chided herself, that's the one question a thief will cave to.

"Of course."

Jill pushed her toes into slippers and led 202 across the plank floors with only the jangle of her key ring and the clomp of his loafers breaking the eerie silence. She was too tired to formulate a refusal, but already regretted the decision. Her only consolation being there wasn't much to steal.

. . .

The next morning, Saturday, when she returned from picking up Fee from her friend Cass's, Jill found Borka at the front desk processing a charge slip.

"Did someone check out?" Jill asked.

"Room 202."

"What? Their reservation was through Sunday."

"He asked if he could check out early." Borka stapled the receipt to a copy of his charges. "You were gone; I couldn't find your mother, so I just took care of it."

A rush of blood, fueled by steam and mixed with a dose of piss, went to Jill's head. She was an idiot. A jumbo-size, Big Gulp of an idiot. There had been something about the guy she hadn't trusted from the start. She'd known, with a creepy kind of third-eye feeling, that the guy was pretending to be something he wasn't. She'd probably have a dozen aliases, a Cessna plane, and a small munitions factory by the time the banks opened on Monday.

"He didn't happen to mention a bracelet, did he?"

"No."

And there it was: confirmation. She'd been had. "Where's Jocelyn?" Jill asked.

"I was going to ask you the same thing. Her bed wasn't slept in."

Jill closed her eyes and tilted back her head. At this point, she thought to herself, she'd take one of those aliases.

CHAPTER TWENTY-ONE

Jill

Sunday

Jill pulled into the Sylvan Golf Course, singing along—albeit badly—with the radio. She liked Sundays. Most guests checked out, and there were rarely arrivals. The third Sunday of the month was her particular favorite, owing to a standing foursome with her three best friends. When storms or biting winds or snowdrifts forced them indoors, they met at Jill's to play cards.

They had long since dispensed with first names, having reduced each of their personalities to a single defining characteristic. Pickle was always in some sort of a jam. Mother Hen, or just Hen, was their counsel, comforter, and all-around protector. And Scoop always had the latest gossip.

Thanks to Jocelyn, Jill was running late. Pickle had canceled earlier due to a sick child. Jocelyn had agreed to fill in, but had backed out at the last minute, claiming a headache and exhaustion. Not only had she deterred Jill, but she hadn't given her time to call anyone else. After showing up with Keith at the wine tasting on Friday and not sleeping in her room, Jocelyn had been gone all Saturday on a clandestine outing. When Jill had asked where she'd been, Jocelyn had the audacity to reply, "A lady never tells." Later on, the "lady" had rubbed her inner thighs and complained of "riding pains." Jill had felt her own groin cinch and pull at the remark.

Sylvan wasn't the sort of fancy country club where you could drop your car and clubs off with a valet. Jill parked, hitched her bag over her shoulder, and scurried through the parking lot. At the side of the clubhouse, she spied two carts lined up and ready to go.

"Sorry, girls. It's been a crazy day," she said, catching her breath and setting down the heavy bag. She put her arm around Hen. "And there was a little mishap with your birthday gift. It's going to be a little late this year." She heaved her bag into the back of the cart. "Looks like it's going to be just the three of us. Jocelyn was going to fill in, but ended up bailing."

"Am I late?"

Jill heard a familiar male voice and turned to see Keith hurrying toward them. She cocked her head in confusion.

Keith approached the group and set his clubs down with a loud *thwomp*. "Jocelyn phoned and said you were desperate for a fourth."

"Desperate?" was all Jill could manage.

He smiled and pushed his hair off his forehead. "Her words, not mine." He spun the golf bag around, inspecting the clubs. "I have no idea what I've got here. They're rentals and look like they've seen hard times."

Hen had been eyeing Keith. She'd only lived in the area for a few years, so had never met him and wasn't aware of his history with the McClouds. "You must be a family member," she said. "There's a real resemblance, especially with Fee."

"Fee's far too pretty to be confused with the likes of me. I'm Keith Fraser." He tossed his head from side to side. "No relation."

Scoop, a lifelong townie, had the audacity to chuckle.

Hen must have understood some misstep on her part. "So sorry. It's just something about your eyes, their shade of brown."

"He's Hester Fraser's nephew," Jill said. "In town for the funeral." Jill gestured toward the two women. "Keith, this is Hen and Scoop."

"Great names," he said.

"We're an informal group." Scoop extended her right hand. "We've met before. Years ago, when you and Jill were dating."

"Wow," Keith said. "You've got a great memory."

Scoop was still holding Keith's hand in a prolonged shake. Jill couldn't tell if it was her proximity to him or the reference to the past that made him seem uncomfortable. He finally pulled his hand away.

"I'm sorry for your loss," Hen said, always one to intuit a situation.

"Thank you, though we weren't close."

Hen nodded with affection. "Sometimes that makes it even harder."

Keith returned her smile and even appeared to relax a little. Hen's calming presence never ceased to amaze Jill.

Scoop reached out and took Jill by the elbow. "I meant to ask you, did you meet with the bank yet?"

Jill colored. "No, not yet."

"There's an article in *Newsweek*. I saved it for you. Lots of people are renegotiating the terms of their loan. After all, the bank wants your payment, not your property."

Jill's eyes darted back and forth from Scoop to Keith. Was he listening? He seemed to be. She wished at the moment, more than she wished for anything—world peace included— that she had never confided in her friend. Though she probably had a better chance of resettling the Kurds than she had at shutting Scoop up. She brushed back a thick clump of unruly curls. "I'm not worried. It'll all work out."

Scoop huffed out loud. "This is not the sort of thing that takes care of itself. You need a plan of action."

Keith gestured toward a bank of gray clouds. "So are we going to get this round in before the downpour? Weatherman seemed pretty sure we're in for quite a storm. It's really cooled off, too."

Jill looked up, grateful for the heavy sky. "Let's get going. Maybe we can beat the rain."

"How about you and I ride together today, Hen," Scoop said. "I want your opinion on what to do about Sammy. I got another call from his teacher. You don't mind, do you, Carrot?"

"Carrot?" Keith asked.

"My nickname." Jill rolled her eyes.

"And don't think it's just for her hair color." Hen poked Jill's shoulder. "This gem is like a ten-carat diamond, highly polished, brilliant, and made of the hardest material known to mankind."

"Makes sense to me," he said.

Jill walked with Keith toward the cart. "I hope you didn't cancel anything on our account. I don't know why Jocelyn would say we were desperate. We've played with three before, and sometimes the clubhouse will just assign us a walk-on."

"I didn't have anything to cancel."

Jill moved toward the driver's side. "Do you mind if I drive?"

Keith wiped his right arm toward the driver's seat. "My pleasure. A day off. A round of golf. And a beautiful chauffeur."

Jill pulled her sun visor down over her hair. She wished she'd taken more time with it. It had a tendency to coil with the humidity and she hated when it stuck out of her visor like dog ears. She shouldn't have worn the pink skort either. Freckled redheads don't look good in pink. She wondered if she looked more like a spotted salmon or a sprinkled cupcake. Jocelyn would have some crazy chakra for pink, like it's the tongue chakra or the menses chakra. And she wished Keith hadn't called her beautiful. She wasn't. She was smart enough and old enough to know as much. Jocelyn inherited Ruby's beauty. Jill got her father's mind and just enough of what remained of Ruby's looks to be known as cute, or attractive, maybe even pretty on a good day, but not beautiful.

Scoop pulled her cart alongside Jill's. "Coolers are loaded and in the back of the cart. Your favorite this time, Boulevard Wheat."

"Thanks," Jill said.

"Are we talking libations?" Keith asked.

"Absolutely."

"I'm liking this more and more."

"Like Scoop said, we're an informal group."

Keith was an awful golfer with a big shank of a swing that sent the ball flying a good two hundred yards left or right, but rarely straight ahead. Jill had a natural swing that was a consistent one hundred right down the middle. Keith kept looking at the rented clubs as if they were warped or bent. Jill knew better. He swung too hard, lifted his head, and had a jerky shoulder rotation, which was responsible for his shots ending up on the neighboring fairway. Most guys she knew would either be mad or mopey by now. Keith just seemed to approach each new hole as a new opportunity to tank.

And despite a resolve not to, Jill found herself laughing and smiling so much her facial muscles quivered like Jell-O. And he, judging by his return grins and guffaws, was having a great time as well. Clever and funny, damn him. And so confoundedly charming and chatty with her friends that they, too, were giggly and flirty. More than once, she steadied herself by visualizing his plane ticket resting atop a packed suitcase.

As they walked off the greens at the fourteenth hole, Keith asked, "So, Carrot, what's up with the names? Scoop and Hen?"

She described how they had earned their monikers.

"Who am I subbing for?"

"Pickle. She stumbles from one calamity to the next."

"Do I get my own?"

Jill shook her head. "Regulars only."

"Darn. You know how I love names."

"I know, but you gotta earn one with us. You know, over time."

He dipped his head into his large hand and brushed the hair off his forehead. "Oh. Over time." He seemed genuinely disappointed.

"You'll be going home soon. Right?"

"Yes." He seemed a little taken back by her comment. "Just one last bit of business regarding the will."

"And Jocelyn will be leaving day after tomorrow, anyway."

"Jocelyn?"

"You two have been seeing quite a bit of each other. Game night. Yesterday."

"Yesterday?" His forehead creased.

Jill's cell phone rang and for once she loved the sound of its jangle. She saw Fee's name in the caller ID box.

"Hi, Fee. What is it?"

Fee's voice sounded anxious. "Mom, there's a problem with the downstairs bathroom."

"What kind of problem?"

"A leak. A big leak."

"Darn," Jill said. "How bad is it?"

"Bad. May-need-a-boat-soon bad."

"Have Jocelyn call the plumber, John Saylor. He's in the book."

"Aunt Jocelyn left."

"Left? Left where? I thought she wasn't feeling well."

"I don't know," Fee said. "She took off all dressed up in a black leather vest and the most killer pair of heels. They actually had a zebra pattern."

"Where's Booboo?" Jill was embarrassed to use any more nicknames, particularly Ruby's, in earshot of Keith.

"I can't find her."

"What do you mean you can't find her?" This was almost more alarming than the leak.

"Well, it's not like I'm her keeper," Fee said. "For all I know, she could be sleeping or something. Except she's not in her room."

"You're going to have to phone the plumber yourself."

"I can't stay and wait for him. I'm getting picked up. I'm babysitting for the Monroes, remember?"

Jill did remember, and also recalled that Ruby had promised to be available for the few guests that remained.

"I'm coming home right now. Call John Saylor and don't leave until I get there." Jill snapped her phone shut and turned to Keith. "I'm sorry, but it looks like I'm the one with the crisis today. There's a plumbing emergency at home. I need to go." She walked quickly toward the cart. "Do you want to jump in with Hen and Scoop to finish the round?"

"Why don't I come with you? I've been under a few sinks in my day."

"Thanks, but it's really not necessary. Fee's calling the plumber."

"How do you know he'll be available with such short notice?"

Jill hadn't thought about that. The guy did service a large area.

"It could be a big mess. Would you know what to do?" He looked down at his khakis and old Nikes. "I'm not afraid of a little water."

"If you wouldn't mind," she said finally. "Plumbing is not my specialty."

They called rushed good-byes to Hen and Scoop and then drove the golf cart back to the clubhouse. Jill tried Jocelyn on her cell phone three times with no answer. Keith agreed to follow her back to the house in his car. If he could keep up; he'd always been a slow driver.

CHAPTER TWENTY-TWO

Jill

Sunday

They found Fee waiting outside; she was barefoot with her jeans rolled to her knees. "Thank God," she said as Jill and Keith walked up the path. She held her phone up. "I can't get hold of the plumber. I've left two messages already. And the Monroes will be here any minute. Am I done here?"

Jill just wanted to get a look at the damage. Fee was a distraction. "Yes. Go."

Once inside, Jill led the way to the bathroom. A steady stream of water gushed from under a bank of three new sinks. The interior designer had talked her into the handblown-glass-vessel–style basins. At over a thousand dollars each, plus the supporting slab of granite, she would have thought they came with plumbing.

"Do you have a wrench?" Keith asked from his crouch under the sinks.

"Out in the shed. I'll be right back."

Jill ran over the flagstone path and sensed, somehow, that the tributary forming under her sinks was not the true source of the crush she felt to her chest. Where the devil was her mother? The toolbox was crazy heavy, but somehow she lugged it back to the bathroom. Keith found what he was looking for and began strong-arming the knob to the left. Fee had had the presence of mind to blanket the tile floor with old towels, and Jill was kept busy arranging them as the eddies of water dictated.

"Would you excuse me a moment?" she asked. "Fee said she didn't know where my mom is. I just want to have a look."

"Sure," Keith grunted. The knob was not budging easily.

Jill hurried to their private quarters and began calling, "Mom? Where are you, Mom?" There was no reply. The usual places were searched: their private family room, Ruby's room, Jill's room, Fee's room. She also checked the public rooms: the lounge, dining room, and library. She then jogged upstairs and, with a master key, opened unoccupied guest rooms. Ruby was nowhere to be found.

When Jill returned, Keith was wiping his soiled hands on a guest towel. "Finished."

Keith followed Jill into the kitchen, where she proceeded to rifle through the deep corners of the large walk-in pantry.

"Did you lose something?" he asked.

"My mother."

"How do you lose a mother?"

Jill tapped her knuckle to her bottom lip. "It's easier than you'd think." She stepped over to the window and looked out to the pond and woods beyond. The sun would be setting soon, and the storms which had threatened earlier were now pressing down in the forms of char-tinged clouds. "More and more, I suspect it's some kind of early dementia. For a long time it was just little things, but it's getting worse. She's always been a character, operating by her own set of rules, but lately . . . And I can't go to the police. Not unless I have something concrete to report."

"It's a missing person, right? They have to help."

"Not for twenty-four hours they don't." She shook her head. "Trust me, I've been here before. About a month ago, I got a call from some guy two miles away. He found her sleeping on his deck chair. And I don't want to describe her fondness for Sam's Bar, or casinos." Jill ran her fingers through her hair and exhaled loudly. She pulled her cell phone out of her pocket, flipped it open, and punched a number into its keypad. She stared ahead for a few moments and then snapped it shut. "Where the hell is Jocelyn?" Hating the fact she needed further assistance, she turned to face Keith. "Would you help me?"

"Of course," he said. "You know I would."

"I'll grab us a couple of flashlights and then I think we should take a walk around the pond."

"Whatever you need."

In the garage, she found a Maglite and a camping lantern. She handed Keith the lantern and directed him to follow her down the path that led from the back of the house to the pond. Hearing a crack of thunder in the distance, she thought maybe they should run back to the house for raincoats, but one look to the murky pond water had her pressing forward.

Fat raindrops began to fall on her bare arms, and she was surprised how quickly the sky was inking over and at the sudden drop in temperature.

"What makes you think she's out here?" Keith spoke loudly to be heard over the sudden spill of rain.

"I've looked all through the house. It's just the next logical place. Sometimes she likes to sit in the Adirondacks and look at the water."

"Would she stay out in this weather, though?" A flash of lightning lit the sky, kindling Keith's face with an eerie incandescence.

"I don't know. She's been acting strange the last couple of days, muttering about broken hearts, and wicked widows, and dead men. Then again, last month she went on a three-day tirade complaining of babies keeping her awake all night and cold doctor's hands." Jill brushed wet bangs off her forehead. "I hope I don't have to tell you that there are no babies or icy-fingered doctors at our place."

They reached the spot where the two chairs faced onto the pond and small wooden dock. An old rowboat was roped to the end of the rickety wooden platform. Jill stepped onto the wooden planks and pulled the boat close. Ruby was not much of a boater, or swimmer for that matter. Jill really didn't think she'd venture onto, or into, the water.

As if reading her mind, Keith asked, "What now?"

Jill shielded her eyes from the rain that was now pouring freely and looked to the thick woods that loomed over the back side of the pond. She pointed. "I see something shiny on the ground over there."

"Is that your property?"

"Technically, no. The owner only comes around during hunting season, though." It was dark enough now that Jill switched on the flashlight.

After a brisk walk, they reached the edge of the trees. Jill bent to retrieve a silver-labeled bottle that lay in the center of a dirt path. "This is one of my wines."

Keith took it from Jill and turned it over in his hand. "But it could have come from any of your guests, right?"

"Except it's new. I only received this case today."

"What about Jocelyn? Where is she?"

Jill shook her head. "She'd drink the wine all right, but Jocelyn's idea of a walk involves a mall and shopping bags. Plus, Fee said she was all dressed up and wearing heels."

"And Fee?"

"No. Definitely not. There's something going on with her, but I don't think it involves drinking."

He gestured behind him with his thumb. "What's back there?"

"Besides trees, just an old hunting lodge, a one-room cabin that hasn't been used in ages. There used to be an interior road from the highway, but its bridge washed out a few years ago. It's only accessible by foot now. And from here, it's a hike."

The rain picked up.

"Why would your mom go there?"

Jill took the bottle back from Keith. She was worried, and irritated, and cold, and just plain old tired of people letting her down. She dropped the bottle. "Probably drunk for starters. And just following the path." Her forearms were wet and she rubbed them in an attempt to generate heat. "Maybe she's just walking that way and we'll overtake her on the path." She looked up, craning her head to see into the dark woods. "But I never know why people do half the things they do. And I've had it with trying to figure them out." There was a bite to her voice and an involuntary roll of her eyes that implicated more than her mother. She could see his surprise and think of no other escape than to follow the path into the woods.

Footsteps crunched urgently behind her. She quickened the pace. Keith pulled on her right arm. "Are you mad at me?"

She pulled her arm back defensively. Had she been the confrontational type, she'd have replied that yes, she was mad, because she had worries enough to fill her sleepless nights without visions of Jocelyn and Keith together again horning in. "I've seen you once in fifteen years. What could I be mad about?"

"It sure sounds like you are." They were under a huge oak with limbs that hovered just above their heads. The tree gave them momentary shelter from the downpour, but the rain was still loud as it pelted the woods around them. "And it's twice actually."

"What?"

"I've seen you twice in fifteen years." Lightning split the sky with a deafening crack and he instinctively pulled her into their small arbor of protection. "I saw you years ago when I was home for Hester's birthday. I came in with my father and we took her out to dinner at the Hitzel Haus. You were there."

"What?"

Twigs crunched under his feet. "I would have said hello, but you were with a date: small guy, big eyes."

Leave it to the big man to size up the little one. "So?"

"I watched him give you a small box wrapped with a big red ribbon. He kissed you and held your hand. I didn't want to intrude."

Jill remembered the night. She and David Skovel were two years into their relationship. She had genuine affection for him, but when she saw the ring-size box, terror had iced her insides.

"It was pearl earrings. For my birthday."

"How nice."

"I lost one within a few weeks of receiving them."

"Oh."

Jill shivered as the dark and cold pressed in around them. "I remember the other time. I met Meredith."

"You remember her name?"

Jill could smack herself, hard, for the gaffe. "She was very striking."

"And controlling, and demanding, and impatient."

Jill was grateful to have the situation with Ruby as a detour. She took a step toward the path. "I think the rain's letting up a little. We really should keep going."

The rain soaked through to her bra and panties, and the silly golf skort kept sticking to her thighs. She could feel, and even hear, the little footies squish inside her golf shoes, and her hair clung to her neck and shoulders in thick, wet ropes.

Finally, a flash of lightning revealed the hunting lodge in a narrow clearing. It was a small log structure with a tin-covered roof. As children, she and Jocelyn had often sneaked out to what they had considered their own secret clubhouse. Jill hadn't been in years, but could still imagine the brick fireplace, simple pine table with mismatched chairs, and sagging bed with tick mattress.

She pushed open the heavy front door and stood peering into the gloom. It was dark and still, and smelled of must and wet wood. About to proclaim Ruby not there, Jill heard something near the hearth groan, and she swept her flashlight over the area.

"Look. What's that on the ground?" she said.

Keith's lantern swung as he strode the few steps it took to reach the prostrate form. Jill followed and reached his elbow just as he rolled Ruby onto her back.

"Oh my God." Jill's free hand covered her mouth.

"She's bleeding. It looks like she fell and cut her head." He whistled low. "It looks bad." Lifting his lantern, he scanned the area. "There's blood on the floor. A lot of it." The light illuminated the shape of several dark logs scattered near the fireplace. "Would she have been trying to make a fire?"

Ruby moaned in pain and slowly opened her eyes. She looked wildly from Keith to Jill, and then back to Keith again. "I knew you'd come," she said through clenched teeth, all the while holding Keith's gaze.

"Mom, it's me, Jill. Tell me, did you fall? Is that why you're bleeding?"

Ruby lifted her hand to her head and winced at the touch. "It got so dark. I couldn't see. Why did you make me wait so long?" She continued to look at Keith. "You're mad at me, aren't you? You know, don't you?" Ruby began to cry. At first it was a small childish whimper, but then it became increasingly despondent. "I kept her close to me. She's always been safe."

Jill shook her head. "She doesn't know what she's saying. Probably a concussion." She flipped open her cell phone. "Shit! No signal." She exhaled in exasperation and looked at her mother, who continued to writhe in pain. "There's no way the two of us can carry her. I'll stay with her. Can you go back and call an ambulance? You'll have to describe the situation to them. She'll need to be carried out on a stretcher." Ruby shivered, also wet with rain, Jill now realized. "She's cold."

Keith set down the lantern, yanked his golf shirt over his head, and threw it to Jill. "Apply pressure." He started toward the door. "Keep her warm while I'm gone. We don't want her going into shock. And don't let her fall asleep."

Keith was gone before Jill could comment. She eased herself down to the ground and wrestled her mother into a sitting position. Propping her back against the raised brick hearth, she pulled her mother up against her outstretched legs trying to make skin-to-skin contact at as many points as she could. Ruby continued to cry off and on. Jill kept Keith's damp shirt, which smelled confoundedly of him, pressed against Ruby's head and tried to shoosh her with comforting words, but Ruby became increasingly restless.

Jill was overcome with exhaustion and felt unwelcome tears come to her own eyes. They'd turned a corner and the view ahead was bleak. There was no way Jill would be able to watch her mother all hours of the day.

Ruby stirred again and her eyes chased through the room. "Has he gone again? Has he left me?"

"Who, Mom?"

"William. William, of course."

Jill caressed her mother's shoulder with her left hand. "That wasn't William, Mom. William's dead. Remember? That was his son, Keith."

"I broke his heart, you know."

Jill realized the need to keep Ruby awake and talking, but didn't want to upset her with difficult memories. "It's okay, Mom. That was a long time ago. You were just a girl."

"I was a looker back then."

Jill couldn't help but smile. "I know. You were the town beauty."

"Hester hated me, of course."

"She hated a lot of people."

"Me most of all." Ruby's body trembled. "I took her fiancé and I took her brother." Ruby seemed to remember her surroundings and gestured toward the fireplace. "This was our meeting place. That's how I knew he'd come here tonight. I was trying to make a fire. William always made us a fire. It was so cold that winter." Ruby stirred and tried to pull up. "I need to make a fire."

Jill managed to resettle her mother, and calm her, and veer the topic to something less troublesome. They spoke of Christmas mornings, and egg hunts, and Fourth of July parades down Main Street. All the while Jill, herself, was disquieted by time lines running through her head. Ruby and Daniel had never hidden the story of their courtship from their children. The summer of Daniel's engagement to Hester and Ruby's relationship with William was common knowledge. But this crazy talk? Jill prayed Ruby was delusional, because if not, the implications were overwhelming and the genesis of the altered course of so many lives—her own included.

When Jill finally heard voices approaching, one of them Keith's, she had to wipe tears of relief from her numbed cheeks.

CHAPTER TWENTY-THREE

Jill

Sunday

From the ambulance, bouncing upon the bench-style seat next to the stretcher and an unconscious Ruby, Jill tried Jocelyn's cell phone again. There was still no answer. This time she opted to leave a message.

"Answer the damn phone, Jocelyn. Where the fuck are you, anyway?"

She noticed the paramedics exchange looks. In their job, they had to see all kinds. Neither her volume nor language could surprise two burly guys who dealt daily with trauma and triage. She supposed, however, she didn't look the type in her little pink golf outfit.

Jill pitched her phone into her purse, thinking that she could surprise them all right. No shit, could she shock them. Her own heart stalled with the recall of events.

. . .

Holding a paint roller in one hand and a screwdriver in the other, Jill lifted them both toward Jocelyn. "Choose your weapon."

Jocelyn stood with hands on her hips. "Neither."

Jill shook her head. "Not an option. You either assemble the crib or paint the room. Take your pick."

"I'm exhausted," Jocelyn said. "You've had me slaving all summer. And I'm a prisoner here. There are laws in this country. I have my rights."

"You agreed to the plan."

"Not to working day in and day out."

"The minute the baby's born, you're free to leave. California, Katmandu, wherever. But until then, just stick to the plan." Jill waved the tools in front of Jocelyn. "Hurry up and pick."

Jocelyn snatched the screwdriver from Jill's left hand. "I'll do the crib." She gestured toward the paint can that lay atop an outstretched tarp. "Because I hate that color you picked for my room."

"It won't be your room anymore. It will be the baby's."

"Poor thing. Who would want to wake up every morning to rubber-chicken yellow slapping them in the face?"

"It's lemon chiffon."

"It's awful," Jocelyn said. "Poor kid's gonna be messed up for life." Holding up a set of assembly directions to the crib, she turned them one way and then another. "Are you kidding me?" she said. "There's like a thousand steps to this thing."

"And what do you have against yellow, anyway? Margaret likes it."

Jocelyn rolled her eyes. "You're paying her to sit around all day doing nothing. It's no wonder she's agreeable."

"Well, we can't go to the local hospital. You know that." Jill bent to pick up a paint stirrer. "And especially these last few weeks, we want to take every precaution. It's best to have the midwife here on call." She pried the lid off the can with a screwdriver. "Anyway, having her here has given me an idea."

"Please. No more of your ideas."

"Oh, stop it." Jill pointed at Jocelyn with the stirrer. "Why do you have to be so difficult?" She dipped the stick into the paint can and mixed in a counterclockwise rotation. "Anyway, Margaret can't stop gushing about the house. How beautiful the downstairs rooms are. How breathtaking the view is. It's really given me a fresh perspective." She lifted the paint can and poured it into the metal rolling tray. "And phase two of the plan."

A growl churned from Jocelyn. "What the hell now?"

"I'm going to turn this place into a bed-and-breakfast. Convert all the upstairs rooms into guest rooms. I'm thinking of calling it the McCloud Inn."

"Are you crazy? You're going to take care of a newborn, and Mom, and run a hotel." Jocelyn shook her head. "Why not cure cancer while you're at it."

"If I could do that, we'd still have Dad here, now, wouldn't we?"

"I wouldn't want him to live through this mess." Jocelyn dropped the directions.

"I think he had his suspicions," Jill said, remembering their last conversation. He had been so serious and had reminded her with such desperation of the hold-fast family motto.

Jocelyn sank to her knees. "You never told me he suspected."

"He never said in so many words, but still . . ."

"I hope you're wrong," Jocelyn said. "To have to worry about such things on your deathbed. It's just not right."

The sisters set to their assigned tasks in silence. Jill's mood was black-hole dark. As much as she was resigned to her chosen course, she was not without reservations. Keith chief among them. He had called again that morning, and his voice had been so confused and plaintive that she'd nearly broken down and confessed everything. Somehow, she'd managed her summer-long refrain of "We're not taking any visitors" and "I can't see you anymore." She could tell he had more to say. She'd cut him off midsentence, knowing it would all come to a head in a week or two. Better to deal with it then.

Ruby shuffled into the room. She wore a tight-fitting nightgown and fuzzy pink slippers. "Thought I'd check on your progress." She stepped toward Jill and peered down at the paint. "What a lovely color."

The groan of a window being opened, and then a boom, sounded in the room next door, Jill's room. The three of them froze and tilted their heads toward the sound. Before they had a chance to react, a voice called out.

"Jill. Where are you, Jill?"

"Oh my God. It's Keith." Jill scanned the room with crazed eyes. "Mom, can you hide?"

"Where?" Ruby looked about with confusion. The doors to the closet had been removed for painting, and Jocelyn's old double bed had already been relocated upstairs.

Jill's gaze came to rest on the open bedroom door. She jogged three steps and was just about to force it shut, when a foot inserted itself between the door and the jamb. Keith's arm, and then head, pushed themselves into the room. "Jill, it's me, for God's sake."

She had no choice but to let him in. He stood in front of her, riveting her with a torrid glare. "Keith, I—"

He cut her off. "Don't worry. I just came to say good-bye." His hands flexed from flat palm to fist to flat palm at his sides. "But I wanted to do it in person."

"Keith . . ." Jill could think of nothing to say. Her hesitation gave him a moment to look past her to the other two in the room. His eyes came to rest on Ruby, and his mouth opened and his head bobbed forward in confusion. Ruby pulled a hand to her distended belly in reaction to his stare.

"What the hell is going on here?" he asked.

"So much for the plan," Jocelyn said. She stood from her crouched position next to the scattered pieces of crib. "Come on, Mom." She took Ruby by the elbow, steering her toward the door. "Maybe we should let these two talk in private." They left the room, closing the door behind them with a jarring thud.

Keith's voice was parched. "Your mom's pregnant?"

Crossing her arms, Jill turned to the window. "You weren't supposed to see that."

"Holy shit! But your dad . . ."

"Was sick. Too sick," Jill finished for him.

It took Keith a long moment to process this information. "Then who?"

"I don't know. She won't say. I don't think I want to know, anyway," Jill said. "It's all been too much for her. She's still in some kind of mourning or depression over my dad. Some days she mopes around worried she will forever have ruined his name. Other days she denies she's even pregnant. And then there are times she thinks she's fifteen again."

"That doesn't sound good." Keith had barely moved since Ruby and Jocelyn left the room. Finally, his whole body slumped forward. "Jesus. What a mess. I don't even know what to say. I thought you met someone else. I thought you were dumping me. No fuckin' way did I think for a moment that—"

"There's something you may as well know right now."

"What?"

"I'm raising the baby."

"What?"

"No one has seen me for months. No one has seen Jocelyn for months. Once word gets out about the baby, people will naturally assume it's mine—or Jocelyn's."

"That's crazy."

"Why?"

"Because it's not your baby."

"I just told you. My mom's not well. She's not competent."

Keith paced in front of Jill. "But why do you have to play this whole charade? Why can't people know it's hers?"

"Her husband just died of prostate cancer. He was impotent and terminal when she conceived." Jill's voice was flat. "You know her history. This town would shun her. Our whole family. The child included. But I'm twenty, and crazy as it sounds, a pregnant single young woman just doesn't have the stigma of a knocked-up, adulterous, past-her-prime woman." She laughed small and hard. "We've come a long way."

"A long way to get where?" He lifted his arms.

Jill pushed her hands deep into the pockets of her denim overalls. "I think my dad knew. He asked me, on his deathbed, to take care of her, to take care of *everything*. I think this is what he meant."

"How do you know for sure?"

"I don't, but I made a promise."

"Couldn't she . . . you know . . . have taken care of it."

"How could you even suggest such a thing. Knowing my dad, his life's work."

"Sorry. It's just . . . Why you? Why not Jocelyn?"

"He knew she wasn't the one for the job."

He snapped his head in anger. "You know what people are going to say, don't you? They're going to say it's mine."

"I know. That's why Jocelyn has kept herself hidden as well. There will be some ambiguity."

He exhaled in exasperation. "They'll still say it's mine."

"Jocelyn had a couple of boyfriends this winter, as you well know. You can say, unequivocally, that you're not the father. I'll invent another guy, someone intentionally vague. And if anyone asks me point-blank if it's you, I'll say no."

Keith took her by the shoulders. "Listen to me, Jill. You're too young for this kind of responsibility. You're ruining your life."

She pulled herself free. "I'm saving a life."

Keith's face twisted in anger. "If you do this, I'm leaving. I can't be a part of it . . . I'm not ready for this." His arms waved as if he were trying to indicate the enormity of the situation.

"I know. I don't blame you."

"You don't care if I go?"

"I do care. More than you know." Jill's bottom lip trembled; there was a fist-size rock in her throat; and her vision was blurry. "But I'm still doing this."

"Why? Jill? Why?" Everything about him was wounded—his voice, his eyes, his stance.

"Answer me this," she said. "Will you manage without me?"

"I don't want to," he said.

"But will you? Will you manage without me?"

"Yes. If I have to."

"That's why," Jill said, stepping back.

A sudden shriek of the sirens as the ambulance sped through an intersection pulled Jill back to the situation at hand. Her ringing phone was another prod.

"Hello."

"What the hell kind of message was that?" Jocelyn asked.

Jill leaned forward to look out the front window. They were pulling into the emergency bay, the paramedics already busy preparing the stretcher for transfer into the hospital.

"It's Mom," Jill said. "Meet me at the hospital."

CHAPTER TWENTY-FOUR

Fee

Sunday

"Time-out," Fee called, slapping her stick down on the carpet and fishing her phone out of her pocket. Dallas (or was it Denver?) seized the opportunity to sail the plastic puck past her head and into the goal. The Monroe twins were a hat trick of trouble: hockey players, trained merchants of pain, and six years old enough to know the difference between a cheap shot and a fair one. Dodging pucks while wearing a too-small face mask had to be worth a lot more than eight bucks an hour. Not to mention the World Wide Wrestling match during which she'd received a nasty rug burn—as referee. She had arrived tired and irritable, not yet recovered from Friday's late-nighter. Since then, she and Cass had only exchanged a series of texts. Both had avoided any mention of anything outside the topic of soccer.

"Hello."

"Fee, it's Mom. I'm at the hospital. Booboo's had an accident."

Feeling the contents of her head drain down her spine, Fee listened in shock to her mom describe her grandmother's situation.

Half an hour later, Mr. Monroe dropped Fee at the entrance to the emergency room.

"Thank you for the ride," Fee said. "And I'm sorry to have ruined your evening."

"Don't worry about us," Mr. Monroe said, implying—Fee couldn't help but notice—that she had other things to worry about.

The waiting room was full of people and it took Fee a few moments to locate her group. It was Aunt Jocelyn's leather vest, which seemed inappropriate in this somber place, that caught her attention. She was startled to see Keith sitting next to her mother, with Jocelyn in the seat facing them.

"What's going on?" Fee rushed to her mother, who pulled her into a hug. "What happened to Booboo?"

"She fell, and hit her head, and maybe went into shock. They've been running some tests. We're waiting for the doctor to update us."

Fee backed out of the embrace. Her mom looked so small in the little pink golf skirt. "But she's going to be okay, right?"

"We hope so, honey." Jill patted Fee's arm. "She was in a lot of pain, but I kept her awake and talking until the paramedics could get to her."

"Could get to her?" Fee asked.

Fee listened as her mom explained the details surrounding Booboo's fall and knew, somehow, she was getting an abbreviated version.

Jocelyn stood. "I'm going crazy waiting here." She took Fee by the arm. "How about you and I check out the gift shop? We could buy Booboo a bunch of useless junk, like teddy bears, and mugs crammed with carnations, and foot-long chocolate bars."

Fee didn't have much choice, because Jocelyn pulled her to a stand. She looked back at her mom and Keith. She just hoped there wasn't any more drama coming out of that department.

"Do you mind if I get a cup of coffee?" Jocelyn asked. "Don't worry about missing anything. They took X-rays and now they're running her through an MRI machine." She stopped at the elevator and pushed the button. "And then they have to read the scans." The door opened and they stepped in. "We could be here for a while."

They found a table at the back of the cafeteria. Fee stared down at a Coke. "So did they find something on the X-ray? Is that why they need an MRI?"

Jocelyn waved her hand dismissively. "We'd have to waterboard 'em to get any real information. We'll know more when the tests are in." She took a sip of her milky-white coffee. The Styrofoam made a scrunching sound. "Let's change the subject for now." She set the cup down. "How's your summer going?"

"Good. I guess. But school's only been out two weeks."

"And soccer?"

"Tryouts for the fall club team are over. The A and B rosters get posted anytime now."

"You're not nervous about that, are you?"

"No."

"Any special guys in your life?"

"Nope." Not unless Coach Yuri was *special* forces with the KGB.

"And your friends? How're your friends?"

Fee had intended a simple exhale, but even she knew it came out as a collapse.

The shiny plane between Jocelyn's eyebrows twitched. "Anything going on?"

"Just normal girl stuff."

"Girl stuff, huh?"

"Yep."

Jocelyn scrunched her cup across the tabletop. "You're giving off something—I'm not sure exactly—I want to say 'wounded.'"

Fee held up her elbow. "I do have this rug burn."

"Not that kind of wounded." Jocelyn traced her finger around the rim of her cup. "Emotionally wounded."

Fee opened her mouth, as if to speak, but found her brain otherwise occupied. Of all people, Aunt Jocelyn had some nerve. She was a hound—a sniffing, slobbering, won't-let-go she-wolf. All the more annoying that Fee *was* hurt, practically hemorrhaging: a nasty slash from Marjory, who chose a couple of Kotex pads over her and Cass; a gash—this one self-inflicted—of worry about the momentum-gathering missing-father story; and sucking air after the gut punch of gossip about Aunt Jocelyn being her real mother.

"Since you're asking, there seems to be something—some secret—surrounding you, my mom, and Keith. People are talking."

Jocelyn broke a chunk of Styrofoam from the cup's rim. "Saying what exactly?"

"Calling me a mystery child . . ."

"Have you talked to your mom about this?"

"I tried, but—"

"No. No. No," Jocelyn interrupted, shaking her head. "You need to talk to your mom. *We* are not talking about this."

"Why not?"

"Because it's a discussion you need to have with your mother."

"But—"

"Look, all I'm gonna say is gossip is evil. Don't listen to it. Beyond that, we either change the subject, or I get up and walk."

There was a just-dare-me quality to Jocelyn's voice that was new to Fee. Fee sat back and crossed her arms.

"Just trust me on this one. There are things better left as they are. If only . . ." Jocelyn wiped the fragments of white foam into what remained of the cup. "It's not my place. And right now we need to focus on Booboo. So how about that gift shop? You wanna help me spend some money?"

Their chat had done squat to console Fee. The only thing Jocelyn had been clear on was Booboo. Now *was* the time to focus on Booboo.

CHAPTER TWENTY-FIVE

Jill

Sunday

Fee and Jocelyn had only been gone a little while, but the awkwardness between Jill and Keith made it seem longer. Jill sensed he was unsure of his role or right to stay and noticed nervous tugs at the too-small Jimmy's Tackle & Feed T-shirt he'd bought en route to the hospital, the bloody golf shirt in a plastic bag at their feet. Before Fee's arrival, Jocelyn had been hyperchatty with questions about the golf game, the plumbing disaster, and their trek through the woods. There had been a goading tone to her comment, "What a turn of events you two have had." Now, without Jocelyn's prattle, worries for her mother cawed for attention. She thought Ruby's head injury was straightforward, but the need for an MRI had her concerned. Also, Ruby's gibberish back at the cabin weighed on her. And compounding everything, Keith's proximity made the air thin and her breath catch.

He sat with his legs open, his arms dangling off his knees, and his head hanging low. "I hate hospitals," he said finally.

Jill was brought out of her reverie. "Were you with your dad when he died?"

"Yes. And my mom, too."

"What happened to your mom?"

A horrific car accident involving Keith's mother, stepfather, and a patch of black ice was described. Keith had spent two weeks at her bedside before she was pulled off life support. He went on to recount a vacation spent visiting his father in Florida. Three hours into a fishing trip, his father had suffered a heart attack. The boat's captain had saved his life with CPR, but a lot of damage had been done. He had open-heart surgery two days later, and passed away four days after that.

"Was he conscious those days in the hospital?"

"In a lot of pain," Keith said. "But, yes, he was aware. We had some good talks."

"About what?" Jill immediately felt she'd gone too far. "If it's not too private."

Keith sat back in the chair. "Choices, I guess. He told me to make good choices." He kneaded the knuckles of his left hand with his right. "I'm not so sure he thought he'd made all the right ones."

"In what way?"

"My parents weren't well suited. I don't think there was a lot of love between them."

"Not even early in their marriage?"

"That I couldn't say."

Jill hesitated for a moment, unsure whether to bring it up. "Did you know your father dated my mother, once upon a time?"

Keith bent his head toward Jill. "I'd heard something to that effect."

"It was the summer before my parents got married." Jill crossed her legs and pulled the once-wet, now-stiff T-shirt in a small nervous gesture. "The summer my father was engaged to Hester." The air-conditioning was too high. Jill wished for a sweater, or even a blanket. "In fact, your father may have been the nudge my dad needed."

"What?"

"We were just kids with silly romantic notions, but Jocelyn and I used to beg my dad, over and over, to tell us the story."

"What story?"

"As it goes, your dad came to town and took a liking to my mom." Jill bounced her feet in an effort to circulate blood. "Have you ever seen a picture of her when she was young? She really was beautiful."

"I could see that."

"Your dad and my mom dated for a few weeks. My mom was my dad's secretary at the time and living at the house, so he had to watch them coming and going. He said it was torture, but at least it forced him to admit his true feelings. He broke things off with your aunt and married my mom in October."

"Are you going somewhere with this?" Keith asked.

Jill squirmed in her seat. "I'm wondering if your dad ever talked about my mom to you. That winter we were dating."

"No."

"Or in the hospital when he was sick?"

"No. Why would he?"

"You said he talked about choices."

Keith opened his hands in a gesture of futility. "It doesn't seem like he had much choice in that one. Sounds like your parents made theirs, and that was pretty much it."

Jill settled back into the chair with her arms crossed. "You're right. I don't know why I brought it up."

A large potted hydrangea wrapped in blue foil and a stuffed Saint Bernard the size of a compact car approached, the first carried by Fee, the latter by Jocelyn.

Jill looked up at the huge dog. "What on earth is that?"

"Mom will get a kick out of it," Jocelyn said. "And she'll love that we're making a fuss."

The swinging door opened at the far side of the room, and a man in a white lab coat walked toward them. "That's Dr. Carver," Jill said.

Keith started to say something, but stopped.

The doctor directed them back through the swinging doors, where they followed him down a long hallway. Jill wondered whether Keith should have remained in the waiting room. It seemed the doctor assumed he was immediate family.

As if tracking her thoughts, Keith said, "Maybe I should go back."

"Nonsense," Jocelyn said. "You've been such a big help and comfort today." She nudged Jill in the ribs. "Hasn't he?"

"Yes. A big comfort." She surprised even herself with the sincerity of the remark.

The doctor led them into his office and switched on a light box, calling their attention to a series of X-rays and MRI scans. His finger floated above an opaque blob. "There is a mass here in your mother's frontal lobe."

"A mass?" Jill asked.

"Yes," the doctor said. "A tumor."

Jocelyn gasped and covered her mouth. Fee reached out to hold Jill's hand.

"I suspect her fall was a symptom," the doctor continued. "Loss of balance is common. Tell me, have you noticed any other changes in your mother? Defective memory? Impaired judgment? Personality changes? Confusion? Headaches? Problems with hearing?"

Jill felt sick to her stomach. Had she really been so blind? "Yes. All of them. She's been a little feisty lately, and impulsive, and drinking more than usual, all things I chalked up to getting older. And a recent funeral had her revisiting the past and a little confused. I guess I attributed those to a kind of funk or depression."

"Don't blame yourself. Symptoms can be difficult to detect, particularly in elderly patients."

"What happens now?" Jill asked.

"We'll admit her and refer you to a team of specialists. A neurologist and a neurosurgeon to begin with. I imagine they will want to operate, and judging by the size of the tumor, fairly soon."

"Admit her?" Jill was surprised.

"Yes. It's a very large mass. We'll want to keep her under observation."

"And it is operable, then?" Jill asked.

"Most likely, yes. If for nothing else than to relieve the pressure the growth of the tumor has created."

Jill didn't like the sound of "if for nothing else."

"Can we see her?" Jocelyn asked.

Dr. Carver checked his watch and then glanced up at the four of them. "It's very late, and we had to sedate her for the MRI." Jill thought he looked with pity at the odd crew, she in her wrinkled golf attire, Keith in the too-tight T-shirt, Jocelyn in her biker-chick getup hugging a gargantuan stuffed dog, and Fee holding the potted plant. "She'll be moved to the third floor. Check in at the nurses' station and I'm sure they'll let you have a quick look in on her."

CHAPTER TWENTY-SIX

Jill

Monday

By the time they filled out the admitting papers and checked in on Ruby, it was four o'clock in the morning. With stiff legs and heads hung, they walked to the parking lot.

"I'll need a ride," Jill said to Jocelyn. "I came in the ambulance."

Jocelyn shook her head. "I got dropped off."

Keith stepped forward. "I'll take you home. I'm not the least bit tired. A drive sounds good."

It was a quiet car ride and Jill couldn't help but be further tumbled by the gloom of black skies.

Jocelyn finally broke the silence. "Is that the sun coming up?" she asked in a croaky voice.

Jill looked to the east. There was nothing but pitch. "Not yet."

"Shit," Jocelyn said.

"What's wrong?"

"I'm seeing lights."

"What?"

"Refracted lights. It's the first sign."

"Oh, no, Jocelyn." Jill knew Jocelyn still suffered from migraines, sometimes lasting days at a time. "Do you have anything with you?"

"Just get me to my room," Jocelyn said, her voice shaky. "I've always got something with me."

Jill helped a hobbling Jocelyn from the car and up the flagstone steps to the house. Jocelyn was wearing sunglasses and holding her temples in a viselike grip. "Do me a favor," Jocelyn said. "Tell Victor I'm sorry, but I'll have to cancel."

"Victor?"

"Yes. Victor."

"Cancel what?"

"Our date."

Jill stopped, forcing Jocelyn to do the same. "My guest Victor?"

"The very same."

"You've been seeing Victor? Since when?" Jill started moving again, ushering Jocelyn through the front door.

"Since Friday night. After I drove Keith home." Jocelyn's voice was still weak, but there was some slight perk to it.

"And what have you been doing?"

"Riding his motorcycle." Jocelyn managed a small laugh. "And riding him."

"I thought—"

"You thought I was with Keith." Jocelyn stumbled. The next spasm of pain brought her to her knees.

"Let's just get you to your room," Jill said, weaving her arm under Jocelyn's. After Jill watched Jocelyn down three pink tablets and a glass of water and curl into a fetal ball, she returned to the kitchen. She found Keith and Fee sitting at the table in silence.

"How's Jocelyn?" he asked.

"Not good, but she took some pills." Jill stood with her arms crossed and back propped up against the marble countertop. If Jocelyn had been with Victor since Friday night, then she'd mistakenly thought that Keith . . . It was too much to think about at the moment. "Looks like we're in for a rough morning, Fee. It's Monday, Borka and Magda's day off."

Fee groaned. "Can't you call them? I'm exhausted."

"No. I can't call them. We'll just have to manage."

"I'll help," Keith said.

"No. Really. We'll be fine."

"Let me help," Keith said. "I couldn't sleep if I tried."

"It's very kind of you, but you've done more than enough already."

"Look." Keith stood and Jill was struck by how he filled the room. "You've got an appointment with the neurologist at eleven, right?"

"Yes."

"And you'll want to visit your mom before that."

"Yes. I suppose."

"What time are your breakfast hours?"

"Seven to nine."

"And what are you serving?"

"Mondays are muffins, coffee cakes, and sliced fruits."

"And guest rooms to clean?" he asked.

"Yes."

Keith gestured about the kitchen. "Then I suggest we get baking."

Fee stifled a laugh.

Keith looked at her with an amused expression. "What? You don't think a guy can bake?"

"You don't look the type," Fee said.

He spied an apron hanging on the back of the pantry door. It was peachy orange with a ruffled edge. He looped the top over his thick neck and tied the strings with three efficient tugs. "Pies are my specialty, but I can do muffins."

A Niagara's worth of mixed feelings pounded at Jill. She wasn't used to being contradicted. She said no, yet he persisted. Nonetheless, with so many responsibilities, his assistance was a welcome relief. And Jocelyn had been with Victor Friday night and all day Saturday, riding his motorcycle, riding him. "Okay. Fine." She corrected the tone. "And thank you. Really. Thank you."

He nodded once. "What kind of muffins?"

She pointed to the fridge. "There are fresh blueberries and raspberries in the bottom drawer. Let me get you a recipe."

"No need."

"You don't need a recipe?"

"You forget, I've been working in restaurants for the past fifteen years."

She opened her hands in a gesture of deference. "You'll find everything else, including the muffin tins, in the pantry or fridge." She turned to Fee. "Honey, how about you set up the dining room. I'll do the rest."

It was wonderful the way they fell into a rhythm. He seemed to move instinctively from one area to the next, just as she thought he might get underfoot. He whistled to himself and tugged at his sunny apron tidily, a Gomer Pyle does June Cleaver moment. A small laugh escaped her lips and he smiled so sheepishly, she momentarily forgot the weight of the day.

Once breakfast was well in hand, she left Fee to serve the few guests. Keith followed her to the large supply closet on the second floor.

"Are you sure you still want to help?" she asked.

"Absolutely."

She pulled a small rolling cart stocked with linens and cleaning supplies into the hallway. "Can you make a good bed?"

"I can make it in a good bed."

She ignored him and rolled the cart toward the first room on the left. "How are you at toilets?"

"I'm better with beds."

She opened the door with a key that hung from the cart and held up a spray bottle of cleaner and a toilet scrubber. "I think I'll start you with toilets."

He took them from her, his hand lingering momentarily and then his pinkie hooked with hers as the spray bottle exchanged hands. A jolt traveled from her shoulders to the arches of her feet, which she was sure he witnessed.

"As long as there's a chance of promotion." He stood dangerously close and his smell, familiar and heady, fell over her.

Emotions, past and present, choked her, and she had to turn and busy herself with the cart until she felt able to breathe again. "Promotion?" She lifted a stack of towels and faced him. "And just what exactly are you looking for in the way of promotion?"

"This has been such a hectic couple of days." The air between them was warm, a microclimate of tropic heat. "First my aunt and now your mom. I'm hoping we can get past all this craziness, and to some degree of normalcy where we can spend time together. Get to know each other again. And ignore all the reasons why we shouldn't."

"I would like that."

"So would I." He smiled and touched her cheek, a gesture so crushingly sweet her whole face ached.

He sucked at both toilets and beds, yet by nine they'd readied the guest rooms and she had even managed fifteen minutes for a shower and change of clothes. It would be an air-dry hair day, which, with humidity, was dicier than a Vegas craps game. They agreed Fee would stay at the inn and be on call for the guests and Jocelyn.

Jill thanked Keith for his help and thought, by his downcast eyes, he was sorry to be dismissed. They walked out the back door together and she felt a pang of regret watching his slouched gait trail away. He had offered to accompany her to the hospital, but she dismissed the idea, insisting he had already gone above and beyond. As much as she'd admit he'd been essential these last eighteen hours, a doctor's appointment to discuss Ruby's condition was a family matter. She promised to call him with an update.

Ruby was asleep when Jill entered the hospital room. There was a nurse at her bedside checking monitors.

"How's my mom?" Jill asked.

"Exhausted. She's hardly moved."

Jill looked at her father's antique watch. "My appointment with the doctor is in twenty minutes. I'm going to have to leave her for a while."

"Honey, she won't know a thing. And don't worry. We'll call you if anything happens."

Jill listened intently as the neurologist rattled his way through a litany of terms and procedures. She'd brought a notebook and pencil, but still had a hard time keeping up. She managed to scribble down a few important details. A battery of tests had ruled out the tumor as secondary, or metastasized from another area of the body. The first step would be a biopsy, which required drilling a small burr hole into the skull and using a needle to remove a tiny sample of the tumor. Those cells would be examined under a microscope to determine the type of cancer, and whether it was benign or malignant. He was referring her to a highly respected neurosurgeon, who would likely want to move things along at an accelerated rate, given the size of the mass.

"Is it that large?" Jill asked.

The doctor motioned to the MRI on the light board. "Yes. And by all indications obstructing the flow of cerebrospinal fluid, which is in turn damaging vital neurological pathways and compressing the brain tissue."

"That doesn't sound good."

"I must be honest with you. We are dealing with a very large mass, which is extremely dangerous, even if it is benign. My guess is your mother didn't simply trip and cut her head; I would guess she lost consciousness."

"When can I see the surgeon?"

"We took the liberty of contacting his office. He just happens to be in the office this morning and in the OR this afternoon. He could fit you in for an appointment, and squeeze your mother onto the operating schedule for a biopsy as his last procedure of the day."

Jill pulled her right hand over her mouth. "Is it that urgent?"

The doctor nodded. "In my opinion it is."

Jill met with the neurosurgeon, Dr. O'Connor, who was very kind, but extremely rushed for time. Today's biopsy would be a preliminary step, from which all treatment would be determined. Dr. O'Connor had already moved Ruby onto Friday's operating schedule, in case it was determined that the best course of action was removal of the tumor. Jill left his office with more questions than answers.

When she returned to Ruby's hospital room, she felt like Rip Van Winkle awakening to an altered world. A small forest had taken root in her absence. There were blooming pots of lilies and tulips, towering sunflowers, fat vases of roses, and bursts of yellow daisies, pink carnations, and red poppies.

Ruby stirred when Jill approached her bedside.

"Where did all these flowers come from?" Jill asked, searching the closest bouquet for a card.

"William was here," Ruby said in a feeble voice.

It didn't seem the time to argue. "How nice. Are these all from him?"

"Yes. He wants to take care of me. He's always been sweet on me, you know."

"When was he here?"

"He just left." Ruby rolled onto her side. Her eyes fluttered and then closed.

Jill stepped into the hallway and looked up and down the corridor. There was no sign of Keith, or William for that matter. She walked over to the nurses' station.

"Did my mom have a visitor?"

The nurse looked up from a thick stack of papers and gestured with her head to a waiting room. "He's in there."

The room was small and sparsely furnished. A wall-mounted

television droned cartoons. Keith sat distractedly rubbing his cheek.

"Keith, what are you doing here?"

"I couldn't sleep and I couldn't stand waiting around in that hotel room. I hope you don't mind."

"No. I mean, thank you for the flowers. They're beautiful, but too much."

"I couldn't decide, so I got a variety." Again, he massaged his jaw.

"Are you all right?"

"A little toothache. No big deal." He dropped his hand. "Tell me about your mom."

Jill told Keith about the biopsy and possibility of surgery on Friday. He listened and asked a few sensible questions. Jill was relieved to have a sturdy net for the burdens she unfurled. She knew stress often triggered Jocelyn's migraines, but was still annoyed by her abdication. And her whole life had been spent protecting Fee. It wouldn't have seemed natural to turn to her for support.

Keith stuttered the start to an obviously difficult topic. "I'm sorry. I think I confused your mom. She thinks I'm my father."

"I know. She told me."

"I hope I didn't upset her. She said something strange." Keith's eyes darted back and forth. "She said she was looking for me, my father I guess, out in the woods."

"I want to talk to you about that."

"About what?"

"That winter when you and your dad came to town, the winter we met." Jill bit her bottom lip. "Do you think my mom and your dad could have rekindled their relationship?"

"What are you trying to say?"

"My mom mentioned the fireplace in the old hunting lodge. She said she and William needed a fire because it was so cold that winter." Jill avoided his eyes. "When they dated, the first time, it was summer."

"The first time?"

"I know it's shocking." Jill rolled her shoulders. "Fee is living proof of my mother's infidelity, so there had to be a partner. I just don't think she was in the frame of mind for a random affair. It would make more sense that it was someone she knew and trusted. Some of my mom's recent comments make me think that your dad was . . ."

"Was what?"

"Fee's father. Do you think . . . ?"

"You're joking, right?"

"No. What my mom said to me was very strange."

"Because she was delirious."

"But she was so specific. As if she were reliving something."

"Come on, Jill. She was out of it. It's hardly credible information."

"He was in town that winter. And they did have a history."

Keith raked a hand across a day's growth of stubble. "It's crazy. That would make Fee my . . . And you my . . . I don't even want to go there."

"It wouldn't change anything between us, bloodwise anyway."

"Wouldn't change anything? It would change everything."

"I'm just trying to say—"

The nurse popped her head into the small waiting room. "Sorry to interrupt, but it's your mother. She's awake and upset. We could use your help calming her down."

Before following the nurse into the hallway, Jill glanced back at Keith. He hadn't moved and there was a faraway look on his face. His attention was elsewhere and she knew from long experience he was closing himself off. Her disclosure had, as he had predicted, changed everything.

CHAPTER TWENTY–SEVEN

Jill

Monday

It took Jill, two nurses, an IV drip, and a solid hour of soothing and supplication to settle Ruby, who was confused and agitated and unable to remember recent events. Ruby's addled state and the way she shrank from the nurses with a wild-eyed terror, yelling "Don't touch me" and "I'll tell Aunt Mabel," gutted Jill, releasing a spill of memories and emotions, some her own and some so tragically Ruby's.

Jill threw the paint roller and watched as a spray of yellow flecked the unassembled crib. She fell to her knees. There was something cold and dark that lingered in the spot where Keith last stood. She muffled a sob into the crook of her elbow, followed by another, and another. She knew there would be some sort of confrontation once the baby's existence became public knowledge, but she'd always been able to tuck it away as some unknowable future. She now realized, with dread, its reality was worse than the fear of it.

"Honey, are you all right?" Ruby padded in, looking fat and grotesque. Could even her nose have widened?

"No. I'm not all right." There was anger and accusation in her voice.

"What did he say?"

"He never wants to see me again."

A protective film glossed over Ruby. A look Jill recognized, all too well, these last few months.

"I'm not surprised," Ruby said. "They do their nasty and then blame you. You'll be on your own once you deliver the baby."

"Once I deliver the baby?"

Ruby, the real Ruby, went somewhere distant and inaccessible. "Did you try and fight him off, honey? Lord knows I did." She pulled a hand to her huge belly. "I told him not to touch me. He was just such a beast, though. At me night and day. He'd have me right on the floor of that dirty old garage. And then make me go out and pump gas for the next car that pulled in, while he tuned in a ball game and stuck his filthy neck under the hood of some old junker. My dresses had oil spots and my elbows were scabbed, but do you think Aunt Mabel would believe me? Not her precious husband."

Ruby's face was drawn and her lips pulled into a white gash. "And he'd be at me again, telling me how pretty I looked. Telling me I smelled like honey and felt like velvet." She spat. "Well, he made me vomit." Ruby's head shook wildly from side to side. "Oh, he was a clever one. Told me I was the only thing worth living for. Told me I was like the sun after a lifetime of darkness." Ruby's eyes rolled back. "He even said I should thank him. That he'd taken me from a wild mustang to a docile mare." Her body went still and then her head hung forward. "He told me it was perfectly natural, but I couldn't tell anyone, 'cause I'd break poor Aunt Mabel's heart. And Mabel was already crazy jealous because I was the prettiest thing, whereas she was uglier than a coon dog. And I owed Mabel that much, her having taken me in and all."

Jill should have stopped her mother a long time ago, but the shock of the tirade rendered her mute.

"When I finally got so big she couldn't help but admit something happened, she blamed me. Said I was a whore and trash, just like my mama. Said I asked for it, probably forced myself on him with my big tits and plump butt. Said bad things happen to bad people. And then she threw me out like yesterday's slops."

Speech still eluded Jill. Her mother had always claimed Janine's father was a childhood sweetheart named Josh, who'd been a good baseball player and wanted to raise horses. His tragic death in a car accident had left her alone to deal with the pregnancy. She'd found the McCloud Home for Wayward Girls through her church, secured her own bus ticket, and arrived on the doorstep unannounced.

Jill rubbed a hand up and down her mom's soft, white forearm. "It's okay. And I'm so proud of you."

"Nobody ever made it easy for me. Not till your father, anyhow. But I always took care of what's mine."

And she had. There had been birthdays when Jill and Jocelyn were pronounced Queen for a Day, complete with crown, scepter, and lady-in-waiting. Closet monsters and keyhole-peeping ghosts had been foiled by an all-night, bed-sharing guardian. And the howling pain of scrapes, and cuts, and black-and-blues had been kissed away with mommy magic. Jill continued to stroke her arm. "And now you've taught me to do the same. Haven't you?"

"And to be strong like me."

"Strong like you." Jill squeezed her mom's arm and let go. She realized that the horrible violation resulting in that first pregnancy couldn't help but taint every other sexual relationship. And her only living relation, her aunt Mabel, had blamed her. "Bad things happen to bad people." It was practically a curse. No wonder Ruby had crumbled following the stillborn death of Janine and a later miscarriage. Whatever the circumstances resulting in her mother's infidelity, Jill knew she was doing the right thing.

"It's never easy to see a loved one like this," the nurse—Barb, according to her name tag—said, snatching a plumed tissue from the bedside table and handing it to Jill.

"There were episodes before," Jill said, following the nurse out into the hallway. "She was abused as a teen. I know we were trying to keep her from hurting herself, but we triggered some sort of relapse."

"Darlin', she's on medication. Not to mention the tumor creeping into corners of her mind she hasn't visited in a while. The important thing is that she's safe and getting help."

"We didn't even warn her about today's procedure," Jill said, propping her elbows on the counter while Barb took a seat at the U-shaped nurses' station.

"That may be for the best," Barb said. "She's frightened enough."

Jill looked to her right, into the wing's empty waiting room.

"Your visitor left a while ago," Barb said.

"I expected as much," Jill said, too tired to mask the disappointment in her voice. "And it's okay, because that's exactly what he is: a visitor."

CHAPTER TWENTY-EIGHT

Fee

Monday

Late Monday afternoon, Fee woke disoriented and sat with a tug to her shoulders. After serving breakfast, she'd collapsed onto her bed still wearing the same clothes the Monroe twins had squirted ketchup on the day before. Her phone alerted her to three new messages from Cass. They hadn't communicated since Fee had texted her from the emergency room with news of Booboo's fall—before the words *brain tumor* had dropped from the sky like bug-eyed aliens.

Booboo's fall. Booboo's tumor. Symptoms going unnoticed. Fee remembered the phone conversation with Marjory's mom. How conveniently Fee had accepted Booboo's confusion with complicity—a deal of sorts. What if Fee had told someone Booboo was acting funny? Would those few days have made a difference? The doctor said the tumor was fast growing.

Two of Cass's texts had the same "Howz Booboo" message.

The third, "The A-team baby," lifted the corners of Fee's mouth, though only briefly. So the roster had been posted on the club's Web site. With everything going on, Fee had completely forgotten about tryouts and even all the business with Marjory. Nothing like stepping on a land mine to take your mind off the pebble in your shoe.

Fee's thumbs quickly typed a reply to Cass. "Booboo not good. Momz at hospital. Good newz about team."

Fee walked down the hall, taking note of Aunt Jocelyn's closed bedroom door. Must be nice, she thought, to have a get-out-of-jail-free card on all the morning's work—especially following an all-nighter at the hospital. And for someone who boasted an ability to read people's emotional auras, Jocelyn sure missed the maintenance-required light that Ruby had been flashing. The dead-lady party had practically buzzed with gossip. Shouldn't Jocelyn have picked that up like some barcode scanner? Furthermore, what was the story with Jocelyn and Keith? Why wouldn't she talk about it at the hospital? What about their special relationship? The way Jocelyn confided things in Fee that she didn't in anyone else, like grumbling about not getting her patch of suburban grass. No way would *anyone* share that kind of regret with the kid they gave up. Still, the whole thing was whacked. And Fee really wished someone would make like a piñata and spill already.

CHAPTER TWENTY-NINE

Jill

Monday Evening

"How are you doing?" Jill asked.

"A little better." The room was full dark, and Jocelyn appeared as nothing more than a tangle of sheets kicked to the foot of the bed.

"Can I get you anything?"

"How about a guillotine? I'd let the damn thing roll at this point."

"At least you still have your sense of humor."

"You think I'm joking?"

"Have you eaten?"

"Couldn't possibly." The form shifted and took shape. A white calf emerged from under the blanket. "How's Mom?"

"They did a biopsy. It involved drilling a hole into her skull."

Jocelyn groaned. "I think I know how she feels."

"They removed a tiny sample and now they're freezing it, and slicing it, and looking at it under a microscope. We'll know more tomorrow." Jill explained about the possibility of a full-scale operation on Friday.

"I'm so sorry I've abandoned you."

"You couldn't help it."

"How's Mom handling it all?"

"She had a bad episode earlier in the day, but she's blissfully drugged for now."

"Thank God for the pioneers of modern pharmaceuticals." Jocelyn scratched herself up the length of the bed. "Did you find Victor for me?"

"Yes. He said he'd take a rain check." Jill dropped into a chair next to the bed. "What are you doing, Jocelyn? The guy at the wake, and then Keith, and now this guy? Why? You're leaving soon, aren't you? What's the point?"

Jocelyn exhaled loudly. "The point? The point is life is short." She rolled to her side. "And to set the record straight, Keith doesn't count."

Jill pursed her lips. "He was your date to my game night."

Jocelyn laughed sharply. "Oh. That was all for your benefit. All the guy could talk about was you. Anyway, I brought him just to pop your cork."

"What? Why?"

"You gotta admit, it made you jealous." Jocelyn pushed into a sitting position, resting against the headboard.

"I was not jealous."

"Oh, please. If you were to pine any more for the guy, we could hang ornaments on you. And he's no better. You should have seen his face when I hinted that Victor fancied you. He went all red and blotchy and changed the subject."

This new information buzzed through Jill's head. "And you and Victor?"

"Oh yes, me and Victor." She rubbed her palms together. "Me and Victor on his motorcycle. Me and Victor in his room. And me and Victor down by the pond."

"Jocelyn!"

"What? He's completely unattached. Not looking for anything more." Jocelyn stretched her legs in front of her. "Anyway, life is short, remember?"

"All too well." Jill opened the curtains. "How about something to drink?"

"Fee brought me some tea."

"That was nice of her."

"Yeah, except she seemed a little pissed at me."

"Welcome to my life."

"She said Keith stayed and helped you out this morning. Made muffins and scoured toilets."

Jill could feel her voice tighten. "He did."

"How much more proof do you need?"

"He wouldn't do it again."

"Why? What's wrong?"

"Some things came up at the hospital. To quote him: 'It changed everything.' I don't think he'll be coming back. Ever."

"What? After all my hard work. How bad could it be?"

"Bad."

"What was it about?"

"Mom's been having episodes, remembering things, reliving the past. When we found her at the cabin, she thought Keith was his father, William. She said it was their secret meeting place. Keith's dad *was* around the winter Mom got pregnant. After I shared my suspicions with Keith, he took off."

Jill shook her curls. "I don't blame him. Somehow we always manage to involve him in our mess."

"Well, if it's true, it's not just our mess anymore."

"Except he doesn't believe it. He said so with his feet."

Jocelyn stroked her eyebrows. "Seriously? You two missed again? I don't understand it. I'm never wrong about these things. And the chemistry is there. You guys were my first, and have always been my strongest, reading."

"Not strong enough, I guess."

Jocelyn crossed her arms. "Maybe too strong, crazy as that sounds."

"Nothing sounds crazy to me anymore," Jill said.

CHAPTER THIRTY

Jill

Tuesday

Jill sat at her desk rummaging through files. She had yet another ream of insurance papers to fill out and couldn't find Ruby's Social Security card. She wondered, with dread, if old 202 had pocketed it. Since Saturday morning, she'd been waiting for the bank or credit-card company to phone her with suspicious activity. Nothing yet, but other things were happening so quickly she barely had a chance to draw breath before something else took it away.

The biopsy results were in and not good. Ruby had a tumor or glioma that was classified as an astrocytoma, so named for its star-shaped cells. Furthermore, given the size and shape of the mass, they suspected it was a glioblastoma multiforme, a grade-four variety of tumor which grew rapidly and spread quickly to other parts of the brain. Ruby was to keep her Friday date with Dr. O'Connor and his operating table. The doctor's remark that he would "remove or debulk as much of the tumor as possible" had not been very comforting. It pained Jill to think of her mother's brain as mere bulk. And the long-term prognosis was bleak. She had been up all night obsessing over the missed symptoms: confusion, unsteady gait, change in personality, and headaches. She wondered how she would manage to care for a sick Ruby along with everything else, and how they'd afford the medical bills.

Jill yawned and bent over the file drawer. She heard a small knock and looked up to see a tall, silver-haired woman in a teal-blue business suit. The woman extended her hand. "Pamela St. John, Homestead Realtors. Pleased to finally meet you."

Recognition filled Jill like a balloon. Her right arm lifted to her forehead. "We had an appointment this morning."

They shook hands.

"You weren't expecting me?"

"I'd forgotten." Jill stood and braced herself against the desk. "My mother's been ill. It's been a crazy couple of days." She breathed a sigh of relief that Jocelyn had already left for the hospital, taking Fee with her.

"Do you have time now? Or would you prefer to reschedule?"

Jill looked at her watch. She had the time, but she wasn't sure she had the necessary concentration. Her recent insomnia was rendering difficult the most basic of functions. "I have a few minutes."

"The exterior is very attractive." Pamela seated herself in the chair opposite Jill's desk. She opened a leather binder and extracted a business card from a small pocket. "Here's my card. And I was so happy to get your call last week." She ran her finger down some handwritten notes. "Now, you say the building was constructed in 1898. Is that right?"

"Yes." Jill sat, too.

"And I understand it has quite a history."

"Yes. It was first built as the center for a plain-living society. It was later converted into a home for unwed teens. I've operated it as an inn for fifteen years now."

"That kind of backstory can be a wonderful selling tool."

Jill opened her hands. "I'm really just interested in having it appraised at this point. I have no plans to sell. It's more of a worst-case contingency." She lowered her eyes. "If you don't mind, I would prefer our discussions be kept private. I hope you understand."

Pamela nodded. "I've been in this business a long time." She closed the folder. "How about we start with a brief tour?"

Jill looked at her watch again. "Sure."

Pamela's high heels clacked along the old plank wooden floors. In the foyer, at the wall of family memorabilia, she stopped and stared at the clan crest. "'Hold Fast,'" she read out loud.

"My great-grandfather Angus McCloud, the builder of the home, came over from Scotland."

"That would explain the skirt."

"Kilt. It's called a kilt."

"Is this Angus?" Pamela pointed to a faded black-and-white photo of a bagpiper in full Highland regalia.

"It is."

"The bagpipes," Pamela said. "Now, there's a lost art."

"Thankfully. What an awful sound. The very definition of caterwaul."

"Obviously the Scots have an eye for design," Pamela said, nodding her head in appreciation. "If no ear for music. This is a lovely home."

Jill led her into the first room off the foyer.

"Was this room always a library?" Pamela asked, testing the sturdiness of the built-in shelves with a tap.

"Yes. The wood is walnut, harvested from the property."

Pamela dragged a finger across a line of book spines. "It's quite a collection."

"My father liked to think it was rivaled only by the city library—locally, anyway."

"You know, the old librarian in town, Delia, was my mother's cousin."

Jill shook her head, as if she didn't recognize the name, but then stopped. "You mean Miss Cordelia?"

"Oh, yes. I suppose she would have had the children call her by her full name. Back in those days libraries were so serious and strict, and librarians had to be proper." Pamela unlatched and lifted a casement window. "Shame because that really wasn't her personality at all. Poor thing even had to hide her sexuality for fear of losing her job."

"I knew her," Jill said. "I even remember her story times from when I was a kid. She was wonderful."

"She died a few years back," Pamela said, closing the window.

"What's going on?" Jocelyn stood in the doorway.

"This is my sister, Jocelyn. And this is Pamela," Jill said quickly. "Pamela's considering hosting a luncheon here."

"In the library?" Jocelyn asked.

"I just love these old buildings." Pamela smiled so convincingly, Jill was reassured she could hold her side of the game. "Your sister was kind enough to show me around."

Jocelyn stepped into the room.

"I thought you were going to stay with Mom," Jill said.

"She got wind of her head being shaved." Jocelyn mimicked the motion of a blade to the scalp. "She sent me to get her wig."

"What?" Jill asked.

"She says she won't see anyone, before or after surgery, unless she has hair."

"Which wig?" Jill asked.

"How many does she have?"

"Three."

"I'll bring them all."

"She doesn't need it until Friday. Besides, she'll be bandaged after," Jill said. "I can't imagine they'll let her wear a wig over her sutures."

Jocelyn raised her hands defensively. "You tell her that. Me, I'm doing as I'm told."

"I should be on my way," Pamela said. "I'm sorry to have detained you. Jill, I'll be in touch and we can arrange a longer tour, if necessary."

A few moments later, Jill waited in the Hummer for Jocelyn. She spied a little pleated paper cup with two oval pills resting in the car's cup holder.

When Jocelyn climbed into the driver's seat, Jill asked, "What are these?" She rattled the pills.

"I took those from the hospital," Jocelyn said. "They're Valium. My migraine's gone for now, but I'm not sleeping well."

"Welcome to the club. I haven't slept since this whole thing with Mom began."

"Want me to swipe some for you, too?"

"No," Jill said. "Absolutely not." She replaced the cup. "Swipe them how? This sounds highly illegal."

"From the nurses' cart. It's easy if you know what you're looking for."

"And how on earth do you know what you're looking for?"

"I have some back in my medicine cabinet at home. I recognize the imprint. Plus, I read the chart of the old lady in the bed next to Mom."

"You're scaring me," Jill said, shaking her head.

"It's just two little pills. Not like I robbed a bank or set fire to a church."

"It's still wrong."

They drove the rest of the way to the hospital, both pretending to listen to the weather report, and then an NPR piece on gay marriage. Jill knew she should confess to Jocelyn the true nature of Pamela's visit. Somehow, all bridges to that conversation were temporarily closed. Instead, the conversation with Pamela about her librarian cousin had Jill traversing her own span of memories.

"I'll push the stroller," Jill said.

"No. I'll push it." Jocelyn grabbed for the handlebar, but Jill held firm.

"Maybe I should," Ruby said.

Both girls turned to glare at their mother. "You are under no circumstances allowed to touch the stroller," Jill said. "Your job is to look grandmotherly. Do you understand?"

Ruby wilted a little, but then cocked her head in protest. "Grandmothers can push strollers."

"We should take turns," Jocelyn said. "It will totally fuck with their minds."

"Jocelyn," Jill said, "don't talk like that in front of the baby."

"It doesn't know the difference between its thumb and my nose. I hardly think it's listening."

"*It?*" Jill asked. "*It?*" She glowered at Jocelyn. "I'm pushing the stroller, you'd probably forget *it* somewhere."

The Indian-summer day was hot and dry, a few early-bird elms had tinges of amber. They had parked at the top of Main Street to purposely walk the entire length. Jill manned the stroller, while Jocelyn and Ruby flanked her on both sides. In an attempt to add a few postpartum pounds, Jill wore baggy overalls padded in the stomach and rear with four layers of undergarments. She felt ridiculous and the bottom layer of shorts cut into her left inner thigh, until she finally had to reach in and give it a good tug. Jocelyn had flat-out refused to wear anything as down-on-the-farm as overalls or pad her ass, but had been talked into a long flowing skirt. The first two acquaintances they passed took a head snap from Jill, to the stroller, to Jocelyn, to Ruby, and back to Jill. The next two whispered spiritedly the moment they were out of hearing range. Jill was a tangle of live wires and she gripped the stroller so tight she could see the ridges in the bones of her knuckles.

Jocelyn, on the other hand, walked with her head high and made loud, inane conversation, suggesting they buy flowers for some "poor Uncle Gus," and insisting all three of them have a double dip of Barker's mint chocolate chip, "the best ice cream ever."

Jill browbeat Jocelyn as she licked the cone and rocked the stroller to soothe the fussy Fee. Jocelyn's car was packed and she was leaving for California in the morning. It's a good thing she's into hair and facials and massage, Jill thought to herself, acting was simply not her calling. There was no gout-stricken Gus, and Mary Beth Barker's mint chip was bitter and runny. Moreover, no one was fooled by their little parade, she was sure of it.

Crunching the point of the cone, Jill recognized Hester's distinctive tall, gaunt figure approaching. She had exited the library and had obviously set her course straight for the McCloud women. She stopped in front of them, clutching two books to her sunken chest.

"I heard there was some sort of commotion out here." Hester peered into the stroller. "And who is this?"

Jill could never get her engine started around Hester. Her hesitation allowed Ruby to answer first. "This is Felicity McCloud."

"McCloud?" Hester asked disapprovingly. "And whose is she?" She looked with accusation from Jill to Jocelyn.

That small gesture of Hester's allowed Jill a tiny pinch of hope. Jill looked to Jocelyn, who tossed her head back defiantly.

"Well?" Hester said.

"She's a McCloud," Jill finally said, looking down at the baby.

"Oh, for goodness' sake," Hester said. "And who's the father?"

"None of your business." Jocelyn lifted her chin and puffed her chest out.

"It just might be," Hester said.

"Let us assure you," Jocelyn said. "It is not." She took a step toward the stroller and stood in front of Jill. "Let's get going. My turn at the wheel."

"I should expect as much from yours, Ruby." Hester's nostrils flared so wide Jill could have attached a vacuum hose. "But as they say, the apple doesn't fall far from the tree, now, does it?"

With fear, Jill watched as Ruby pushed her shoulders back, angling her head forward in a ram-ready position.

"*They* say a lot of things, don't *they*?" Ruby said. "They miss the point, though, don't *they*? Isn't *fall* just another word for *harvest*, life's wondrous cycle of renewal and bounty. And isn't *bounty* another way of expressing the diversity of life."

With each fully enunciated syllable of Ruby's, Jill swelled with relief. She hadn't seen her mother this clear-eyed and quick-of-tongue in months.

"Tell us, Hester," Ruby said. "What are you reading these days? Nothing banned, I hope."

"Of course not," Hester snapped.

"Certainly not you, the consummate friend of the library." Ruby charaded quotation marks around the semiofficial-sounding organization.

With her mention of the library, Ruby straightened, while, ironically, Hester shrank back, retracing her steps, one behind another.

"Do give my regards to Miss Cordelia," Ruby said.

After which, Hester huffed and turned abruptly, marching away with angry slaps of her sensible brown shoes.

CHAPTER THIRTY-ONE

Jill

Thursday

Jill jammed the file drawer closed. Where could she have put that box of checks? Like the past two days, they were gone, vanished. She brought the heel of her palm to her forehead and pressed her eyes shut.

"Lose something?" Jocelyn stood in the doorway of Jill's office.

"Some checks."

"Where did you put them?"

Jill turned and smacked a stack of files onto the desktop. "Seriously, Jocelyn."

"I think I know your problem. You're too organized. There's no contingency for failure." Jocelyn stepped into the room and sat in the chair opposite Jill's desk. "Now me, for instance, I have a problem with sunglasses. I lose a pair a week." She sat back and crossed her legs. "So now I keep backups stashed all over: in my glove compartment, my gym bag, my briefcase."

"You have a briefcase?"

"It's not technically a briefcase. More like a tote. Gucci. To die for. But the point is, I have a system."

"So you want me to leave blank checkbooks all over the place?"

"I didn't say to use my exact system. Create one of your own."

"Is this why you came in here?" The lost checks had her inventing all kinds of worst-case scenarios, all of which ended with her footing the bill for 202's highfalutin lifestyle. Jocelyn and her nut job of a squirrel's filing system were not helping. "Because now's not a good time."

"I'm worried about tomorrow. How Mom will do," Jocelyn said. "Her long-term chances don't sound good. And I'm freaking out a little. I needed a diversion, and company."

"Me, too." Jill exhaled in a show of sympathy, although she was certain her ticker tape of worries was longer. So long, in fact, she figured she might as well hire a grand marshal. Besides Ruby's situation, the lost checks, and her ongoing money problems, Fee was sullen and moody. Keith hadn't responded to the "can we talk?" text she wished—with all her heart—she hadn't sent. She imagined he was busy, traveling and maybe even back to work by now. And she still wasn't sleeping. Nonetheless, Jocelyn was a welcome diversion. "Let's talk about something else."

"Like what?"

"Like Hester," Jill said. "Do you remember that awful day? The first time we took Fee into town?"

"Of course. Why do you ask?"

"Funny enough, that woman, Pamela, told me her mother was a cousin of Miss Cordelia, the librarian."

"And?"

"Pamela called her Delia," Jill said.

"So?"

"So, it got me thinking about what Mom meant that day. We were so caught up in our own drama, I never really processed it." Jill scrunched her mouth as she thought. "I think Mom's odd bounty-of-life speech, about diversity and banned books, was outing Hester and Cordelia, or threatening to anyway."

"You think Hester was gay?"

"Think about the way Hester totally shut up when Mom called her the consummate friend of the library. And today Pamela mentioned that Cordelia, as a proper librarian, had felt she needed to hide her sexuality. It all makes sense."

Jocelyn rubbed her palms together. "I love it."

"And the three books Keith returned to us. 'To H., with all my love, D.' The *D* was Delia, not Daniel." Jill placed her palm on the stack of hardcovers. "*The Confessions of Nat Turner* was published in '67, I checked. Mom and Dad were married in '65. Those books were not from him."

"The smoking gun." Jocelyn bounced up and down in the chair.

"Actually, I find it all a little sad."

"How so?"

"Think about it. Hester was obviously closeted. And judging by the selection of books, their relationship went way back. They lived in a time when a lesbian relationship would have been scandalous; the town matriarch and librarian, no less."

"I didn't think about it like that," Jocelyn said.

"And Miss Cordelia was a sweetheart. If they'd been together for years, there must have been a side to Hester, a softer side, she never dared show."

"I suppose."

Jill shook her head. "More damn secrets. Think of all the girls who came here pretending to be at Aunt Mary's for the summer, or taking care of their sick grandmother, or at some vocational school. And then there's Mom, so fractured by abuse that she rewrote sections of her life too unpleasant to deal with. And Dad sensing a breakdown and scrambling for a way for Fee to be raised a McCloud. Pile on my grand finale of a fib and my own naïveté in wanting to do the right thing, in thinking there is a right thing to begin with."

"Ugh." Jocelyn dropped her hands over the sides of the chair. "I really hate thinking that Dad knew."

"He was the one to encourage her to go out with her girl-friend, remember?"

"A girlfriend is one thing," Jocelyn said.

"That's why William makes sense," Jill said. "He was some-one she knew and trusted. I think she probably reached out to him for comfort during a difficult time, a time during which her grasp on reality was slipping."

"I had always gone with an immaculate conception theory, myself," Jocelyn said, gathering to a stand. "Comfort sex with an old boyfriend, huh? It just doesn't have the same wow factor."

"I doubt it ever had much of a wow factor," Jill said. "Even back then."

CHAPTER THIRTY-TWO

Ruby

December 1995–January 1996

"I'll have another Seven and Seven, Sam." Ruby slid her empty highball glass toward the bartender.

"May as well make it two." Glenda rattled the cubes in the bottom of her drink. "How's Daniel?" She turned to Ruby; her dangly reindeer earrings darted back and forth.

"Not good. We have another appointment with the doctor day after tomorrow. I'm not expecting much, though."

"I don't know how you're coping with all this so close to Christmas." Glenda shook her head. "But you stay strong somehow." She tapped her Marlboro against the bar's rough wooden surface before lighting it with a snap of her Bic. "Lord knows we've had our share of knocks, but we always answer the door, now, don't we?" Glenda nudged Ruby with an elbow and laughed with a deep hack.

Ruby had recently rekindled a relationship with Glenda, who had been a girl at the home the summer before Ruby and Daniel had married. Ruby always knew Glenda had stayed local, after adopting out the child, but their lives had taken different paths. Ruby had busied herself raising her girls and seeing to her administrative duties at the home. Glenda had worked dispatch for a trucking company and barreled through two unsuccessful marriages. A few weeks ago, Ruby ran into her at the oncologist's office, where Glenda was waiting with her first husband, who was battling lung cancer.

The door opened and Ruby shivered as eddies of cold air blew across the backs of her arms. The wintry wind rattled the silver tinsel Sam had strung along the shelf of liquor bottles. A man in a long woolen coat with a thick argyle scarf wrapped around his face and ears took the seat two stools down from Ruby. He ordered a scotch on the rocks with a splash of soda, and Ruby was instantly transported to a different time and place. It was summertime. She was young and naive and had never tasted anything as perfectly awful as scotch. Her date had laughed, until almost asthmatic, as she gasped and then licked her tongue on the back of her hand in an attempt to clear her burning palate. The fleeting memory of that summer, *her* summer, poked her with such a sudden stab of melancholy that she had to press a hand to her side.

"William?" she said. He was much thicker about the neck and jowls than she remembered, and his woolly hair, which had been chestnut brown, was now full silver.

It took a moment, but then his eyes sparkled and his mouth curled into a handsome smile. "Ruby," he said, as if it were the one-word reply to a game-show question. "What's a gem like you doing in a dump like this?" he asked, as if remembering the game's phrase-it-as-a-question format.

"Don't let Sam hear you talk that way about his place," Glenda said. "He'll cut you off." She leaned over the bar to get a good look at him. "And I mean at the knees."

William laughed long and hard. "I've had my legs go out from under me a time or two, but they always seem to show back up in the morning." He raised his glass to the two women. "Along with a killer headache."

"Aren't you going to introduce your friend?" Glenda poked Ruby in the side.

"Sorry," Ruby said. "Glenda Tippett-Mason-Pardini meet William Fraser."

Glenda leaned across Ruby and extended her right hand out to William. Ruby couldn't help but notice the muffin tops spilling from Glenda's low-cut blouse.

William scooted over one seat to occupy the bar stool next to Ruby. "Tippett-Mason-Pardini? That's a mouthful."

From the ashtray, Glenda lifted her cigarette; an inch of ash hung precariously from its tip. "Maiden-Married-Married," she said. "I earned 'em all and I use 'em all." She lifted her cocktail and shook it at William. "And in case you're interested, I'm in the market for a new one."

"I'll keep that in mind," William said.

Ruby was reminded of the way he had so easily blended with anyone and everyone. His wool coat was expensive and the button-down pegged him as white collar, something Sam didn't attract too much of, yet there he was mixing it up with Glenda without airs or pretensions.

William was surprised to hear about Daniel's illness and

showed genuine concern. Ruby, in turn, was sorry to hear William's marriage had recently fallen apart. After a second scotch, William shared the story of his wife's infidelity. Glenda, who had just recently been scamping around town with the very married chief of police, took that opportunity to powder her nose.

William ordered another scotch and turned to Ruby. "You're lovely as ever."

"Oh, stop. I'm old and I'm fat."

He tilted back in his seat, taking in a full view. "You look good to me. I never did like skinny women. And what are you, fifty?"

"Not until February."

"You see? Still just a young thing."

Ruby shook her head. "It's been so stressful lately. I've aged a hundred years."

"Have I been gone that long?" William asked.

"Long enough," Ruby said. "In the meantime, your son's been making himself known around town. He's all my daughter Jocelyn talks about."

"Really." William stroked his chin. "I'll be darned. Well, if she's anything like you, then I don't blame him."

"People say she looks just like me when I was her age."

"Here's to it." William raised his glass. "Gorgeous at any age."

Ruby turned her head from him. Lately she'd only thought of herself in terms of Daniel's wife and the girls' mother. She couldn't even remember the last time anyone had complimented her. Most conversations regarding appearance began with "Jocelyn the beauty" and finished with "Jill, cute as a button." Not that Ruby would begrudge them their time in youth's flush; it was, rather, that more and more she could barely remember hers, short as it was.

A week later, Ruby sat at the same bar stool, her head hung low and her lashes wet with tears.

Glenda patted her on the arm. "You'll get through this."

Ruby lifted her head. "Daniel won't."

"How long did they give him?"

"A couple of months."

Glenda stuck her bottom lip out and exhaled; her bangs lifted and then fell back into place. "What you need is another drink, a double oughta do it." She motioned toward Sam, who promptly set another Seven and Seven in front of Ruby.

Ruby swirled the ice around the frosted glass and took a big sip. The amber liquid seared her throat and leaked a warm trail down her gullet. She had never been much of a drinker. Daniel didn't like to keep spirits around the house; he thought it set a bad example for the girls. He was, however, uncharacteristically supportive of these nights out with Glenda, ushering her out the door with an "enjoy life while you can." She was beginning to like the kaleidoscope effect of alcohol on objects, animate or inanimate. One tweak of the cylinder and it all shifted and resettled into new possibilities.

There was a rustle from behind and William eased himself onto the stool next to her. "Back again?" he asked.

Glenda leaned forward and spoke over Ruby. "She had a tough day. They don't get much tougher."

William asked about Daniel and grew ashen with the news of his prognosis. "I'm sorry. If there's anything I can do?"

"The woman just needs a few good friends right now," Glenda said.

William bought them another round and they sat in glum solidarity for a long spell.

"What we need is the Boss," Glenda finally said. She bounded off her seat and set off toward the jukebox. She dropped a few coins into the machine and "Born to Run" enlivened the small bar. Glenda stayed and swayed to the music, gripping the glass box with her hands. She obviously knew one or two of the bristled pool players, who catcalled their appreciation of her improvisational dance. Moments later, she was slow-dancing with a guy who hadn't even bothered to put down his pool stick.

"You're much too young to think about being widowed," William said, signaling to Sam for two fresh drinks.

Ruby played with the lobe of her left ear, heavy hoops having long ago stretched her piercings into two long gashes. She looked at a spot on the wall behind William. "For all intents and purposes, I was widowed as a child. My first boyfriend, Josh."

"I remember the story."

"We were just kids, had our whole lives in front of us. He dropped me at my parents', kissed me good-bye, and then next thing I knew," she said, snapping her fingers. "I must be the kiss of death," she said, still focusing on something behind him.

"Of course not," he said. "Don't let yourself think that."

Ruby took another big gulp of her drink. "If I were you, I'd keep my distance."

"I'm not afraid." He patted her arm. "Not one bit."

Glenda returned to order another drink and grab her cigarettes, advising them she had fifty bucks riding on the next game of pool.

"She's quite a character." William pointed to her as she rejoined the small group at the pool table.

"I guess I just needed to know there was someone like her out there."

"Like what?"

"Someone who lives by her own rules. Someone who first and foremost lives."

"You live." William's eyes always had a way of keeping Ruby, their brackish brown shading with the situation.

"Barely."

"You need to do something about that, Ruby." Espresso now, his eyes flicked back and forth. "The Ruby I once knew had more life in her than all of New York, the outside boroughs included."

"Soon," Ruby said. She looked at her watch and then over at the pool table, the surface of which still held quite a few balls. "Looks like my ride won't be ready for a while."

William glanced toward the game and back at Ruby. "I'll drive you."

"No," she said quickly. "I wouldn't want to put you out."

"No bother. I should quit now anyway. Lord knows Hester will chew my head off already. I'm a drunken mess according to her."

"I'll let Glenda know."

Ruby felt a little wobbly as she walked through the icy parking lot. Just as he always had, William knew just when to step in with a handrail of a right arm. He eased her into a Cadillac with a front seat so expansive you could bowl a frame or two across it. Daniel had been driving secondhand station wagons for the past twenty years. What they lacked in style, they made up for in affordability and passenger capacity. Ruby looked out to the frozen landscape as William turned onto the county road that led to the McCloud Home.

"Some days I wish I'd never shown up that summer when Hester and Daniel were engaged." He broke the stillness of the ride with the foggy exhalation of his words.

"I beg your pardon?"

"I wish I'd just waited for the wedding. I've always wondered if my presence, my interest in you, wasn't the catalyst Daniel needed. Maybe had I waited, he'd have been too far down the aisle."

"I don't believe in what-ifs," Ruby said. "I don't like to think about them, anyway."

"I like to," he said. "They can be fun. Take you somewhere you didn't get to go."

Ruby leaned her head against the frosty window. The cornfield to her right was shorn to a ragged patch of snow-covered stubs. "There're lots of places I didn't get to go."

"Ruby." He turned his head to her. "You're not the one who's terminal."

"I know."

"You're going to be okay."

"It doesn't feel that way."

William pulled to the shoulder of the road and put the car in park. He scooted over toward Ruby. "Come here." He pulled her into an embrace.

Ruby stiffened, remembering a scene so painfully familiar she felt something within her detach from time and place itself, and hurry back across the years to be, once again, young and vital.

Four weeks later, Ruby and Glenda sat at the bar. Tuesday night had become Ruby's favorite. Not only were well drinks a buck, but she and William had established a pattern. Ruby was careful to arrive with Glenda and depart with Glenda, but she and William had found a little tryst in the trees. William called it his Ruby Tuesday. Ruby had even caught herself humming the tune as she went about duties—formerly Daniel's—while he lay weak and moaning, or in those moments when the crush of worries about continuing without him were too much to bear. One time—through a spasm of pain—he'd asked what she was singing. "The Stones, I heard them on the radio," she'd replied, after which Daniel had commented how the music brought back "memories." At that last remark, Ruby had blushed and hurried out of the room.

"Is something wrong?" Ruby asked Glenda, who was unusually quiet.

"Is he coming?"

"You mean William?"

"Of course, William."

"He's coming," Ruby said. "Why?"

"Nothing," Glenda said.

William arrived, and as was custom, Glenda slid down a stool so he could sit between them. His eyes were already bloodshot, a sure sign he'd started without them.

"You're a little late," Ruby said. She had started to worry he wouldn't come.

"Hester." He gagged on the word. "She's on my case day and night."

"Why are you still staying with her, then?" Glenda asked.

"Because I'm broke and broken," he said. "Hester may be hell-dog mean, but at least she's putting a roof over my head."

"You're a lawyer," Glenda said. "Get yourself a job. Get

yourself a place of your own." She paused and then continued, her tone more serious, "Get yourself a life of your own."

William sat back and exhaled. "Point taken."

In need of the facilities, Ruby stood and excused herself. It gave her a moment to compose herself. Glenda coming down hard on William like that was uncalled for. The last thing Ruby needed was more heaviness in her life. She had plenty of that at home. William, at least, understood this. No pressure. No burden. Just an overall lightness of being. When guilt squirmed in her belly like a coiled snake, he charmed it away. When she felt herself fading, he was bellows to her smoldering ashes.

Moreover, she was helping William, too. By his own admission, he'd lost interest in his career, lost self-confidence, lost his battle with the bottle, but was now—thanks to her—finding himself. Despite all that, Glenda's rebuke weighed on her.

When she returned from the bathroom, Glenda was alone and wiping her eyes with a tissue. Sam stood at the other end of the bar with his arms crossed and an angry look on his face.

"I hope you're happy," Glenda said.

"Why?" Ruby looked around for William.

"Hester was just here. She gave William a public drumming you wouldn't believe. Called him a no-good drunk, lazy-ass loser, and a whoremonger."

"What?" Ruby sank onto the stool.

"The last comment was directed at me." Glenda blew her nose with a big gander of a honk. "Said she heard he'd been slumming down here with the local trash."

"But—"

"I'd already heard the rumors," Glenda said. "My name's been joined so tightly with his lately, we may as well be Siamese."

"Glenda, I'm sorry. I didn't know."

"You're just lucky you timed your pit stop so perfectly. Hester wasn't letting anyone off lightly. Told Sam this place was a blight on the town."

"Oh God," Ruby said.

"Yeah, well, if I were you, I'd get outta here. And I'd be careful."

Ruby drove around for a while, too agitated by what Glenda had said to go home. Twice she missed the unmarked turnoff from the blacktop, but she needed to see William and there was only one place where she could think to go. She had never driven her own car down the property's narrow interior dirt road, the only access to the cabin. She feared her old wagon would mire in the snow and mud, and she'd just as soon die there before she'd call attention to the hideaway. Hester was onto them, she was sure of it. Simply using Glenda as a lure for Ruby, the bigger fish. Her temples were pounding and her heartbeat ragged when she pulled in front of the cabin. She was overcome with relief to see smoke curling up the chimney and a suffused interior light spilling onto the inky-black ground.

"I'm so glad to see you." William rushed to her as she opened the door. "I was afraid you wouldn't come." He held her in an embrace.

"I had to see you after I heard about the scene at the bar."

"I'm sorry," he said. "Hester had no right to insult Glenda like that."

She pulled away. "I didn't know about the rumors."

William held her hand and directed her to the small table and mismatched chairs, the cabin being much too practical for anything like a sofa. "There's more. Hester has booked me into an alcohol treatment facility."

They gripped hands over the rough wooden surface of the table and it wobbled unsteadily. "What? Rehab? But that's not her decision to make."

"She's got me over a barrel on this one. If I refuse, I'm gone, and so is Keith."

"What does Keith have to do with it?"

"Nothing. Just a bargaining chip."

"She still can't force you to go."

"Keith's her only heir," William said. "If I don't do this, she's threatening to change her will."

"It's a bluff," Ruby said. "Even she wouldn't be that mean."

William raised his eyebrows. "I wouldn't be so sure."

"Is your drinking really a problem?"

William removed his hand and rubbed both his hands up and down his thighs. "The divorce petition mentions my drinking."

"I didn't know," Ruby said, chewing at the side of her cheek. "Then, Hester's right. You should go."

"It will just be for a few weeks."

She stood, turning from him and flattening a palm over the icicle-laced windowpane. Its crystalline perspective was lovely and dazzling, but ultimately obscured.

"It's for the best," she said. "Daniel needs me more than ever. We've been wrong. This is wrong."

William sprang to his feet, knocking the chair to the floor. "Don't say that."

"What if Hester had found you with me instead of Glenda?"

"To hell with Hester."

"It's not Hester I'm worried about. It's not you either. I couldn't live with myself if Daniel found out. If I did anything to hurt him."

"Okay. Okay," he said, grabbing her still-turned shoulder. "You're right. The timing is all wrong. I'll get sober while you take care of Daniel. A temporary separation."

Ruby pulled her coat over her shoulders. *Temporary*, she remembered, was the word the school counselor had used the day she'd placed the pamphlet for the McCloud Home for Wayward Girls in Ruby's hand.

"It's not temporary, William. You won't come back."

"How can you say that? Of course I will."

"You won't." She threaded her arm through her purse strap. "But I can't think about that right now."

She was out the door and running to her car before he could respond. The cold winter air was so brittle its shards tinkled as she gasped for air. And, later, she would remember nothing of the drive home.

"Ruby, is that you?"

She'd hoped to find Daniel sleeping, though nights were his most difficult, pain and discomfort supplanting sleep.

"I didn't mean to wake you." She removed a bracelet, placing it on a dresser-top tray.

"You didn't. I was up," he said through a groan. "How was your evening?"

"It was okay." Earrings joined the bracelet.

"And Glenda?"

"Oh, you know Glenda."

"What's wrong? You sound sad. These nights out are supposed to be a break."

"I don't need a break. Glenda and I won't be going out anymore. I'm needed here."

Daniel scrambled to a sitting position and switched on the bedside lamp, the effort leaving him winded. "I want you to know, Ruby, that I understand. *Glen-da*"—he pulled on the first syllable, altering the word into something almost unrecognizable—"is a distraction, a diversion, a bit of cheer in bleak times."

"No she's not. I mean . . . I don't need to be distracted. I'm fine."

"I want you to be, Ruby. No matter what, I want you to be fine."

"How could I?" she asked, dropping next to him on his side of the bed.

"Because I'm asking you to be," he said, his voice choked with emotion.

That he was giving her permission, begging her no less, to be fine, given what and who she had just come from, brought her to tears.

CHAPTER THIRTY-THREE

Jill

Friday

Jill stretched her legs in front of her, the hospital waiting-room chair shrinking in size and hardening with every passing hour.

Jocelyn looked at her watch. "Didn't they say they'd be done like an hour ago? Longer is bad, right?"

"Let's not jump to conclusions. Not yet." Jill hugged her arms to her chest. Exhaustion had brought her to an altered state of consciousness, one where she could actually hear her brain crackle. And if she had another night of insomnia, she might as well welcome its sidekicks: snap and pop. She watched as Fee walked back into the waiting room after getting "the air" she had claimed she needed. Jill hoped she was in a better mood.

"If everything goes okay with Booboo, can I have a sleepover at Cass's tonight? I haven't seen her all week." Fee could have sweetened tea with the voice she was affecting.

"I don't think so," Jill said. "I'm sorry, but there's just too much going on right now. For a little while longer, I want you close by."

"Figures," Fee said, all the syrup tapped from her voice. She reached down and opened her backpack to drop in her cell phone, when the corner of an envelope caught Jill's eye.

"Fee!" Jill said, already feeling her voice screech with panic. "Are those the letters I asked you to mail when you ran errands with Borka?"

Fee looked down. "Sorry. I forgot."

"That was Tuesday. Three days ago."

"I said I was sorry."

Jill stood and paced in front of the chairs. "Do you think the bank is going to care when I say you're sorry our mortgage is late?" Jill had a meeting with the bank next week. She hoped to renegotiate the interest rate. Should that fail, she would request a reduced monthly payment made possible by an extension to the payment schedule. She certainly didn't want to start off the negotiations with another late payment to address. "I thought I could trust you."

"Come on, Jill. Lighten up," Jocelyn said. "It's been crazy these past couple of days. It's a wonder we've all remembered to piss."

"Easy for you to say. You took a sick day at the worst possible time." She turned and pointed at Fee. "And I told you how important those letters were. How could you forget?"

"She's human, for God's sake," Jocelyn said. "We all screw up from time to time."

Just as Jill was about to respond, the door to the waiting room pushed open and Dr. O'Connor stood before them in his blue scrubs with a mask still dangling from strings tied around his neck. They stood and gathered in front of him. He seemed to sense the tension in the room and took a long look at the three of them before speaking.

"Your mother's a very strong woman." He squared his shoulders. "She came through surgery better than I had hoped."

"That's good, right?" Jocelyn said.

"For the immediate future, yes, that's good," he said. "We were able to remove a large portion of the tumor. This should allow your mother some relief from the symptoms that have been plaguing her."

"A large portion?" Jill asked. "Not all of it?"

"As I had explained prior, its shape and location rendered a clean resection virtually impossible."

"So it will likely regrow, then?" Jill said.

"Radiation and chemotherapy are still options. We'll just have to see how strong she is." Dr. O'Connor looked old and tired. Everything about him appeared gray—his hair, his eyes, even the chalkiness of his skin. It was almost eight P.M. and he had accommodated Ruby into an already full operating schedule.

"Thank you," Jill said. "Thank you for everything." Her head pitched from side to side with questions and concerns, but for now she was relieved Ruby had made it.

It was nine P.M. by the time they got back to the house. Borka had everything clean as a monk's soul and had served wine and cheese to that night's crowd, though parlor games had been canceled. She also left three messages from guests requiring concierge services for the next day. Jill phoned in a Saturday dinner reservation for one of the parties before she even had her purse off her shoulder. She'd have to wait until the morning to set another couple off on a hike with a bird-watching book and picnic lunch. The third request was puzzling. The message, scribbled in Borka's cramped hand, stated, "Jepsen—Room 209—anniversary cake—Fee."

Jill quickly changed into her favorite pj's, silky lilac drawstring bottoms with a matching button-up tank, and slid her aching arches into pink fuzzy slippers. She walked through to their private family room and dropped into the chair next to the old Shaker sideboard. Jocelyn was watching TV. "Did Fee go to bed?"

"She's getting ready to go on that sleepover," Jocelyn said.

"What?"

"You were on the phone." Jocelyn turned the volume up with the remote. "I told her to go ahead and scram while she could."

"You did what?" Jill asked.

"She said if she asked you, you'd say no again."

"Oh, did she?"

"And you would have," Jocelyn said with a shrug. "Probably still will."

"How do you know?"

"Because I know."

"Really? What else do you know?"

"I know we've all been through a lot," Jocelyn said. "And that you were pretty tough on her before."

"I was tough on her because she screwed up."

"She's been helping out a lot. And is just as worried as the rest of us. She needs to get out, let loose a little. Just let her go."

"You have no right."

"No right to what?" Jocelyn asked. "Is she grounded? Why can't she have a night off?"

"She's not grounded, but like I said, I want her close by for now. Anyway, it seems there's something regarding a cake she must know about."

Jocelyn waved her hand dismissively. "It can wait till morning."

"We're all going back to the hospital in the morning."

"She can take care of the cake thing when we get back."

"Like she took care of the mortgage check?"

Jocelyn powered off the TV. "What the hell is going on with this place anyway? Are you in some kind of money trouble?"

"Nothing I can't handle."

"What was that phone call from the bank about? And that was a real-estate agent looking at the place. I know one when I see one."

"I'm just having it appraised," Jill said.

"Appraised for what?"

"None of your business." Jill instantly regretted the remark. Her recent insomnia had her temper idling high.

"It is my business. It's all of our business. The place still belongs to Mom. And as far as I know, I'm still an equal to you and Fee in her will. This place is my inheritance, too."

The word *inheritance* was the final gust that blew Jill away. She had inherited all of it. The house. Fee. And the history between Keith's family and hers. Not one piece of what currently constituted her life had been a real choice. It had all been dumped on her like a load of gravel.

"You're right," Jill said. "You should be an equal, so it's about time you stepped up, because, you know what, it's overdue. And yes, I fucked up. I'm behind on some loans and in deep shit." Jill knew she was gesturing wildly with her arms. With an orange vest and a whistle, she probably could have directed traffic. "And the more I think about it, the more I say, have at it. Have it all, for that matter." She gestured a full loop of the room. Her imaginary intersection would have been a multicar pileup by now. "Mom. Fee. She was never mine to rightfully claim. So if you think you can do better—"

There was a crash in the doorway and Jill looked up to see Fee staring at the two of them with shards of a water glass and a puddle at her feet.

"How is it that I'm not really yours? And what does that mean—it's Jocelyn's turn? You two must think I'm some sort of idiot, like I wouldn't figure this out." Fee's face was puffy and tears pooled in her eyes. "I'm Jocelyn's, aren't I? That's what those two old ladies were talking about at the wake. That's why they called me a mystery child."

Jill's stomach lurched as if in free fall. "Fee." She took a step toward her. "It's not what you think."

"Yeah. Right." Fee flicked her hair over her shoulder. "What is it, then? More lies? *Mom?* Why would you do this to me?" She looked from one sister to the other. "Jocelyn, why wouldn't you tell me?"

Jocelyn lifted her hands in supplication. "Oh God. This is a mess." She turned to Jill. "You gotta help me out here."

Fee kicked her foot back, slamming the open door back against the wall. Picture frames rattled. "Just tell me the truth. How hard can it be?"

"Fee, it's complicated," Jill said.

"No, it's not," Fee shouted.

Jill and Jocelyn exchanged looks.

"Just answer the question!" Fee yelled. "Who had me?"

"Now's not the time for this conversation," Jill replied. "I'm sorry for what you heard. It was said in the heat of the moment. We all just need to calm down."

Drops streamed down Fee's face. "Too late for that. You've basically told me, anyway."

"No. I didn't. Honey, it's honestly not what you think."

"So, for once and for all, then, tell me," Fee said through tear-soaked words. "Am I your biological child?"

There was a long pause, Jill scrambling for a loophole or deferment. Finding none, she said, expressing the words like steam, "Will you sit down, at least?"

Fee, a knob of hard angles, sat on the arm of the sofa.

"I never wanted to tell you like this," Jill began.

"Tell me what?"

"It was a difficult time. Dad had just passed away and she wasn't well, detached and out of touch with reality. She simply wasn't capable of taking care of you."

"Who wasn't?" Fee asked.

Jill took a deep breath. "Booboo."

The room went boneyard still.

Fee rounded on Jill. "You're a liar. And that's sick."

"She was fifty, and you were the result of an affair." Jill's head was screaming at her to stop, that it was enough for now, yet words kept falling around her. "She was not in her right mind. The guilt of it all triggered some sort of breakdown. She wasn't competent."

Fee tossed her head violently from side to side. "It's not true."

Jocelyn stepped forward. "I'm sorry, Fee. It is. It's true. But no one ever meant to hurt you."

"I don't believe it," Fee repeated.

"It was a terrible situation," Jocelyn said. "Your mom did what needed to be done. She did the right thing."

"The right thing." Fee brought both hands to her head.

"How is lying to me the right thing? How is keeping me in the dark about something as important as my own birth the right thing?"

The eyes that turned on Jill weren't Fee's, weren't—more to the point—her *daughter* Fee's.

"I promised my dad I'd take care of my mom, of everything. And I kept that promise. But it was at a cost, and for that, I'm sorry."

"Sorry isn't good enough," Fee said. "Sorry is bullshit as far as I'm concerned. What about me? Where did I fit into that promise?"

"Fee," Jill said. "It was so complicated. It still is."

Fee took two steps backward. "No one thought about me. Did they?"

"I know it's hard right now to think of it in this way, but, honey, it was all for you."

"Bullshit!"

"Fee, lower your voice."

"No," she said, louder still. "And you don't get to tell me what to do anymore, because you're not my mom. You're my sister. And that's all you'll ever be to me from here on. My older sister. My *bitchy* older sister." Fee turned and ran to her room, slamming the door behind her.

There was a long silence. Jill heard only the clock on the wall and her own labored breathing.

"Well, we fucked that one up," Jocelyn finally said. "Do you want me to talk to her?"

Speech wouldn't come. Her vocal cords were in knots, permanent damage likely. It couldn't have gone any worse. Everything was ruined. There was not one thing, not one fucking thing, in her life that was not ruined. Jill spied Jocelyn's car keys lying on top of the sideboard and grabbed them. "She's all yours." Tears washed makeup, mascara, and the day's grime into her eyes as she stormed through the kitchen, out the backdoor, and across the path to the Hummer. The last thing she remembered seeing was Jocelyn waving frantically in her rearview mirror, and then she was barreling down the long driveway, gunning for the road.

She drove for about an hour with the darkest of reels looping through her mind. All she'd said was wrong. All she hadn't said, also wrong. There was a tugging sensation at the back of her head. Some sort of border war had been declared between her lack of sleep and the adrenaline of fleeing, an east-versus-west battle for control of her two hemispheres. And from the south came marching in the emotions, a million strong and growing. She finally pulled over to the shoulder of the road, thinking she couldn't even run away without screwing up. She'd taken Jocelyn's keys, but nothing else.

When she had squealed out of the driveway, the gas had been half full. Now at a quarter tank, she could either turn back or continue and face the consequences. She levered back the seat and stared straight ahead. Wouldn't it be nice, she thought, to drive through life without the hindrance of a rearview mirror? The joy of an open road and clear mind without ever having to look back. Jocelyn had that gift, the ability to shed people and places.

After their father's death and Fee's birth, Jill had been rent open by Jocelyn's decision to leave and had always harbored a secret hope that Jocelyn lived with regret. She remembered those first few weeks with newborn Fee, after the breakup with Keith and Jocelyn's departure. Fee had been colicky, as if sensing the grift perpetrated against her. It had taken Jill a long time to establish a bond, after which it seemed they both clung desperately to each other, aware of the tenuousness of the claim. Jocelyn had called only once during those weeks, keeping the conversation brief and pretending a bad connection. She wondered now if Jocelyn—and her mother, for that matter—had ever paused, even momentarily, to question their direction. Interesting how often choices were represented as a fork in the road. Jill thought it more often came down to the decision she now faced: go forward or go back. What if Jocelyn had stayed to help? What if her mother had remained faithful?

She glanced down at her father's watch. Stopped. She lifted it to her ear. No little *tick-tick*. She tapped it. Nothing. She tapped it harder. Nothing. She stared at it again. The sub-second hand frozen midtock just past the three-quarters marker. She fingered its leather strap for a moment. It had always been loose, a man's watch, after all. Of all moments, she thought, and then resigned herself to operating without it.

She had instinctively turned left out of the driveway, which meant that the sun would rise behind her. She hoped she had enough gas to get her to daylight, though doubted it. She then uprighted the seat and put the car in drive. "To hell with it," she said, and continued straight ahead.

CHAPTER THIRTY-FOUR

Fee

Friday Night

There was a knock on the door again. Fee ignored it. Jocelyn had established a pattern. First came three raps with the knuckle. Those had a sharp pitch to them. Next came three pounds with the side of her fist. Those were dull in tone, but delivered with more force. Then came the speech, usually something along the lines of "I know you're in there. You can't ignore me forever," or "Come on, Fee. Let's talk." Finally, the slaps with the flat of her hand. Those were just pathetic. As was the whole situation. Jocelyn had been at it for about an hour, the cycle having repeated itself numerous times, with an occasional "Your mom took off, so it's just us," thrown in to break the monotony.

Finally came the *click-click-click* of heels down the hallway. Jocelyn off to pee, or to call a locksmith, or to conspire in the ruin of someone else's life. Fee wanted to bolt. Problem being, she'd first have to get past Jocelyn. And then somewhere out there, her mom. Her mom—ha. Not her mom, her sister— and technically only half. It felt like a demotion. Like a back-door deal. Like a con, a lowdown dirty trick. She pulled out her cell phone and punched in Cass's number.

"What's up?"

"Cass, I need your help."

"What's wrong? You sound funny. Have you been crying?"

"I'll tell you later. Can you and Mel come pick me up?"

"You sound terrible. Where are you?"

"I'm at home. Meet me at the top of my driveway? Don't pull down."

"Fee, you sound really weird. Is everything all right?"

"No. It's not all right. Just pick me up and I'll explain then."

Fee waited an agonizing twenty minutes, then grabbed her backpack and lifted the window as quietly as she could, resting the pop-out screen against the side of the house. She hoofed it up the long gravel driveway and waited by the side of the road until she saw their car and flagged it down.

"Fee, what happened? It's your grandma, isn't it? She didn't make it." Cass swiveled in her seat to get a better look at Fee, who'd scrambled into the back.

Fee leaned down and put her face in her hands. "She's okay for now. Just drive."

The car was spooky quiet for a few minutes before Cass broke the silence. "Are you going to tell me what's going on? Are you hurt? Your face is all puffy."

She wiped tears from her eyes and snot from her nose. "I've been sobbing my heart out, that's what's wrong."

"Why?"

Fee lowered her face into the crook of her elbow and felt her whole body rack in the most pathetic, soap-opera-worthy flood of tears. Neither Cass nor Mel dared speak. They probably didn't dare breathe either. Who could blame them? Fee was freaking herself out. She became aware of her labored breathing and the wet hairs at the nape of her neck. Having a whole family rearrange itself into something unrecognizable, like some bizarre Mr. Potato Head with lips for eyes and foot for a nose, was a workout.

She finally found a pocket of air and managed to gasp her way through a boiled-down version of events.

"Whoa," Mel said. "That's fucked up."

Fee dug through her bag for Kleenex. "I know." Finding none, she rewiped on her sleeve.

"Wait, I don't get it," Cass said. "What about the guy from Turkey?"

"I invented that. To shut Marjory up."

"That was a lie?" Cass's tone was as much accusation as it was question.

Fee turned her head to the window. "Just my luck. The truth is even more twisted." *Luck.* Fee gargled the word, remembering Cass's firmly held we-make-our-own belief.

"So where are we headed?" Mel asked. Fee could tell that she was trying to change the subject. Cass didn't turn around again. She sat motionless, her eyes fixed straight ahead. A bad sign, Fee knew.

"I can't go home right now," Fee said. "I don't have to either. My parental unit is in intensive care."

They drove in silence. Fee was out-of-body quiet. She kept thinking about "her parental unit," Booboo. *What the hell?*

The whole thing had her realizing there was a Booboo she never knew existed.

When they pulled into Cass's driveway, Fee didn't remember getting there. And moments later, when she found herself on the basement couch, she had much the same sensation.

"I know I should probably feel sorry for you right now," Cass said. "But at the moment I'm more mad than anything else."

"Don't be mad at me," Fee said, tears choking her words. "I've always told you everything."

"I know."

"So why would you suck me into that stupid lie, then? I've been defending you and that bogus story."

"I'm sorry. I wanted to tell you. It's just . . ."

"Just what?"

"I only said it to mess with Marjory, but then it kind of snowballed and I was too embarrassed to take it back. Besides, I was so tired of not having a dad that even that dumb story felt better, even though I felt guilty about it every day."

"Yeah, well, you should have."

"If it makes you feel any better, look what it got me: still no dad, just a new mother." Fee lowered her eyes at her friend. "Can you forgive me?"

"I really don't know." Cass fluffed the pillow behind her head and stretched out on the love seat, closing her eyes.

Fee powered on the TV, but not even Comedy Central could dislodge the stone in her chest. She channel-surfed, watching a string of half-hour shows, one after another. With every mutation of family passing before her eyes—two gay dads and an Asian baby, a houseful of orphaned siblings, cash-strapped divorced parents forced to occupy the same home—not one of them was nearly as outrageous as her own. She decided her family could be a sitcom, except all they had was the situation—no comedy.

Sometime later, Fee's cell phone rang—yet again—and even the air seemed to grow still. This time she fished the phone out of her pile of things.

"Fee, it's Aunt Jocelyn."

"What?" Fee moved toward the stairs, not wanting to wake the sleeping Cass.

"Have you talked to your mom since you took off tonight?"

"You mean my sister?"

"I mean Jill, *your* mom, *my* sister."

"No. Why would I?"

"I need you to come home. Right away." Jocelyn's voice seemed tight.

"Did something happen with Booboo?"

"No. It's your mom I'm worried about."

"What? You're worried about *her*?"

"I already talked to her golf friends. And I've driven all through town. No one's seen her."

"So? What's it to me?"

"Cut the crap, Fee," Jocelyn said. "We'll all apologize like a million more times, and then you can still disown us, but right now I'm worried about her. Has she ever done anything like this before?"

"Like what?"

"Like lose it in any way?"

"No. I guess not."

"That's why I'm going out of my flippin' head here," Jocelyn said.

"She's a big girl," Fee said.

"She's been gone for hours."

"So?"

"So. She didn't take her purse or her cell phone. She's in her pj's and out there freaking out about you, about Booboo, about money, and who knows what else. I really need you to come home."

"What good would it do?"

"Listen, Fee, your mom has her faults. God knows I've done my best to shake that stick out of her ass over the years. And, yes, she's wound tighter than a tourniquet. But she did what she did out of duty, and to protect you." Fee could hear the lather in Jocelyn's voice. "And she loves you like any mother loves their kid: fiercely, and blindly, and at great personal sacrifice."

"What sacrifice?"

"Keith, for starters."

"I'm what split them up?"

"Don't hold it against the guy. It was all such a mess."

"I'm at Cass's," Fee said. "Three-twenty Elm Street. Come get me."

"Thank you."

"But let's get one thing straight."

"What's that?" Jocelyn asked.

"I still hate you."

"Fair enough."

Fee watched as Aunt Jocelyn, driving Fee's mom's car, pulled up the scary-movie-dark street. For the second time that night, Fee snuck out of a home. As she lowered herself into the car, Jocelyn lifted three hardcover books from the passenger seat and placed them in Fee's lap.

"What are these?" Fee asked.

"First stop is to return them."

"You're not serious. A library run? I thought this was an emergency?"

"It is. And we're not returning them to the library; we're returning them to their owner, or owner's nephew, anyway."

"You think she's with him?" Fee asked.

"No. But I think he'll help us find her."

Jocelyn pulled out of the driveway and headed into town. She drove fast, way faster than Fee's mom ever did. The poor old Subaru rattled and bucked in defiance of such treatment. She ran two stop signs, flipped off three other drivers, and parked in the loading zone in front of the Graystock Bed and Breakfast. She bounded up the steps, two at a time, with Fee following as best she could. Jocelyn then slowed and approached the front desk almost languidly. Fee saw the young man straighten with his eyes fixated on Jocelyn's advance. Fee marveled at the way Jocelyn could turn it on like a switch.

"Good evening," Jocelyn said. "Could you ring Keith Fraser's room for us?"

"Sorry." The guy shook his head of long dark hair. "He checked out."

"That can't be." Jocelyn's body shrank by several inches.

"Oh, wait," he said, tapping his head. "He's still here. Had a dental emergency that kept him another day. Broken crown."

Jocelyn plumped and quickly fished inside her purse. She extracted a prescription bottle of pills; holding them up, she gave them a little shake. "He called me and asked me to bring these over. He's in a lot of pain after the procedure. That's why I was so surprised when you said he checked out. He's expecting us." Jocelyn leaned over the desk, squashing her boobs against the wooden surface and giving the clerk a little wake-up call of his own. "He told me the room number over the phone, but I've always been terrible with numbers."

The guy was flustered. He lowered his eyes and typed a series of computer commands. "You sure he's expecting you?"

She rattled the pill bottle again. "And these."

"Room 103."

"Thank you," Jocelyn said in a voice sticky with honey.

Fee was impressed, deeply impressed. Jocelyn didn't bend rules; it was more like she coaxed them and curled them into something that she could coyly tuck behind an ear.

"What's going on?" Keith answered the door in a white T-shirt and plaid pajama bottoms. His hair was mussed and patchy stubble darkened his cheeks and chin.

Jocelyn shoved the books at Keith. He received them awkwardly. "I'm returning these. The *D* stands for Delia, or Miss Cordelia, as we used to call her. She was the librarian in town for many years."

The books started to slip from his hand and he scrambled to secure them against his chest. "What?"

"Your aunt Hester dedicated all her love to someone named Delia, not Daniel. One of those books was published after my parents married." She took a few steps past him into the room and Fee followed. "But that's not really why we're here. We need your help."

Keith seemed confused. "What time is it?" He closed the door.

"Late," Jocelyn replied.

"Help with what?"

"Jill. I was hoping you'd heard from her, but judging by

your condition, I'd guess not." Jocelyn cocked her head at him. "How's the tooth?"

"Hurts." Keith put a hand to his right cheek. "What about Jill?"

"We had a fight." Fee could tell Jocelyn didn't know how much to say. "Fee overheard." Jocelyn made a clawing gesture out of her right hand. "Cat got out of the bag. And then Jill took off."

"What's all this got to do with me?" Keith asked.

Jocelyn huffed. "You let her down."

"I've been out of commission." He pointed to his mouth.

"No excuse." Jocelyn then pulled her fist to her own chest and rapped lightly. "But I let her down, too, and so did Fee."

"What did I do?" Fee asked.

"The mortgage check for starters." Jocelyn walked to the middle of the hotel room. The bed was mussed, and the room was lit by a single bedside lamp. "She's in some sort of financial mess and you forgetting to mail that check somehow made it worse. Plus, something's going on with your friends, and like any mom, she's worried about you."

Fee crossed her arms.

"I still don't know why you're here," Keith said.

Jocelyn looked like she was going to haul off and slug him, but she managed to calm herself into a huge lolling roll of the eyes. "Do I need to hit you over the head with one of those books?" she asked. "Your aunt Hester was closeted. She had a special friend at the library, one whose lipstick matched her own. And I, for one, say 'hallelujah, Sister Hester.'" Jocelyn was working herself up into some sort of frenzy. "Don't you get it? People are multifaceted, families are complicated, and yours is no exception. Now, shall we move on to your father?"

Keith rubbed his jaw, but Fee could see it was more than his tooth that was smarting.

He stacked the three books on a desk and then blocked access to them with his body. "At the risk of getting clobbered, I still don't know why you're here."

Jocelyn shook her head from side to side wildly. "Because you two are a fit. An off-the-color-chart, pheromonal flood of fated fidelity." She stopped and looked him over, lingering on his tousled bed head. "Though I honestly don't know what she still sees in you." Jocelyn tapped her left knuckle to her mouth. "Just goes to show you how damned constant she is." She opened her hands up plaintively. "So this running away is big. Call-out-the-dogs big. Have you ever seen her lose her cool, ever?"

"No." Keith's shoulders hunched forward.

"Nor has Fee, and nor have I, and I've known her longer than the two of you. And let me tell you, she's a rock. A big, solid, stubborn boulder of dependability." Had foam poured from Jocelyn's mouth, Fee wouldn't have been all that surprised. "Her mother is lying in a hospital bed after having a chunk of her head removed. She's got money problems. The secret she dedicated her life to is blown, as is the promise she made to our father. She thinks the guy she's still nuts for has left town—again. She probably thinks Fee will hate her forever. And she's a control queen and neat freak mired in one huge, stinkin' pile of shit." Jocelyn pushed her bangs from her forehead.

Keith cleared his throat. "You seriously think she's still nuts for me?"

"Oh, for God's sake," Jocelyn yelled. "Just go find her, you idiot!"

CHAPTER THIRTY-FIVE

Jill

Saturday

Jill tuned in the AM radio show, *Sleepless on the Prairie*. A regular, Jack from Waterloo, called to share that he had been awake for fifty-two straight hours and referred to himself as the walking dead. Jill wondered how many hours she'd actually slept in the past six nights. When she tried to add the single-digit figures, one to another, she found she couldn't run even the most simple of tallies. Her brain felt cottony and even scrunched with the most rudimentary of tasks. She reached to change the station, when her gaze flitted over the little pill cup Jocelyn had taken from the hospital. Valium. Wouldn't the root of a word like *Valium* be *valor* or *valiant*, as in *strong*? An old can of Diet Mountain Dew sat in the cup holder next to the pills. Jill lifted it and shook, a swallow at the most. She gulped the first pill with spit and the second with the slags of Jocelyn's pop.

Dawn from Dubuque reported that she suffered from hyp-
nagogic hallucinations, something Jill had never heard of, but
that sounded like a terrifying state of paranoia in the moments
before sleep. If she had a phone, she might have called to
describe her own current situation, a zombie zone where you
become your own worst nightmare. She doubted, though,
she'd even get past the screener. Who'd believe her story?

A bell sounded from the Hummer's control panel and Jill
glanced down to read a message, the crux of which was "refuel."
About fifteen minutes later, the car resorted to intermittent
belches as it sucked in air with the dregs of the tank. She pulled
onto the shoulder as it rolled to a stop with a concluding
shudder.

"Well, that's that," she said out loud.

Her lids had been heavy with sleep for the past few miles,
and had it not been for the racking of the car's engine, she
might have dozed off. Her movements were slow, as if her body
were contending with something other than gravity, some
counterforce which had her trapped between a state of tran-
scendence and a state of oppression. She turned off the head-
lights and marveled at the dark surrounding her. The two-lane
highway was deserted and void of lights, save the stars above.

Once again, she was aware of a battle within. The car was
a cocoon of warm night air and she thought of lying down on
the backseat, her silky pajama bottoms sliding over the tan
leather bench. Somehow the adrenaline of her flight champi-
oned and she pulled the keys from the ignition, thinking Jocelyn might just be onto something in her appreciation of
modern pharmaceuticals.

Within a hundred steps of the car, she was aware of the
jingling sound the keys made in her hand. What good were

they now? The car—not hers, not her responsibility—was use-less. Anything behind her was useless. She lifted the keys in her right hand, weighing their heft, and then jettisoned them into the field of corn that lay north of the road. She loved the way they arched through the air, rustled the stalks, and then settled with a muffled *thud*, with no mile marker, or sign, or distinctive feature to mark the spot. She kept on walking.

The recent rains had brought with them air so heavy Jill's shoulders sagged. Fee would never speak to her again. That much was clear. She'd screwed up: tolerable when it was your own life, intolerable when you dragged someone else down with you. The secret, the lie upon which she'd so foolishly erected a life, was a blunder of a size and scale defying ratio-nal thought.

The backless slippers were impractical walking shoes, designed to shuffle from bedside to bathroom with carpeted stairs or kitchen tile representing the apex of their ability. They hobbled her gait and she was in no mood for delay. She pulled off one and then the other and threw them into what she thought, given the sightless soil of night, was a bean field. The first few barefoot steps were painful and a shock. She was unable, in the dark, to avoid rocks or glass or whatever it was that pierced her stride. She was soon able to strike a compro-mise. She found that if she concentrated on the very top of her scalp, fixating on the lifting sensation, which felt like an inversion of hair follicles, her feet in turn went numb. Jill was definitely going to ask Jocelyn what else she had in her little medicine cabinet.

She continued this way for several miles until she spied a neon sign for Idabelle's twenty-four-hour truck stop. A huge black truck, with more wheels than there were inhabitants in the county, was the only vehicle in the lot. It was remarkably clean with bright chrome trim and a loopy purple script on the driver-side door that read MIG'S RIG. She trekked across the blacktop to the restaurant, pausing only briefly at the door to read the "No shoes, No shirt, No service" sign. The door chimes tinkled as she walked in.

A waitress carrying a coffeepot stopped to look her up and down. "Honey, you're bleeding," she said, pointing to the ground behind Jill.

Jill turned and was shocked to see a trail of bloody footprints leading from the door to the spot where she stood. She lifted her right foot, and then her left, noticing several cuts on each.

"You need shoes to come in here, plus you're not dressed," the waitress said irritably.

Jill pushed through the haze that held her in its mist. She spied a solitary figure at one of the booths along the window. "I'm with Mig."

She walked with all the determination she could collect and scooted into the booth across from the man she hoped was indeed the Mig of MIG'S RIG. He was clearly startled by her appearance and juggled his coffee mug from one hand to the other before setting it down on the sparkly laminate surface. He was younger than Jill, probably in his late twenties, but hard-looking with small black eyes, long dark hair, a sweat-stained white tank top, and a large eagle tattoo the wings of which spanned his entire back and folded up over his shoulders.

"What the hell do you want?" he said.

"I need a lift," Jill said. "Which way are you going?"

Mig looked at her for a long time, taking in the silk pajama top and even ducking his head under the booth to her swollen and bloody feet. "Sioux City, and then Casper, but I ain't no damn Greyhound Bus."

Jill ran her left hand through the back of her hair. She could feel wet tangles that clumped at the nape of her neck. Even though the Valium had rendered everything cheerier and easier, the gash on her right toe was starting to throb. She looked down to her hands folded across her lap. Her pj bottoms were ripped at the knee. She vaguely remembered falling. She fingered her father's watch, flipping it one full rotation and then lifting its clasp. The door chime sounded again and another trucker, an old guy with gray hair and muttonchops, took a seat in the booth next to them.

"I don't have any money, but I could pay you with this." She slid the watch across to Mig's side of the booth. "It's Swiss and vintage. I admit it's not working at the moment." She bit her lip. "But it's valuable, very valuable."

Mig lifted the watch and turned it over in his hand. There was black grit under his nails and deep in the crescents of his cuticles. He stood and dropped the watch into the front pocket of his jeans. "We leave in five. I'm hitting the head. I suggest you do the same." He strode off toward the back of the restaurant.

"You want a cup of coffee?" The waitress stood over her with a steaming pot and a clean mug.

"I don't have anything to pay you with."

"I'll stand you one," the waitress said, her tone softer than before.

"Could I also trouble you for the time?" Jill asked. It was still full dark. "My watch stopped and I lost track."

The waitress looked down to Jill's bare arms. A question seemed to be forming, but then she said, "Almost three-thirty."

Jill's head felt gaseous, as if tiny blasts of air or vapors were popping randomly. This time tomorrow, she thought, I'll be in Wyoming, a state she'd never visited. Of course, there were scads of places she'd never visited given the endless demands of motherhood and the inn, and compounded by finances. She didn't know how much of the road she'd see this trip, though; she needed sleep badly, very badly.

"Wake up."

Jill tried to ignore the intrusion.

"Wake up."

There were sandbags pressing down on Jill's chest and she shielded her eyes from the sun streaming through the window. Her cheek pressed into a small puddle of drool she'd left on the vinyl surface.

"Your name Jill?" The waitress looked down at her, resting the ever-present coffeepot on the table.

"Where am I?"

"Exactly where you were three hours ago when you showed up here in nothing but your slinky little nighty-night." The waitress gave her a long look: not harsh, more puzzled. "Are you one of those crazy sleepwalkers?"

"No," Jill said. She was still too muddled to sit up.

"Well, if you're looking to be found, there's a guy here looking for someone named Jill. You fit the description."

A headache was brewing at the base of her skull; with the pain came memory. "Where did the trucker go?"

The waitress laughed. "He took off hours ago. You were passed out by the time he got out of the can. Anyway, I told him he had no business giving you a ride anywhere. You were in no condition."

"Oh."

"He left you this." The waitress pulled Jill's watch from her apron pocket and placed it on the table. "You're lucky. He may look like trouble, but he's as honest as the road is long. Still, whatever game you're playing at, it's dangerous."

Jill heard the door chimes, but she was still too groggy to pull up.

"You didn't answer my question," the waitress said. "Are you looking to be found?"

Jill poked her head up over the booth. She saw Keith standing near the counter and talking on his cell phone. Their eyes met and a look she couldn't read washed over his face. He walked fast in her direction.

The waitress lifted the steaming pot and walked off, saying, "Looks like you've been found."

Icy terror pained Jill's throat. She looked down at her embarrassing attire and blood dried hard and black on her feet and knees.

"Jill. Thank God." Keith stood looking down at her as she pulled to an upright position.

She had no reply. Was completely bereft of strength. She turned to the window, drawing her legs tightly up to her chest. She knew it was a ridiculous head-in-the-sand response, but she couldn't help herself. Facing Keith in such a state was beyond her current capacity. Within moments, her knees were wet and she could feel her body convulsing. The padded bench depressed as Keith took a seat next to her.

"Thank God you're okay," he said. His arms encircled her

back. "You don't know how scared you had us." He matched her shaking with a rocking embrace. "I just woke up some trucker in his cab and he said he saw you sitting with some long-hauler who took off a couple of hours ago." He patted her back and then tried to turn her face toward him with his hand. She resisted, keeping her face to the window. "Jill, what is it? Are you hurt?"

"No." Her voice was blubbery.

Keith took a handful of napkins from the tabletop dispenser and pushed them into her hand. "Where were you going?"

She wiped at her face and noticed the paper napkin went brown with grime. "Nowhere. Just turned left." She still had her face to the window.

"I know, or I guessed anyway. You went west. Due west. That's how I found you."

"I can't even run away right," she said flatly.

He turned her head toward him and this time she didn't stop him. She faced forward and lowered her feet to the floor. He took the napkin from Jill's hand and wiped gently at her cheeks. "Oh, I don't know," he said. "Looks like you've done a pretty good job from where I sit." Unblinking, he held her gaze; two of the lashes above his right eye were crossed. "How about I take you home?"

"What's the point? It'd be empty. My mom's in the hospital, and I've screwed up with Fee—probably lost her forever."

"She's not lost. She was with Jocelyn. I'm sure there were some unpleasant words, but she's not lost. As a matter of fact, she was worried about you. So, how about I take you home?"

"I don't have a home. I gave it to Jocelyn, but the bank will probably take it from her."

He nodded his head in appreciation. "We make quite the

pair. Jack and Jill at the bottom of the hill." He leaned back against the booth's padding with crossed arms. "You've got nowhere to go, and I've got no one to go to." He scooted toward her, looping an arm over her shoulders. It was warm and heavy, and she felt herself sag under its heft. "Why don't you be my someone and we'll work out the somewhere."

"Why would you burden yourself with me and my troubles?" Jill asked. "I've screwed up in every way."

Keith straightened in his seat. "A long time ago you asked me a question. You asked if I could manage without you. Do you remember?"

"Yes."

"It turns out I can't. I thought I could, or should, but I can't." He lifted his arm from her shoulder, taking her hand and pulling it into his lap. "Besides, knowing now that Fee is my half sister, I think I should stick around."

"Knowing?" Jill felt it needed repeating.

"She does look like a Fraser."

"She hates me."

"Give it time. She'll come around. You'll get past this. We'll *all* get past this."

"*We'll?*"

"I want to try again."

Jill could think of no reply. She lowered her eyes, spying her left hand in his right, but viewing it as something foreign and unfamiliar. "I missed you so much."

"I asked Jasper to contact you about the wake," Keith said. "I needed an excuse to be near you. And I wasn't sure you'd come to the funeral. I took one step inside the town limits and all I could think about was you."

"Really?"

"Yes. Really."

"I died the day you left," Jill said, looking into his eyes.

"And I'm alive for the first time in years."

Jill felt fresh tears trail down her face. Keith put a finger under her chin. He kissed one cheek and then the other. When he finally kissed her mouth, she tasted a warm mixture of salt and sweetness with just a slight crunch of road dust.

CHAPTER THIRTY-SIX

Jill

Saturday

"Why did you let me sleep so long?" The events of the past twenty-four hours buzzed about Jill's wet head like a bothersome gnat.

"Because you needed it." Keith closed a magazine and replaced it on the coffee table. "You showered. Good."

"I was filthy. Caked in blood and dirt." A bandage covered her left kneecap.

"I cleaned you up a little bit, but figured the rest could wait."

"But it's five o'clock. I've missed the whole day." She pulled her hands to the sides of her cheeks. "My mom. What's going on with my mom?"

"She's fine. Still in intensive care, but doing better."

"But I should have been there." Jill's voice was panicked.

"Jocelyn's there. And Fee's been back and forth."

"You've spoken to them?"

He nodded his head.

"About us?"

He patted the spot on the couch next to him. Jill took a deep breath and shuffled across the room. Had he really come to find her? Had he really held her and said he loved her, had always loved her? She eased herself onto the sofa. He pulled her hand into his lap. The cotton of his faded Levi's was warm and smooth.

"Jocelyn said we belong together because there're no two bigger blockheads on earth." Keith rubbed the top of her hand with his thumb.

"She's said worse."

"I censored that a bit," he said. "Suffice it to say, she's certain we were made for each other."

"And Fee?"

"She was kind of quiet. I think she was mostly relieved you were okay."

Jill dropped her head into her hand. "I can't believe I took off like that. It was really stupid."

Keith swung his arm over her shoulder and pulled her into the crook of his underarm. "What it lacked in subtlety, it made up for in efficiency."

"What did?"

"Your request for help."

"How pathetic."

He rested his chin on her wet hair. "Not at all. Somewhat brilliant, if you really think about it. You got Jocelyn taking care of things. You've given your daughter the truth, which she deserved. And you got me so worried for a few minutes there"—he thumped his chest—"that I remembered there's still a vital organ in here." He kissed the top of her head.

"When you put it that way." Jill turned his wrist to read his watch. "I should get to the hospital."

"Visiting hours are almost over for the day," he said. "Plus, Jocelyn's got it covered. She said to take the day off and rest up."

"That was nice of her."

"Technically, I think she said something more along the lines of 'Tell Joyride Jill to cool her engines for a while.'"

"That sounds more like her."

"And that's the part I feel comfortable repeating."

"I couldn't sit around here, anyway." Jill stood.

"Before you go, then," Keith said. "There's someone waiting to talk to you. Fee's in her room."

Jill knocked on Fee's door. There was no answer. She opened it a crack and spied Fee lying on the bed, listening to her iPod.

"May I come in?" Jill asked.

Fee removed the earbuds, but didn't reply.

"I'd like to apologize," Jill said. "It was stupid of me to run off like that."

Fee shrugged. It wasn't much of an invitation, but Jill took the few steps into the room and seated herself on the edge of the mattress. "I caused everyone a lot of worry at a time when we should be focusing on Booboo."

"You mean my mom?"

"I'm your mom," Jill said. "I'm not done apologizing either. I'm sorry to have kept this from you. I shouldn't have; you deserved the truth. Maybe not as a girl, but certainly as a teen. I want you to know, though, that none of this was done to hurt or deceive you. You should know that Booboo loves you. I do, too."

Fee steepled her legs, her arms clamped over them, and her head dropped forward. "So what happens now? What do I say to Booboo?"

"I've been thinking about that. Nothing for now, I think. We have to focus on getting her stronger. I wouldn't want to upset her. And even before you, her way of protecting herself was to rewrite certain pieces of history—the difficult ones. There never was a boyfriend named Josh. Booboo was abused, probably by her own uncle."

Fee gasped.

"I know," Jill said. "This home is the proverbial house of cards. And it probably goes even further back. No one would say what happened to your great-aunt Rose, in whose honor the home was founded." Jill ran her fingers through her still-wet hair. "And here's the thing. There's more to this whole saga."

"What now?" Fee asked.

"I never knew who your father was. Booboo would never say and I guess I didn't want to know."

"And?"

"She was incoherent when I found her in the woods. It triggered something and she spoke of him, of your father."

"And?"

"I suspect it was William Fraser, Keith's father."

"You gotta be kidding me," Fee said.

"Keith never knew. Sounds like William never did either."

"So that makes Keith my—"

"Half brother."

"And the dead lady my—"

"Aunt."

"This settles it." Fee pulled her knees to her chest. "We're freaks and con artists. And I hate to say it, but I'm right in there with you all."

"What? Why?"

"I made up a story about my dad. To shut Marjory up about him being a deadbeat."

"You did?"

"Yep."

"Was it a good one?"

"No. It was stupid."

Jill was quiet for many moments. "Your birthright, I suppose." She exhaled, jutting her bottom lip forward. "What a mess. And I've had my hand in it. There's more."

Fee's head popped up. "There's more?"

"I'm having some financial problems. I owe the bank more than I can pay. I've even had a real-estate agent appraise the place, just in case. I don't know what's going to happen, but you should know that it's bad. And I'm scared."

"Oh." Fee quietly bobbed her head up and down. "That *is* something I should know."

"At least I've learned my lesson," Jill said. "No more secrets." She stood and straightened the crimp in Fee's comforter. "I'm going to the hospital. You want to come?"

"I can't. I'm getting picked up soon for that soccer party. It's okay if I go, right?"

"Yes. Of course. You should. Have fun."

"Tell Booboo I love her."

"I will."

"And, for the record, I love you back."

"Thank you. It's nice to hear."

Smiling, Jill closed the door to Fee's room. Theirs wasn't a family that said it often. After everything Fee had been through in the past few days, Jill was touched by her willingness to forgive. They'd obviously done something right.

CHAPTER THIRTY-SEVEN

Fee

Saturday

Cass bowled a strike, her second in a row. Fee high-fived her.

The first few minutes of the party had been awkward. Non-text-returning Cass was obviously still pissed, but she was too sweet and their friendship too strong to let a fight fester. When Cass had finally walked over and asked about Booboo, Fee knew it was code for a long list of things, first and foremost being "We're still friends."

"Not bad," said Logan, who was watching from the neighboring alley.

Coach Yuri had not been happy about the presence of boys at their team party, but there wasn't much he could do about the six guys who had *coincidentally* booked lanes at the same time.

"Thanks," Cass said, tucking a never-been-flatironed curl behind an ear.

For a moment, Fee stood super-glued to the spot. Even allowing for Memory Lanes' blinding fluorescent lighting, there was something odd about Cass. It was the weirdest thing, but she was buzzing—literally crackling—with energy. And even her white T-shirt gave off a greenish tint. *Huh?*

Fee spun to where Logan stood still watching Cass as she sashayed back to the viewing area. He, too, was giving off strange vibes. Logan stepped into their lane and Fee smelled . . . lime sherbet. *What the?*

"You're up, Fee," Logan said, pointing to the overhead scoreboard. "But looks like Cass is kicking your butt. Everyone's, for that matter." He offered Cass a celebratory fist bump.

A Katy Perry song came over the loudspeaker. Logan groaned.

"You don't like this song?" Cass asked.

"It was okay the first hundred times I heard it, but it's my sister's current favorite, and when she likes something, she *really* likes something. It's cool, though. My mom does a lot of at-home physical therapy with her and music helps to motivate her."

Again, Fee remembered holding the door for Logan's special-needs sister at a basketball game.

Marjory—returning from the snack stand with a pop, probably diet—took in the scene through slitted lids.

Fee knocked down eight pins, leaving a split. Her second try only connected with one pin. Marjory, up next, blocked Fee's path.

"I can't go anywhere these days without hearing about you."

Something circled Fee's tummy and then drained with a glug.

"The craziest shit," Marjory continued, hands on hips.

"Missing Turks, love triangles, sisters hiding for nine months. Don't think I don't know what you're up to."

Uh-oh?

"You'd do anything for attention. It's pathetic really. You're so boring that even invented scandals are better than your insignificant life. Except no one's falling for it."

Fee broke into a smile so out of practice her lips stuck to her teeth. At least a pregnant granny wasn't on the list, yet. She looked to where Cass and Logan were chatting, both with big smiles and bright eyes. *Speaking of falling,* Fee thought to herself. She dragged her left foot behind her right, tripping and having to catch herself against the small scoring table.

Marjory snorted with laughter. "Got your retard shoes on again, Fee?" she asked in her loudest, could-cause-permanent-damage voice of hers.

Fee glanced quickly at Cass and Logan, their conversation momentarily on pause. Logan's eyes narrowed at Marjory.

"Your turn, Marjory," Fee said. "And watch out for that gutter." She pointed down the wooden lane. "It's a trap."

Feeling pleased with herself, Fee took a seat and a big swig of Coke. Judging by the vibes sparking between Cass and Logan, Marjory and Logan's breakup was inevitable; provoking Marjory had just sped things up a little. But it was her first reading. And she was exploring. And holy crap, it was fun.

A little while later, she and Cass sat in chairs against the wall of the party room. Fee took a big bite of pepperoni pizza and wiped her mouth with a napkin. "So what's up with Logan?"

"Nothing."

"Yet," Fee corrected. She jerked her head to where Marjory, ingesting only air, sat with two other team members. "He took off without her, didn't he?"

"Yeah."

"Did he say anything?"

"Kind of."

Fee's eyes got fat-baby big. "What?"

"Just that she was sort of . . ."

"Sort of what?"

"A bitch." Cass brought her hand to her mouth, trying to hide the grin. Her eyes, though, sparkled with mischief.

The door to the party room swung open and Borka's gaunt frame jutted into the room.

"Crap," Fee said. "My ride."

Coach Yuri approached the unexpressive Czech. "May I help you?"

"I'm here for Fee," was Borka's all-business reply.

"Ah. Our Velicity," Yuri said.

Fee had no idea if Coach Yuri had meant Felicity or Velocity, but she did notice the way Borka's shoulders snapped to right angles and her cheeks colored with pink spheres.

"If there's no hurry and you're hungry, we have food." Coach Yuri pointed to a table where boxes of half-eaten pizzas were open and scattered.

"What, me?" Borka asked, her head bobbing back.

"What? You eat? No?"

"No, thank you," Borka said flatly.

In the parking lot, Fee scrambled after Borka. "That was nice of Coach Yuri to offer you pizza."

"Was leftovers," Borka said.

"He kind of sounds like you—doesn't he?"

Borka halted her march. "He's no Czech. Is Russian." She spat the last of those words out like a bad nut.

"Is that bad?"

"To be hungry is bad. To be lonely is bad. To be Russian is curse."

Alrighty, then. Though Fee couldn't help but notice that everything about Borka was crisper, humming, and shining with a coral-pink glow.

CHAPTER THIRTY-EIGHT

Jill

Sunday

"Wake up." Jocelyn stood over Jill with a newspaper in hand. "Wake up. You're never gonna believe this." Jocelyn nudged Keith's shoulder. "You, too, Romeo. Get up."

"Jeez, Jocelyn, a little privacy would be nice." Jill rubbed her eyes. "Believe what?"

"You're in the paper. The inn is in the *New York Times*."

"Oh my God. What's happened now?" It had to be bad news, Jill thought. Something about her finances. She sat up straight.

"You made Miles Bartlett's column." Jocelyn waved the paper in her face. "*Inn Search of America*. The whole thing is about you."

"What?" Jill reached for the *Times*, but Jocelyn held it over her head. "Allow me. And I quote." She took a step back, out of Jill's reach. " 'In a word, imperturbable. Such is the nature of Jill McCloud, innkeeper extraordinaire.' "

"It does not say that." Jill swiped at the paper, but Jocelyn proved too quick.

"Oh yes it does. And there's more."

"What's going on?" Fee stood in the doorway.

"Look," said Jocelyn. "Your mom is in two places at once." She pointed at Keith. "In bed with a man, and in print with another."

Keith pulled the sheet up over his bare chest.

"Give me that paper," Jill said.

Jocelyn took another step backward. "Let me continue." She snapped the paper to its full length. "'With an unflappable nature and the keenest of anticipatory talents, Jill McCloud manages the McCloud Inn of Scotch Derry, Iowa, with proficiency and aplomb. No request is too small, no hour of the day an inconvenience.'"

"Oh my God," Jill said. "It's 202. Who else would talk like that? And I let him use my office in the middle of the night."

"Who?" Keith asked.

"That overbearing fusspot who drove me crazy. It has to be him. It all makes sense now."

"Which guest?" Jocelyn asked.

"He was at that wine tasting. Bad toupee, thick glasses. It was his wife's birthday that night."

Jocelyn examined the photo. "Bald as a cue ball here."

"Let me see that thing." Jill finally managed to snatch it out of Jocelyn's hand. It was him, even without hair and without glasses she recognized his smirk of a smile. She read the piece and couldn't believe what it said. It was all complimentary, every single word. She passed the article to Keith and sat rubbing her head. "He liked everything. The house. The grounds. The area. And the service."

"That's great, Mom," Fee said.

"The *New York Times*," Jocelyn said, "that's a big readership."

Keith held the paper against his chest. "That guy's syndicated. It'll be more than just New Yorkers reading this thing."

Still unable to process the information, Jill looked from Fee to Jocelyn to Keith. The phone rang. Fee answered Jill's bedside cordless.

"McCloud Inn. How can I help you?" Fee listened for a moment. "A reservation? Certainly. Just let me get to a computer." She placed her hand over the mouthpiece and whispered, "He mentioned the article." She hurried out the room with the phone at her ear.

Jocelyn cocked her head at Keith. "Boxers, eh? Go figure." She threw him his jeans. "Better get your pants on. Looks like things are gonna get interesting." She stopped and pointed her finger at Jill. "And do me a favor, would you?"

"What?"

"Wear purple today." Jocelyn pointed to her head. "Purple is the crown chakra."

CHAPTER THIRTY-NINE

Jill

Sunday

Jill paused at the threshold, eavesdropping.

"We really need you to get up, Mrs. McCloud."

"Mom, please. It's for your own good," Jocelyn said.

"You can both go to hell," Ruby said with as much force as her weakened state could muster.

Jill took a deep breath and stepped into the hospital room. "What's going on?"

"Thank God you're here. She's impossible." Jocelyn's eyes flashed with relief.

Jill had been delayed at the inn with new reservations, calls from local reporters, and a follow-up phone conversation from none other than 202 himself. He had apologized for his performance, most of it acting, except the requirement of her office. A rewrite, deadline, and crashed computer really had put him at her door that night. Forgetting his wife's birthday

hadn't been acting either. He offered to pay her for the bracelet, which she politely declined.

Ruby's nurse, an iron-faced, fiftysomething rock of determination, was not happy. "Your mother must get up, even if
just for a few steps, a trip to the bathroom if nothing else. We
need to get her blood circulating. There's a risk of infection
and clots if we don't."

Jill surveyed the scene. Fee sat in the bedside chair. Jocelyn
and the nurse hovered over Ruby, who looked small and
opaque with the huge turbanlike bandage swaddling her head
and the standard-issue gown bunched loosely over her shoulders. Jill spoke briefly to Keith, who had shadowed her into
the room, after which he discreetly exited.

Jill stepped toward the bed, rustling a shopping bag. "Look,
Mom, your favorite color." She pulled a poppy-red housecoat
from the tote. She motioned with her hand toward Jocelyn
and the nurse. "They didn't honestly expect you to be seen in
that hospital gown?" She reached into the bag again. "And
here, a new head scarf." The scarf was black with big red polka
dots. "Your Grace Kelly look. Everyone will think you're a
movie star."

Ruby lifted her head slightly. "I could have been, you
know."

Jill nodded. "Everyone said so. Dad always claimed you
were the most beautiful woman he'd ever seen, in real life or
on-screen."

Ruby's hand went to her throat. "Well, he took an oath to
say so, now, didn't he?"

"But he wasn't the only one." Jill stepped toward her mother.
"Sit up a little so I can get this on you." Jill quickly slipped
the silky fabric over her mother's bandaged head and tied an

expert bow under her chin. "Why don't you swing your legs over the bed?" She held the red housecoat over Ruby expectantly. "Let's see if I got the right size."

Ruby pushed to a sitting position and slowly eased her legs over the bed. Jocelyn's eyes flared momentarily, and then she shook her head in amazement.

"That's good," Jill said, slipping the cotton robe over her mom's shoulders. "Here, take my arm." She nodded to the nurse, who instinctively knew to flank Ruby's other side. The two of them lifted her to a standing position. "We won't do too much, Mom," Jill said. "You've been through a lot." She talked slowly and calmly, as if to a child.

"You're darn right I have," Ruby said.

"You're a fighter, though. Aren't you?"

"Always have been."

"If you think you can make it to the bathroom," Jill said, looking at the nurse's name tag. "Then Betty here will tell you about all the eligible widowers on the ward."

"What, the half dead?" Ruby said. "I can do better than that."

Jill left her in the bathroom with the nurse and stepped back into the hospital room. Jocelyn stood glaring at her with her fists on her hips. "Fuck you," she said to Jill playfully. "I couldn't even get her to lift a cheek for the bedpan and you've got her signed up with a dating service."

"Experience. And maybe I borrowed the color thing from you."

"See," Jocelyn said. "It works. Hard—cold—science."

Fee turned to her mother. "Will Booboo be okay? She looks so weak."

"Don't worry. I'm going to take care of Booboo," Jill said.

"She's coming home with me as soon as she can. She'll still need radiation and chemo, but she's resilient." She turned to her sister. "I could use some assistance. How about it, Jocelyn?"

"Wow," Jocelyn said. "A request for help. This is new."

"I'm learning," Jill said. "So?"

"Why not," Jocelyn said. "L.A.'s great and all, but I'm getting a little tired of all that sunshine."

"We can definitely guarantee a few rainy days around here," Jill said.

"And you're gonna need some help now that you got all that free advertising." Jocelyn rubbed her chin. "I think we need to offer a few spa services."

"Color therapy?" Jill asked.

"Among other things." Jocelyn perched on the arm of Fee's chair. "And Victor will be glad to hear I'm only a few hours away."

There was a rap at the door and the three of them looked up to see Keith. "I got some magazines for your mom," he said, his thumb trailing the corners of a stack of at least five. He hung uneasily in the doorway.

"Well, get your butt in here," Jocelyn said. "Put them on her nightstand. And fluff her pillow while you're at it."

"Jocelyn!" Jill said.

"Oh, please," Jocelyn replied. "He wants to be useful. He's practically dripping with it."

The nurse and Ruby emerged from the bathroom and slowly started making their way toward the bed.

"She's doing great," the nurse said. "I can barely keep up."

"I was always a step ahead," Ruby said with labored breathing.

The nurse eased her into a reclining position and settled the sheets over her, her scarf and housecoat still intact.

"Maybe that's what makes the McCloud girls such a great catch," Jocelyn said, after a small pause. "We don't make it easy."

"Ruby Jolene Renard McCloud never had anything easy in her life." Ruby swatted at some imaginary foe.

"Renard," Keith said. "Renard was your maiden name? *Renard* is French for 'fox.'" A knowing look passed between Keith and Jill.

"I think he's calling you a foxy lady, Mom," Jocelyn said. "Careful, Casanova. One of us at a time."

"I had the looks," Ruby said.

"You still got 'em," Jill said.

"Red's a good color for me." Ruby straightened her head scarf.

They all agreed. Even Jill. Especially Jill.

CHAPTER FORTY

Jill

August

Rubbing her temples, Jill watched the circus unfolding before her. A tent worthy of Barnum & Bailey flapped in the late summer breeze. Odd people scrambled about with purpose. A slip of a woman juggled a tray of wineglasses. A tall man hurried past with a vase the size of a dunk tank filled with sweet peas. Sweet peas! Jill had heard nothing of sweet peas. So far as she knew, the flowers—all of them—were roses. And she ought to know; she was, after all, the bride.

How had she let it come to this? How had she allowed her mother to wrest control of the event, *the event*. A fat man lumbered by under a stack of folded chairs.

Early in the planning stage, Jill had been under the now-laughable assumption that she would have an active role and deciding voice in the arrangements. She had been wrong. She had also thought that, as a chosen life partner, Keith would be her consummate supporter and confidant. Wrong there, too. Much to Jill's ire, not only had Keith given Ruby carte blanche to "go big," he was her accomplice, as well as banker.

"What the hell are you doing?"

Jill was dragged from her reverie by a frowning Jocelyn.

"Why?"

"You're sitting for hair and makeup . . ." Jocelyn looked at her watch. "Five minutes ago."

"I thought you were doing it?"

"The makeup. Yes. The hair? God no. I'd need an electrician's license to handle all that wiring."

"Some maid of honor you are?"

"Co—maid of honor. I'm sharing the marquee with Fee, remember?"

How could Jill forget? The two of them were worthless puppets to Ruby's madness.

"Have you seen Keith?" Jill asked.

"He went for a run."

"What? Now?" Jill was certain that his recent exercise regimen was new. His complaints of aching calf muscles and an empty tube of IcyHot were evidence to this theory.

"Last-minute tone-up."

Did Jocelyn say "tone-up" or "tune-up"? Neither made any sense. It wasn't as if Keith needed some beach-ready physique. With all that had happened in the last two months—their engagement, Keith moving in, Jocelyn moving in, Ruby's follow-up medical appointments—there had been more than enough to coordinate. The honeymoon, it had been decided, could wait.

"Honestly, Jill." Jocelyn again checked the time. "Move it. After hair and makeup, we have to get you into that dress."

The dress. Another sore subject. She had chosen a blue so pale and crystalline it reflected light, and attention. Later, she'd been pressured into an ecru, a light creamy vanilla. She had no idea exactly when the conspiracy against her had been hatched, but the end result was a dress so incandescently white it was probably viewable from space, and possibly already being tracked by NORAD. And don't get her started on the train, a ridiculous ankle-buster of an invention. Or the veil. Because impaired vision was the perfect complement to floor-length ball gowns, high heels, and an audience.

Jocelyn applied a final brush to Jill's eyelid and stepped back to examine her work. An end result, Jill had to admit, she couldn't have achieved herself. And her hair. What a transformation. The stylist had had to tug until her biceps rippled and resort to a straightening product that could strip the Pacific of its waves, but it was all worth the effort. Jill's hair was as sleek as copper sheeting.

"Wow, Mom," Fee said. "You look hot."

Jill allowed herself a smile. "I feel hot."

"No time for a weather report," Jocelyn said. "We've got a schedule to keep. Come on, let's spoon you into that dress."

The dress. If the color was all wrong, at least the style and fit were not. The simple silk bodice, Empire waist, and billowy tulle skirt were heavenly. And maybe Jocelyn did know a thing or two about color. The shade she chose for the bridesmaids' dresses was a perfect green: heart-chakra green, as she called it.

Jocelyn zipped Jill from behind while Fee held a strand of pearls out for her mother.

"Are these Booboo's?" Fee asked.

"Yes. My something borrowed."

"How're we doing in here?" Ruby poked her wigged head through the door. Her chemo-ravaged hair had yet to grow in, so, on this occasion, the wig was a necessity. It was a new one, however: ash-blond, cropped, and—for Ruby—decidedly matronly. As was her dress, an elegant jacketed raw silk in dusty rose. Ruby padded across the room, coming to a stop in front of the bride. "You look beautiful." She brought her clasped hands to her mouth. "I can't tell you how long I've dreamed of a wedding, a *perfect* wedding."

"Are the guests all here?" Jill asked.

"Seated and waiting," Ruby said. "Did you know Borka was bringing a date?"

"I did," Jill said, exchanging a look with Fee.

From the garden, a long baleful screech filled the air.

"What was that?" Jill asked.

Ruby smiled. "Part of your surprise."

The sound continued. A trapped animal couldn't produce a more pitiful sound or evoke such melancholy.

"Is that what I think it is?"

"Yes, dear," Ruby said. "Your father so wanted bagpipes at our own ceremony. It was his only regret. Well, that and . . . oh, never mind. I'll ruin everything if I blabber on." She clapped her hands. "Jocelyn, Fee! Off you go."

Something Ruby had just said needled Jill. And as much as there were times, Jill supposed, when surprises were welcome, expected even, as much as surprises could be—birthdays and Christmases, for instance—but your wedding day? Moments before the march down the aisle?

"Mom. Honestly. Tell me what's up."

She wouldn't. Was, in fact, a lockjawed, rock-faced autom-
aton with eyes fixed determinedly ahead. One look at Ruby,
though—so giddy with the day and so honored to be the
down-the-aisle escort—and Jill resolved to weather the unfore-
seen. Besides, it couldn't be any worse than the bagpipes,
which, thankfully, had been replaced by an instrumental ren-
dition of "Greensleeves": the musical signal for Keith and his
groomsmen to take their places, for Jocelyn and Fee to begin
the procession, and for Ruby and Jill to be in position under
the floral archway.

Mendelssohn's traditional march began. Judging by the
tremble in Ruby's hand and the slightest of tiny catches in her
breathing, Jill knew her mom was crying. She didn't dare look.
Tears, she knew, were more contagious than Ebola. She did,
however, have several tissues tucked into her bouquet. Just as
she retrieved one, out of the corner of her eye, she saw Ruby
scratch up and under her wig and emerge with her own han-
kie. She could now hazard a look, and broad smile, at Ruby.
Giggles: the antidote to tears.

"You ready, Mom?"

"Been waiting a long time," Ruby said, dabbing at her
cheeks.

They got about halfway down the aisle, when a flash
of color caught Jill's eye. She blinked, cursing the veil and
its foglike cover. A few more steps, though, and her breath
caught.

There stood Keith in full Highland dress. As any good
Scottish girl could, Jill recognized the obligatory parts: the
Prince Charlie jacket with brass buttons, lace-up Jacobite shirt,
shaggy sheepskin sporran, ghillie brogue shoes, thick woolen

hose, and the kilt—not just any kilt, her father's kilt, the McCloud clan tartan.

"Nice legs," she said upon reaching the altar.

He twisted his calf to the side. "You like?"

And as she would again but a short while later, Jill said, "I do."

The
McCloud Home
for Wayward Girls

Discussion Questions

1. Consider the purpose of the McCloud Home before it became the McCloud Inn. Why do you think the McCloud women raised Fee as a secret? Was it out of respect for Daniel or something more?

2. There are numerous weather analogies throughout the novel. Do you think the author uses these as a metaphor for the McCloud family history? Discuss.

3. Do you think Hester was mean and vindictive because she had to suppress her true sexuality, or do you think she was angry for other reasons?

4. In a confused moment, Ruby proclaims that she "killed" William. Do you think William's failures in life (his alcoholism, loss of employment, and divorce) were due to a broken heart?

5. Discuss the significance of Jill's golf girlfriends' nicknames: Pickle, Hen, Scoop, and Jill's nickname, Carrot. Jill seems mostly serious, so why do you think she indulges in this?

6. Why do you think Fee created such a preposterous tale about her missing father?

7. Discuss what you think Jill was running from, and why, after the truth comes out about Fee's birthright.

8. Discuss Jill's quote in the Hummer during her flight from Scotch Derry: "Wouldn't it be nice to drive through life without the hindrance of a rear-view mirror?" (p. 279) How is this especially significant to her?

9. Why does Jill bear most of the responsibility for her family? Do you think it's because of her deathbed promise to her father, or something more?

10. When Jill is running away, she notices that her father's watch has stopped. Do you see any irony in this?

11. Why do you think Jill turned west out of the driveway? Do you think she knew Keith would come searching for her if she went that way?

12. Delsol uses gemstone references throughout the novel to signify diamonds in the rough. Discuss her different uses, including both people and places.

13. Right before the Hummer runs out of gas, Jill ponders calling in to the AM radio station and explains that in her current position she has become her own worst nightmare. What do you think she means by that?

14. Why do you think people always thought the worst of Ruby?

15. Do you think it's fair that Jill was saddled with the burden of caring for the home, Ruby, and Fee, and giving up a future with Keith while Jocelyn was able to live her life as she chose? Why or why not?

16. We find out in the end that Fee is only a half sister to Jocelyn and Jill, but she displays character traits from both of them. Do you think nature or nurture has more to do with this?

17. Keith has a sixth sense about names and Jocelyn makes a living from her ability to read auras. Do you think there's some validity to this?

18. In the end, Jill ends up with the wedding she very well could have had in her twenties to Keith. Do you think in this case the wait was worth it? Did she do right by her family and herself by raising Fee as her own and exemplifying the McCloud family motto "Hold Fast"?